Praise for *Hush*, by Jude Sierra

"In her debut novel, Sierra explores Cam's emotional confinement and burgeoning self-discovery with poetic delicacy... Sierra skillfully captures the frustration of navigating identity and interpersonal relationships for those to whom it doesn't come easy. The subtle twist of fantasy enhances the narrative while also complicating the notion of consent... a worthy read and a valuable addition to the genre."
  - Library Journal

"The writing itself is full of flowing words and beautiful prose with precisely chosen phrases. The entire book has a specific cadence and tone that indeed compels you to read on."
  - Joyfully Jay Book Reviews

AND COMING SOON FROM JUDE SIERRA, *IDLEWILD*

WHAT IT TAKES

what it takes

Jude Sierra

interlude press • new york

For Lex.
Thank you for helping to make my dreams come true.

part one

chapter one

MILES GRAHAM IS EIGHT YEARS OLD WHEN THEY MOVE TO Santuit, Massachusetts. Simmering in the backseat of the car from Logan Airport, Milo pouts and keeps careful eyes on his father. He looks away at the slightest hint that his father might look back at him. He answers his mother's mindless chatter meant to fill the space in the car. Still, the knowledge rolls inside him: nothing is ever going to be the same. *Nothing.* Things suck enough in his life; he doesn't need this.

They left behind the glow-in-the-dark stars his mother had put up on the ceiling for him—the ones he used to navigate the dark that presses on him and scares him when he's left alone in it. They left his friends and the tree he loved to hide under where drooping willow branches and delicate leaves created a perfect refuge.

Once they turn onto Route 28 and ribbon their way along the Cape, his anger only increases. Who wants to live here, where sand blows over the road and the scrubby trees are spindly and strange? The scattered houses lack the comfort of suburban uniformity: orderly and easily navigated streets and pretty, neat lawns clipped into standard perfection.

1

This is gross. And awful. And so, so unfair.

Despite all this, Milo knows better than to ever, ever voice his anger. When his father's eyes flicker up so Milo can see them in the rearview mirror, he wipes his face as clean of complaint as he can.

o o o

MILES RUNS into Andrew the third day there, when he's lumbering down Chickopee Beach, kicking up sand that he knows will pool in his shoes and ruin his socks. Milo's mother will have something to say about that, but he doesn't care. He doesn't care at all, because he's running away and he's never going back and he is never, *ever* letting his father near him again. With his breath tearing through his lungs and his snail-slow pace across the sand, he knows he has to go back. But he still makes himself empty promises. He's kept himself going in a sprint across an unfamiliar town, past the marina and the tiny shops lining Main Street. By the time he hit this beach he was winded but determined.

Milo is so focused on his belabored progress and the anger and hurt inside that he doesn't see the boy until he's tripped over him, flies and then tumbles into the sand and scrapes his knees impressively.

"What the fuck?" he yells, turning back to glare at the offending boy.

"That's a grown-up word," the boy says, pressing his lips together primly. "And you ruined my picture."

Milo stands, shakes sand from his clothes carelessly and tries to ignore the way the boy shields his eyes to avoid the sand. "*Fuck,*" he says deliberately.

The boy watches him for a few seconds. His hair is light brown shot through with blond, and his skin is tan. From what Milo can tell, he's about his age.

"I'm Andrew Witherell," the boy says, standing up and holding his hand out.

Milo's cheeks burn. He looks down at scattered shells and bits of sea flotsam in disarray; some carved lines in sand are still visible despite the skid marks he made in his fall.

"I'm Miles Graham." Miles takes his hand politely, then gestures toward the ground. "Did I... is this yours?"

"Well, it was."

Milo looks away. The sun is low against the water and the wind is picking up, unexpectedly chilly. His parents barely paused in Boston when they arrived, but it was sweltering compared to this. The air here is crisp; heat is whisked away by winds and a clean open bay. He wants to offer to help Andrew fix it, or to sit, or to find a distraction of some sort before he has to face the music and trudge home. He doesn't want to risk a *no*, though.

"How old are you?" Andrew asks.

Milo pulls himself up to his full height, which isn't much. "I'm almost nine." It sounds better than eight.

"I'm eight too. Wanna play?" Andrew says it easily; his smile comes fast and natural, and everything relaxes.

"Yes," Milo says gratefully before plopping onto the sand.

o

"Cats or dogs?" Andrew asks.

"How is that a question?" Milo bites his lip, concentrating on tracing the same pattern Andrew drew on the sand.

"Because cats are awesome and I don't think I can be friends with a dog person."

Milo's pretty sure Andrew is joking, because he's smiling again.

3

"But dogs are way more awesome," Milo explains.

"Hmm. Well, okay. Pizza or broccoli?"

Milo laughs. "Pizza of course."

"Okay, good. We'll be friends then."

"You're messing with me, aren't you?"

Andrew laughs, nodding, and Milo feels himself relax a little.

"Well then," Milo says as he clears his throat, "only friends can do this." He pauses for effect so that the gravity of the moment can sink in. "You can call me Milo."

"What kind of name is Miles anyway?"

"A lame one." Milo's squiggles on the sand are awkward and sloppy compared to Andrew's. "But don't... I mean if you ever meet my parents, call me Miles, please."

"Okay, whatever." Andrew sweeps away Milo's lines in the sand and hands him the stick. "Try again."

"What, are you an artist or something?"

"Maybe one day." Andrew shrugs. "Who knows?"

Milo works carefully, biting his lip in concentration.

"What do you want to be?" Andrew asks.

"A grown-up."

"That's a stupid answer. Everyone wants to be a grown-up."

"Well, grown-ups can live anywhere they want. And they don't have to answer to anyone. They make their own rules." *No one can hurt you.*

"Like ice cream before dinner?" Andrew asks.

"Exactly." Milo gives up on his attempt at drawing like Andrew.

"Well then, let's go." Andrew stands, sand showering from his creased shorts. He gestures toward the sand dunes and the lurking woods past them. "I live right by here."

"What?"

"My parents aren't home." Andrew holds a hand out. "Come on." He tugs Milo up and takes off up the beach. Milo follows, although his stomach knots at the idea of breaking rules. But *ice cream*. What his parents don't know might not hurt him.

∘ ∘ ∘

"Come on." Andrew tugs Milo through the woods, pushes aside low branches and hops over logs easily, leaves him stumbling behind and getting slapped by those same branches. "It's so cool."

"It's a pond. Like all the other ponds," Milo points out, slapping a mosquito on his arm.

"No. It's not. No one is ever here. It's a secret pond."

"Oh? How did you find it?"

"Exploring, stupid."

"Are you sure it wasn't the fleeting hummingbird, whispering secrets in your ear?" Milo teases.

"Oh my god, shut up. I wrote that poem when I was like, nine."

"Drew, that was only like, a year ago. Plus it will never stop being funny."

"I'm never telling you a secret again," Andrew says. Milo forces a laugh. He knows Andrew doesn't mean it, and that sucks because in the two years they've known each other, all Milo has done is keep secrets.

They work their way to the edge of the woods and onto boggy ground. The pond is small, lined with grasses and littered with lily pads. The bluest sky reflects on the still water.

"We're explorers," Andrew says with reverence that reflects the hush of their surroundings. "Discovering new land. Looking for gold in sunken ships."

Milo raises an eyebrow and stops himself from pointing out that a pond is no place for a ship. He isn't as good at pretending as Andrew is, but it's fun once he gets into it.

"Last one to the treasure buys the candy," Andrew shouts, whipping off his shirt and making a dash for the water.

"You suck," Milo yells, struggling out of his own. "No fair!" He splashes into the water and his feet sink into the sticky mud. Once he's in, though, he takes off; despite not having grown up by the water, he's a much better swimmer than Andrew. He reaches the middle with ease, then, panting, waits for Andrew to paddle his way toward him. Weeds brush his legs, which is creepy. He flips onto his back, floating and warming in the sun. He yelps and swallows water when Andrew suddenly pushes him down.

"Fuck you!" he coughs out when he surfaces, splashing Andrew full in his laughing face.

"Ugh." Andrew flails in the weeds. "This is so gross."

"Maybe the treasure is in the woods," Milo offers, already working his way to the shore.

Andrew follows without complaint. The best part of the hunt is the hunt, not the discovery, he's explained to Milo many times. Milo doesn't complain, ever, when Andrew takes him on adventures, because it's so much fun, pretending to be someone else for a few hours.

"*Milo.*" Milo whips around at the sound of Andrew's shocked whisper, tangled half into his shirt.

"What, where?" Milo scans the clearing for whatever has scared him. Only Andrew isn't looking around, but at him.

At his back.

"Shit." Milo scrabbles his shirt on. *Shit*, how could he have forgotten?

"What—" Andrew pushes Milo's shirt up. His hands are cold from the water, and his voice is scared when he asks, "What happened?"

WHAT IT TAKES

Milo closes his eyes against the sick feeling in his stomach, pushes Andrew away hard enough that he trips and falls onto his butt and then runs.

o

Of course, he gets lost. These are Andrew's woods; this is the stretch of adventure they brave only with Andrew as head explorer, as the leader of whatever dumb enterprise he's dreamed up that day.

Stupid Andrew and his *stupid* adventures and Milo's stupid, *stupid* willingness to play baby games he knows he's too old for.

He runs until he's out of breath. Off the beach the heat sits wet and heavy, and the woods shift and chirp around him, full of things that creep him out when he's here alone. He has no idea where he is, though, so he sits by a tree and closes his eyes and tries to slow his heart the way he used to when he was very little, closed into his closet, the darkest, safest space he had. He pushes down the fear of being lost, and tries his hardest to forget the look on Andrew's face and the sick feeling in his stomach at knowing he's been found out. He's going to be in so much trouble if Andrew tells. Milo tries so hard to be perfect; tries everything he can think of. The worst is when it's been so long he almost forgets what it's like—when he lets himself believe that he's earned his father's love. It's a long time before he hears Andrew's voice calling for him, distorted through the rustling leaves and singing birds around him. Milo doesn't want to answer, but he'll never find his way out alone.

For one heart-stopping moment, the very idea that maybe he *could* stay here and lose himself forever feels good.

And that scares him more.

"I'm here," he shouts. And then again, hearing Andrew's approach.

o

Milo takes off faster than Andrew can get up. By the time he has his shirt on, he can't hear Milo anymore. He headed east, and so Andrew does too. At first he's not worried; these are his woods; he'd never get lost in them. Milo will, though. He hopes it will only be a matter of time till he finds him. He heads east and tries to imagine what path Milo might take, running in a panic through the woods.

Andrew stops after a bit, closes his eyes and tries to listen for Milo, but finds that his own heart is beating so hard it's pounding in his ears. What he'd seen… that couldn't be an accident, could it? Andrew isn't dumb. There's always been something weird about Milo's family. Teddy even asked him about it once.

"You ever notice that we can never go to Milo's house?"

"Yeah. So?" Andrew said. He had none of Milo's secrets to protect, but knew that Milo did have them. Teddy was cool, but he wasn't Milo's best friend.

"It's just weird. His dad is weird, right? Like super weird. Have you ever met his mom?"

"*God*, Teddy, it's not a conspiracy theory."

Andrew has wondered too, though, and hoped that one day Milo would talk to him about it. But never once in two years has Andrew thought those secrets might be *these* kinds of secrets.

Around him the birds are calling, and he can hear a frog singing somewhere to his left. Milo probably didn't go that way, then. Andrew smooths his shirt; his hands are shaking. He needs to calm down in order to find Milo. Maybe, once he realizes how lost he is, he'll have the good sense to sit down the way Andrew taught him. He seems to have headed deeper into the woods, and not toward Andrew's house.

Andrew finds Milo about half a mile from the pond; he must have been running in a loop without meaning to. Huddled against the trunk of a big maple tree with his arms around his legs, looking into the verdant and shifting hues of the forest, Milo rests with his cheek on one knee. His hair is drying in wild tufts, dark enough to look brown where it's plastered down. Maybe it's the contrast, but it makes the dried clumps look more red than usual. Milo is always pale—more than Andrew at least—but right now he's positively white, making his freckles stand out in sharp contrast.

"Hey," Andrew approaches carefully. He doesn't want Milo to run away, but he has no idea what to do. He's not sure what he saw, but whatever it was, it's the sort of thing grown-ups are supposed to take care of.

As if he's reading Andrew's mind, Milo speaks up. "You *cannot* tell anyone."

"Milo." Andrew kneels in front of him; the sharp poke of twigs and leaves scrape his already scraped knees.

"I know—" Milo looks at him. His eyes are dark and too serious, and Andrew's stomach is doing this flipping thing and he might throw up. "I know this is the kind of thing you think you have to tell someone about. But..." He presses his lips together and looks away. The face he's been making, scary and intense, falls apart as his lips quiver and his dark blue eyes tear up.

Andrew starts to put his hand on Milo's shoulder, then changes his mind and sits next to him and wonders if he should, like, hug him or something.

"It will be so much worse if you tell," Milo says with a cracking voice. "I'll work harder, and it won't happen again. It's not that bad. It's not like that. He'll be so mad if he finds out I told."

"It's not like what? What happened?"

"I don't want to talk about it." Milo averts his face, scrubbing tears off his cheeks on the material of his board shorts, as if he thinks Andrew won't see. Andrew takes a chance and scoots a little closer, until their shoulders are touching.

"Milo," he says, helpless and confused.

Milo leans into him suddenly, shaking a little. "Please don't tell, please, *please.*"

"But if he's hurting you, they'll make him stop."

"*No.* Everyone will believe him; he lies. He's a really good liar. Besides, no one cares when it's like once or twice."

"That's not true," Andrew says.

"This was an accident; there's not going to be any proof."

"We'll take a picture."

"Stop it," Milo says, too loud for the quiet trees around them. "*Shut up,* you don't understand anything!"

Andrew grabs him by the hand when he pushes him away and starts to stand. "No, no, I won't tell, I promise, don't go." He'll think of something, later. When he's not here, with Milo shaking and scared and angry, with no one else to talk to or share his secret with.

Milo stands for a few long seconds, not looking at Andrew, then tugs him up too. "Can we go?"

"Milo," Andrew says, then hesitates. "Can I see?"

"What?" Milo pulls away. "No! Why—?"

"I want to be sure it's okay, it looked—" Andrew swallows. Milo blinks and his eyes are red and his lashes are clumped. Andrew moves around him slowly, then carefully pushes up the hem of his damp shirt. Milo doesn't move. One shocking welt runs from the top of Milo's shoulder blade halfway down his upper back. Andrew doesn't touch it, although he is tempted.

"How much does it hurt?" he whispers.

"Not that much anymore." Milo shrugs his shirt back down and steps away. "It'll be fine in a few days."

"Milo—"

"No. Let's go, I don't wanna say any more."

Andrew wants to press for more—for more what, he has no idea. Something. Something to help, some way to convince Milo it would be okay to get help from a grown-up.

"Fine," Andrew finally says. Milo doesn't move and it takes Andrew a second to realize it's because he's waiting for Andrew to lead them home.

"My house?" he offers, setting off toward the east. He picks the only fix he can think of. "Ice cream?" It's stupid, maybe, but he's a kid. It's pretty much all he has.

"Yeah." Milo smiles. "Totally."

○ ○ ○

HE TRIES. Andrew sits on it and sits on it, but he wants nothing more than to tell his mom, because this secret is way too big for him. When he has Milo over or when they are with friends or in the woods, it's as if he can suddenly really *see* his friend. Milo gets nervous or upset a lot. All the times Andrew has had to talk him into things, he understands now, are because he's afraid.

After a sleepover, when he's tired from staying up late with Milo and Teddy telling ghost stories and playing the newest Zeus and Co. video game, Andrew finally cracks. He's been holding on to it *forever*. It's been two whole weeks; he's too tired to ignore how exhausted Milo has seemed lately, and he just wants to help.

"Mom," he starts, sitting at the breakfast bar and rolling an apple back and forth from hand to hand, not looking at her. "I need to tell you something."

"Confessions?" She smiles. "Let me guess, you guys ate all the candy last night?"

"No." He looks up. Her blonde hair is extra light in the sun, and the knowing smile she gives him makes him feel safe. "I

11

mean, yes, we ate the candy, but that's not what I want to tell you."

She leans onto her elbows on the kitchen counter. "All right. What other trouble did you boys get into?"

Andrew takes a deep breath and fiddles with the stem of his apple until it comes off. "Um, well. I—how do I help...?"

"Help...?" She prompts when he doesn't say anything. He swallows hard and tries not to think about how mad Milo is going to be.

"Mom, I think Milo's dad is um, well. Like, mean."

"Okay." She comes around to sit next to him; her demeanor becomes more serious. She runs a hand through his hair. "Do you mean like he's strict and yells?"

Andrew shakes his head. "No like... hits him? Maybe?" For some reason Andrew thinks if he softens the truth Milo maybe won't be that mad. His mom doesn't say anything, just clears her throat and looks away.

"Did he tell you that, honey?"

Andrew nods, then rethinks it and shrugs. "Well, I saw something, once. Like on his back? But he made me promise not to tell. He said it's only happened a few times."

"Okay. Okay." She takes another breath, then pulls him into a hug. "You did the right thing, telling me."

"He said it will make his dad more mad if people know, and I don't want to—"

"I know, honey." She turns and takes him into her arms. He lets her hug him for longer than usual, and when she runs a hand through his hair he doesn't want to squirm away at all. And he'd never admit it, not when he's almost eleven and too old for this, but he loves the way she smells and how soft she is and how it feels to be hugged like this. He's not sure what she's going to do, but it feels so much better not to be holding this inside and not knowing how to help his friend.

o

Whatever his mom does, Milo is right. It does make things worse. At least that's the last thing Milo says to him—well, yells.

"Why would you do that?" Milo's voice carries, snatched by the wind. Andrew's been out on the beach for an hour, staring morosely at the water. He's been going all the way down to Graylock for days, hoping to run into Milo. Andrew knows Milo rarely comes here, despite it being just south of his house and so much closer than Chickopee and even Pine.

"I didn't know what to do!" Andrew feels miserable and small. Milo hasn't talked to him in a few weeks, and until now he didn't know what happened. All he knows is that after his mom promised to try to take care of it, Milo dropped off the face of the earth. "Can you tell me what happened?"

"It was so *dumb*. This dumbass lady showed up. She asked some questions and did stuff and then it was over. There's nothing for them to do because it *is* nothing!"

"How can you say that?" Andrew can feel his own voice getting louder. He cannot fathom a world where his parents would ever do something like that to him.

"Well, it *wasn't* anything," Milo says acidly.

"Has he done it again? We can tell for sure this time!"

"No, of course not, asshole." Milo has never, ever called Andrew a name. His face is all twisted up, and his eyes are scrunched up and angry. "Why would he do that after some fucking person comes to our house asking about abuse and neglect and—" Milo presses his hands to his eyes. But when he looks at Andrew again, he's not crying. "He's mad. He's really mad, and that's worse. And you won't ever get that. And you won't ever know more because I am never, *ever* trusting you again."

"Milo, no, please. I'm sorry."

"I don't care." Milo walks back toward the parking lot, and doesn't turn around. Andrew wants to follow him, but it will only make things worse.

o o o

MILO DOESN'T speak to Andrew for months after that. And that sucks and Andrew wishes he maybe hadn't told because it didn't help Milo anyway. Milo never talked to him that much about anything else that happened with his father, so Andrew doesn't know how bad things were, or what Milo meant when he said it was worse after he told. He has no way of knowing, now. Constant guilt and fear sit in his stomach, along with the ache of missing his best friend deeply. He still has friends, but no one gets him like Milo.

It's the first day of school after Christmas break when Milo finally talks to him again. They're in the same social studies class and were paired up for a project, so it's not as if Milo actually wants to. Andrew closed his eyes and groaned when Mrs. Kluzinsky read off their names, unsure if he was happy or mad or if he should get his hopes up. For a while after Milo stopped talking to him, Andrew tried to convince himself it was fine, that he didn't *need* Milo and that he didn't care. But that only lasted so long. Andrew isn't stubborn enough to hold onto anger for long, and he's never really been that great at being angry anyway.

He has Milo come to his house, because there is no way he'll go to Milo's, and no way his mom and dad would let him. It's a flat and uncomfortable conversation, with Milo looking anywhere but at him and shrugging it off as though this is the biggest burden ever. But he still agrees to meet Andrew after school.

When he gets to Andrew's house, Milo takes off his shoes and puts them where they go. He's always been welcome here, but once that's done he pauses in the entry instead of thundering up to Andrew's room.

"Um..." Andrew fiddles with his binder, shoving loose papers back in and crumpling them hopelessly. "We can work at the table. My mom is working there too. Or in my room."

Milo's eyes are a little hard, and he looks angry, but he shrugs. "Your room is fine, whatever."

"Want something to drink, or a snack?"

Milo sighs. "No, I want to get this over with already."

Andrew swallows hard and turns without a word to go up the stairs.

They divide their work quickly, splitting the European countries they have to do their report on, then start shuffling through their books. After a while Andrew opens his laptop to search for information on the geography of Italy. The quiet is unnerving and makes him feel twitchy.

"You shouldn't have told," Milo says suddenly. He doesn't yell, but Andrew's never heard someone so angry before.

"I..." Andrew turns to look at him. "I didn't know what to do, and I didn't want him to hurt you anymore."

"Well, I'd tell you if he did, only you can't keep your fucking mouth shut."

Andrews stomach drops. "Is he?"

"Like I'd ever tell you." Milo gets up on his knees and squeezes his pencil so hard it breaks. He looks down in surprise, then throws it. "You said you'd keep it a secret. You're a liar and you suck."

"I'm sorry, I'm sorry," is all he says, because he doesn't know what else to say. Andrew's throat is tight and scratchy. He is sorry because he knows that telling had consequences Milo is paying for, but also selfishly because he misses Milo so much.

15

Andrew would be mortified to play pretend with other friends the way they used to—it's way uncool, but Milo never cared about that. None of his other friends try to draw with him or understand the things Andrew likes to do. No one else would think to memorize the constellations Andrew invents, or pretend along with him that they're maps to navigate by. And he can see how alone Milo has been, because his friends were Andrew's friends and Milo stopped talking to all of them when Andrew told.

"Whatever, it's not like anyone believed you anyway," Milo says.

"Because you lied!"

"What was I supposed to do? My dad said I had to and that if I didn't everything would fall apart and he'd leave us. He was going to leave us with nothing, and then my mom would be all alone. Where would we live?"

"I..." Andrew swallows. "I didn't—" He'd never thought of Milo's mom. He barely knows her actually, only that she's quiet and reserved and stays home all day, which is weird. His stomach turns when he thinks how he would feel if one of his parents decided to leave.

"Yeah well, whatever." Milo begins stuffing his books back into his bag. "I don't care if we fail this, I don't care, *I don't care.*"

"But your grade—" Andrew says. Milo's parents are *really* strict about doing well in school. And now that he knows more, he has an idea that bad grades mean worse things than yelling in his house. Milo's shoulders drop. "Milo..." Andrew kicks the carpet lightly. "What if I promise to keep your secrets?"

"Are you kidding?" Milo's eyebrows rise so high it's almost comical, but there's nothing funny about the disbelief and anger on his face.

"It didn't help, did it? I know that now," Andrew points out. "And we could be friends. You could come here when you need to and not be alone. I know you have been alone. We could do stuff again and have *fun*."

Milo is quiet for a while. "And you'd really promise not to tell this time?"

"Cross my heart."

Milo looks down at where his hands still grip his book bag. He finishes putting his stuff away, more carefully this time. "I don't know. I'll think about it."

"Yeah?" Andrew tries not to smile too wide. It's not a promise, but it gives him hope.

Milo zips up his bag. "But I have to go. Can we do this tomorrow?"

"Sure, yeah." Andrew has his lame piano lessons before dinner, and he reminds Milo, who nods.

"After school then. If we look at our parts tonight, maybe it'll go faster."

"Okay," Andrew says. He stands when Milo does, but Milo gestures with his hand.

"It's fine, I know my way out." He leaves Andrew's door open and clomps down the stairs. Andrew winces when he hears the front door slam. It's not a good sound, but there's a chance it means good things. It may have been months since they've been friends, but Andrew knows Milo's face and he's pretty sure the way Milo's lips relaxed—not in a smile, but also far from the angry lines they had been in—means forgiveness is near.

chapter two

MILO KICKS THE DOOR TO ANDREW'S ROOM OPEN WITHOUT knocking, startling him. "I got the new Timewarp." Andrew throws the magazine he's been flipping through onto the floor and tries to catch the video game Milo tosses at him.

"We have to play," Milo says.

"Milo, you know those aren't really—"

"Yeah, yeah, blood and guts, shut up; we're playing."

"They make me nauseated." It's not just the gore, which Andrew admittedly isn't a fan of, but also because the graphics make him feel carsick. He scans the cover. "Besides, this is rated M. How did you get this past your parents?"

"First," Milo says, counting off his fingers, "Ted got it for me. He has some lame family thing tonight, so you are my victim. Second, we're thirteen, not three; who cares. Third..." Milo plops his bedside trash basket next to him. "Puke in here if you need to. Come on, man, I need something to do."

"All right." Andrew pulls out the controls to his console and flips his TV to the right channel. There's an edge to Milo's voice and his shoulders are tense the way he gets when something is up at home. There's not much Andrew wouldn't do to give Milo what he needs when he gets like this.

"Compromise," Milo says, settling against the headboard of Andrew's bed next to him. Andrew's skin heats up and he tries his best to ignore it. "We'll play for a while, then we can do something you want."

"Build pillow forts and paint our nails?" Andrew jokes. Milo smirks at him. It's unspoken that Andrew wouldn't really mind a good game of play pretend.

"Shut up and try to keep up, son," Andrew says, button-smashing the crap out of his controller, taking down zombies as if he's actually got skills. It makes Milo crazy that Andrew manages to button-smash bullshit his way through games.

It takes half an hour for Andrew to start feeling sick, which fortunately coincides with a short fuse on Milo's part. After being soundly killed by zombie forces—again—he throws his controller to the foot of the bed and flops down, moaning.

"Oh thank god." Andrew puts his own controller down and rubs his eyes. Milo rolls off the bed gracelessly.

"I'm hungry, wanna—" Milo picks up the magazine Andrew dropped earlier. "Is this—"

"Oh shit!" Andrew snatches it back and covers his face, which is flaming red; he really thinks he might puke now. He scrambles off the bed and trips over the garbage can.

"Oh, this totally explains that," Milo says at the spill of tissues, winking at Andrew, then pretends to flip through the magazine. "Oh, Freddie, you are *so dreamy.*"

"*Stop.*" Andrew feels as if he's about to cry, which would be the absolute worst reaction right now. "Listen, just go, get out."

"Oh hey." Milo's face sobers. "No, come on, I'm kidding around."

Andrew looks away. "Go."

"No, no." Milo climbs over the bed and tugs Andrew's hands from his face. "Dude, it's like, it's not like I didn't think—"

"What—"

"Well, you're kind of obvious, sometimes."

"*What?!*"

"I mean to me, because I know you." Milo explains. "Hey, *whoa*, just like, breathe."

"I—" Andrew realizes he's almost hyperventilating. "I wasn't expecting—"

Milo looks him in the eye steadily. "Okay, let's calm down. Take a deep breath."

"Stop stealing my mojo," Andrew jokes, because this is totally the thing *he* usually does: calm Milo down. But he does what Milo says and takes a deep breath and then another. He shifts away.

"You better? You look like you might hurl."

Andrew nods, sits back and crosses his legs, and Milo does the same so they're facing each other.

After a long minute of averted eye contact and smothering silence, Andrew says, "You're going to stop being my friend now, aren't you?"

"What? Shut up, no." Milo's voice is certain and strong. Andrew closes his eyes and takes a shuddering breath and wonders.

"Why not? Isn't this—don't you think I'm some sort of freak or gross or something?" Andrew's not stupid and neither is Milo. They both know the slurs that get tossed around when they're playing ball with their friends or on teams where any sign of weakness or ineptitude will get you called a fag or a pussy or homo. Now that they've outgrown the gray area of hugs, if affection is given it has to be followed by the saving grace of a "no homo" moment.

"Drew, really, it's not surprising," Milo says. "And..."

"And?"

"You're my best friend. You've been my best friend forever. Nothing's gonna change that."

Andrew bites his lip because he really thinks he might cry now, and it's not from fear like before, but because for a small, blinding moment he loves Milo so much. It feels strange, though—different—more than gratitude and care and understanding and the safety of knowing another person so well. He wants to hug him and cry, which, despite Milo apparently being okay with things, might actually get him a "no homo."

"Okay," Andrew says, barely managing to keep his voice from catching.

"Oh, come here, you asshole." Milo tugs him forward in a hug that Andrew sinks into, relieved beyond bearing. "Let's get some ice cream and set off on some really stupid adventure."

"Keep wording it like you're doing it for my sake, and maybe one day you'll believe you're not the total dweeb here."

Milo snorts and gets up, then opens the door for Andrew. Ice cream beckons.

o

"So, do your parents know?" Milo is tossing Cheezits into the air and trying to catch them in his mouth. He only seems to be achieving a fifty percent success rate, which means there are crumbs and Cheezits everywhere. The lack of ice cream in his house—shocking really—was quickly remedied with a box of crackers Andrew found stashed in the cereal cupboard. It's a poor substitute, but Andrew is working with what he has.

"No. Well, I don't know." Andrew shrugs and, like a civilized person, eats some Cheezits by putting them directly into his mouth. "Do you think I need to?"

"I don't know?" Milo shrugs. "I don't know the rules for this. Only if you want to." He bumps his shoulder against Andrew's.

"Do what you want when you think it's the right time? Your parents are cool; I'm pretty sure it'll be okay."

"Damn what have you been reading? Grown-up shrink books?"

"Yes," Milo deadpans. A Cheezit takes a bad bounce and hits Andrew on the cheek. "Better than gazing adoringly at Freddie McKay."

"Shut up." Andrew smiles though and feels it all the way in his bones. He tells himself he's smart enough to know that's not a crush sort of feeling.

○ ○ ○

UNFORTUNATELY FOR Andrew, that love thing stays, despite his best intentions. Part of it is the realization that, as they get older, Milo is definitely going to be hot. He's sort of hot right now and he's only started to grow. In the last year he's magically shot up, surpassing Andrew's height by at least three inches. His hair admittedly needs a little work, with the way he wears it flopping around and too long, thick and with the slightest curl, but that's totally acceptable considering the color, which is a deep auburn Andrew is obsessed with. But not as obsessed as he is with Milo's eyes. Andrew tries not to be totally obvious about how often he tries to sneak looks at Milo, because he doesn't want to be a creeper or scare Milo away, but still, most of the time his eyes are really deep blue, like the water when it's overcast but not too dark. You really have to look to see the blue. Andrew loves that.

But more than anything it's *Milo* himself whom Andrew likes. Some of his feelings are the same as they've always been— wanting to help him, protect him from everything in his life that's hurting him. Andrew loves that he's Milo's *person*, the person who knows him best. Milo lets Andrew see him at his most vulnerable.

It's the *worst*. It's horrible and unfair and not right because Milo is straight and his best friend, and being in love is *awful*; it feels as if he can't breathe when Milo smiles his brightest *Andrew only* smile, and when Milo laughs Andrew's stomach turns funny but *good*. But it's not good; there's no chance Milo will ever feel the same. Being in love is one thing, and maybe he could deal with it, but the worst part is all the other things Milo makes him feel: tingling and too hot in his body and completely out of control. Morning after morning he wakes up from dreams about Milo, embarrassed and wondering if he can get away with changing his sheets and washing them several times a week without drawing suspicion from his parents.

o

"Drew." As soon as he walks in the door Milo shuts off Andrew's iPod where it's perched on the speaker dock. "What is with you? All you do lately is sit in here listening to emo music with the blinds closed."

"I like it," Andrew says.

"Well, you're turning into a hermit, you look like you haven't seen the sun in days, and you're being boring. Let's go do something. Bike down to Spikes. Play ball, go swimming."

"No."

"Yes." Milo starts to pull Andrew out of his bed.

"Milo, I suck at all of those things."

"Well, you're never going to get better at anything other than lying around being dramatic about whatever it is you're being dramatic about if you don't get out of here. You aren't bad at swimming. You're being a lump."

"Ugh." Andrew looks down at his clothes. They're comfortable but gross, because he's been in them since the afternoon before. "I have to change. Go downstairs or something?"

"What, you're suddenly shy?" Milo teases.

"Shut up and get out," Andrew says, trying for a joking tone. There is no way he's going to let Milo sit around while he gets sort of naked, not with his too skinny and not-right body.

"You're so weird. You're getting weirder." Milo laughs and slams the door behind him.

Andrew gives the shut door the middle finger, as if that will help, and then flips hopelessly through his minimal and depressingly similar clothing choices. He checks the weather on his phone—not warm enough for shorts. He pulls out a maroon and white striped shirt that he hopes won't scream *gaygaygay,* because other than Milo and his parents no one knows, and he's happy with that for now.

o

Milo settles in to wait at the kitchen counter, pilfered apple in hand. Something about the crunching noise in the soothing silence and familiarity of Andrew's place is comforting. It's often quiet at his own house, but it always seems like an unfinished silence, menacing. Sometimes Milo prefers his father's anger, and the fighting and turmoil, over the silence, because he knows what's happening. It's the waiting that kills him, the anxiety of waiting for the other shoe to drop.

"All right, whatever, let's go." Andrew stomps into the kitchen. Well, as much as a tiny person who weighs nothing soaking wet can stomp. It's cute. Milo winces internally, then turns away and swallows his last bite of apple, which feels stuck in his throat.

"Go where?" he manages to ask.

"I don't know." Andrew throws his hands up, then starts poking around in the snack cupboard his mom keeps stocked.

He grabs a granola bar and tears into it. "This is your idea. You tell me."

"You are so dramatic. You should join drama club this year."

"Eww," Andrew says around a mouthful of chocolate chips and granola.

"Well, you don't like anything lately. You're not dressed for swimming. Let's ride up to Spikes and play pinball."

"I thought you wanted me to get sun?" Andrew says.

"This isn't an evil plan or anything. You'll get sun on the way; I biked over. You'll get to destroy me at arcade games. It's a win all around."

"Well," Andrew tosses the wrapper into the pull-out garbage can. "Okay. I could go for that."

"Sweet."

○

Because everything in his life is a competition, Milo always pushes his own limits. Usually he would try to bike into town as fast as possible, but Andrew is not like that, and Milo doesn't want to hurt his feelings. Milo keeps pace with him as they head east into town, trying to take in their surroundings in a way he usually doesn't. He remembers hating this place, and although his bitterness has abated, he'll never love Santuit. Other than Andrew and Ted and Sarah and their families, there's nothing here that makes him want to stay. He can't wait until he can grow up and escape. Once he's old enough, he'll never have to talk to his father again. He'll never have to endure this place, where too many people know his secrets. Where what happens in their home—even if people don't know everything—is a secret the town keeps without speaking in anything more than pitying glances and whispers when his back is turned.

College is a lifetime away, and thinking about it makes him feel twisty and hopeless, so he avoids it. The truth is, although it's annoyingly dramatic, he understands Andrew's urge to hole up and get away from everything. He has no idea why Andrew is being like this—maybe he's working on the whole coming out thing—but Milo resents it, because Andrew's pulled away from him, though Milo totally told him he was okay with everything and he *is*.

But he has Andrew outside now; he is laughing because a gust of wind has almost blown him over. The sun is brilliant today, and Milo knows if they go down to the beach it will be dazzling over the water. But the beach is where he goes to escape; it's his temporary runaway place, and that's not what he wants now. So he laughs at Andrew and squints his eyes and throws his arms out to the side, showing off his skills.

o

Andrew does kick his ass at Star Wars pinball, and when Ted comes, it's a slaughter so pathetic they don't speak of it. It makes Milo happy to see Andrew happy and doing things, but also rubs him the wrong way because Milo always wants to be the best at everything.

"I'm starving." Andrew bumps Milo away from the claw machine he's been fucking around with. He doesn't want anything, but he wants to grab a prize because no one ever wins with this machine.

"What do you want?" Milo says, still distracted.

"Food," Andrew says.

"No joke." Milo turns away from the machine. "You're always hungry. Where does it all go? How are you not getting fat, lying around all day stuffing your face?"

"I doubt I'll ever be fat." Andrew is usually self-conscious about how skinny he is, but he soldiers on with an only slightly strained smile. "But hopefully it will go to the magical growth-spurt machine you are hogging."

Milo's new height advantage is totally cool because he's always been the shorter one. Andrew doesn't seem in danger of being short. He's always been really skinny; they're all growing, but with Andrew it's kind of like he's being stretched.

"Good luck with that one," Ted chimes in. Like Milo, he's shot up recently too, leaving Andrew behind in a genetic race for height. They might both be brown-haired and brown-eyed, but Andrew's hair naturally highlights and his eyes are lighter and much more expressive. Ted's a really chill guy who doesn't care about such things; he saves his energy for mischief he ropes them all into. He's focusing on a racing game, throwing his weight behind a sticking wheel in a booth too small for him.

"Shut up. Let's get some burgers." Andrew grabs Milo's hand to pull him toward the restaurant portion of the arcade, then drops it quickly with an apology, flustered and blushing. "So sorry, I, I didn't... sorry."

"Chill, it's cool," Milo says. Andrew looks away and walks ahead of him. It's not as if Milo cares, because he's thought Andrew might be gay for, like, ages now. Milo's used to the idea and he doesn't care and a part of him likes the familiarity they've had with each other. Yeah, maybe it's uncool and the other kids will make fun of them. But they're not here and every kid who uses the word fag as if it's funny can fuck off, because he doesn't want anyone to make Andrew feel bad, *ever*. He has to be careful, though, because word getting around that he's holding hands with Andrew would be a thing that his father might actually kill him over.

o

They're in the woods one day in July when they come into a small clearing. Milo has been keeping complaints about the humidity and bugs to himself. He wants to hang out with Andrew and if this is the best he can get, he'll take it. Andrew comes alive when they're out here, which is awesome. God knows Milo could use some happiness too.

"You good?" Andrew asks. He looks around the clearing, then sits carefully on what's left of a fallen tree. Milo kicks at a tuft of grass.

"I'm fine."

"Milo," Andrew says in that voice he gets, the one that's knowing and superior.

"I'm *fine*. Looking forward to school. Less time at home, you know? It's close but not close enough, and it's making me crazy."

Andrew looks at him for a long moment, then away. His eyes explore the fringe of woods, and the scraggly wildflowers in the sunlight. "We should build something out here."

"Huh?" Milo gives up and stands next to him. A line of sweat slides down his temple, and he wipes it away.

"Like a fort?" Andrew shoots him a shy and hopeful look. Milo resists the urge to point out that they aren't kids anymore and that they're too old for that kind of play, because he doesn't want to hurt Andrew's feelings. "I know it's lame. But come on, it'll be fun!"

"How will we do that? We need wood and supplies and, like, to know how to build stuff."

"We'll figure it out." Andrew's face brightens; Milo is terrible at resisting this sort of persuasion. "And then we'll have a place no one knows about. It'll be our thing." Andrew looks away then and shrugs. "That sounded wrong. I didn't mean—"

"No! No, that's cool." The thought of a secret place is appealing. If they do this, it'll be somewhere Milo can go when everyone is busy and he can't go to their houses. Plus, the thought of planning something to build is exciting. "So we'll need a plan."

"Blah," Andrew complains. He starts circling the clearing.

"How do you plan to accomplish this without—"

"A plan? I'm kidding. Come on, let's find a spot. We can go home and make the best plan ever and it'll be like a little wet dream for you."

Milo blushes and laughs and only looks away for a second before looking for an ideal spot.

о

The fort takes longer to build than Andrew anticipated. The wood was expensive, and they had to figure out how to pay for it, and also, come on, they aren't master builders yet. Despite all of Milo's drawn plans—the first drafts roughly scratched into dirt, then, as they sat on the beach, into shifting sands that proved to be a terrible sketch pad, and finally on paper—the process was a whole lot of trial and error.

"It's not all that big," Milo says when they're finally, for the first time, seated inside their little creation.

"It's fine." Andrew is unpacking a cooler of snacks and pop he brought for the occasion.

Milo inspects their handiwork. "There's a huge gap over here."

"Oh my god, Mr. Perfection, enjoy the moment." Andrew kicks him in the ankle.

"No wait, there's an exposed nail; let me find the hammer—"

"Milo," Andrew says in his most stern voice, which isn't that stern at all when it cracks. He clears his throat. "Shut up, sit down and drink your Coke. We can fix that later."

Milo sighs and sits down. Andrew can tell he's working very hard not to examine the fort for more flaws.

"We'll be here again, you know," Andrew says. "We have time to fix things up if we want. For now, it's mostly done; it's awesome. *We're* awesome."

"Yeah. True." Milo smiles; his hair is a shaggy mess and his face is spotted with pimples that have come and gone as they've started to hit puberty. His shirt is dirty, they're both sweating

29

and it's sweltering in the fort—even though it's in the shade, the heat of their bodies in the confined space is driving the temperature up to uncomfortable. Milo is right—it is small, and being so close to Milo makes a completely different heat suffuse his body. It's confusing and new and unwelcome, and, if he doesn't distract himself immediately, will be very obvious.

Andrew distracts himself by looking over their creation. The wooden floor is rough enough to need more sanding. The walls are made of mismatched wooden boards—some bought and some scavenged—that don't fit together perfectly, especially around the small window and door. One day, when it's not about a billion degrees, Andrew wants to paint the walls inside. Milo looks up to examine the roof while they finish lunch, and Andrew contemplates whether making some sort of sign outside the fort would be too childish.

It's far from perfect, but still, for that moment, Andrew can't imagine that he's ever been happier.

chapter Three

JUNIOR YEAR OF HIGH SCHOOL IS THE WORST YEAR OF MILO'S life to date. Between balancing swim team, National Honor Society, the volunteer hours he has to do and his grades in AP classes, Milo is always strained and overwhelmed. Disappointment and anger sit like a constant, suffocating blanket over his home.

Two weeks into his fall semester, Milo comes home to a pile of messy papers from his room on the kitchen table. The house is dead quiet, silence so menacing Milo has to swallow down rising nausea.

His room is turned upside down. His mattress is flipped off the bed. Every drawer in his dresser has been removed and emptied.

Privacy in his home is an illusion; there is always the threat that his father might decide to search his room. He is required to turn in homework and assignments randomly when asked, so his father can keep tabs on his progress.

But this—this is new. There's not a clue in the house, no squeaking floorboard or the ping of a phone chiming. He has no idea if anyone is home. But a cold sweat dews, and his heart

31

begins to race. Panic nips at his heels, ugly and familiar but monstrous, as he struggles to think of what might have set this off, if he left anything incriminating in his room.

He can't think of anything though, and that's the worst.

There are no instructions in his room. Down at the table, he finds leftover assignments, papers he turned in, notes from friends at school, all piled up. Milo doesn't dare read the notes; he knows his shaking hands would find some conversation or joke he's going to pay for. There are no instructions in the kitchen either. No one is home, there's no one to tell him what to do, or how to beg to make it well. Any course of action he can think of carries the weight of repercussion, because it won't be the right one. Nothing he does now is going to be right.

So he sits. He sits at the kitchen table and waits. The shadows grow long, and after a while he silences his phone so Andrew's texts stop interrupting the punishment he's taking right now—a sentence of anxiety and fear and anticipation.

His father comes home late from work and deposits his briefcase by the door. He takes off his shoes and carries them in and up to his room, walking past Milo without speaking a word. The sun is setting, and the room has grown very dim, but he doesn't dare turn up the lights.

When his father finally comes back, the first thing he does is get a garbage bag from under the sink. He snaps it open and holds it next to the table.

"Am I supposed to throw this away?" Milo fidgets. He's scared of speaking, but holding his tongue when he's meant to reply is just as bad.

"Read them all. Every grade and every note."

John Graham is an imposing man, over six feet tall and well built. A life of leadership in the communities they've lived in have taught him how to project. When he speaks, people listen. His eyes, a lighter version of Milo's, are incredibly changeable.

Milo has seen him use them to charm and disarm people. His father is good at manipulating people and knows how to change his expression to fit each situation.

At home, he doesn't need to change anything. Here, he's himself first; the look in his eyes, steel and disappointment, is as natural as his breath.

Milo swallows and forces himself to maintain eye contact as long as he can. The last thing he wants to do now is to show his father his fear or any weakness. He can't help that he's flushed, because his coloring always gives him away, but he'll be damned if he'll let his hands or his voice shake. He knows that for every poor grade and every conversation deemed inappropriate, he'll be punished. The least he can do is take it like a man.

o

He can't tell if his father has become harder over the years, or if his expectations are more demanding, or if it's just that Milo can grasp how awful his home life is in a different way because he's older, but everything feels like too much, all the time. Some days he wakes up feeling as though he can't breathe, days when his heart hurts from beating so hard, days when it's almost impossible to get out of bed.

The free time he does get, scant as it is, he tries to spend at Andrew's house. Andrew's family knows that Milo's home life sucks. His parents are kind and make room for him every way they can. But as things escalate in his house, and as his father becomes rougher, Milo finds himself keeping secrets from Andrew again. When he was a kid, his father rarely bruised him; his words and anger and booming voice and threats had been too much and enough to keep both Milo and his mother cowed. Sometimes now he has bruises from his father grabbing his arms, and a couple of times he's been slapped, but that doesn't leave marks.

What he can't hide is his fear, the overwhelming anxiety that comes over him—not from Andrew, because it always hits him when he's with Andrew. Andrew says he thinks it's because Milo feels safe with him. All Milo knows is that after it happens; when his breath comes so short it feels like his heart will come out of his chest, when his vision goes dark with panic, he feels weak and embarrassed.

One day Andrew pulls him into his closet and closes the door, so that his voice is the only thing guiding Milo through breathing and calming, and eventually crawls out to get Milo tissues. Milo cries into his own arms, folded up on his knees, shaking and wishing the floor would swallow him for being so childish and fucked up. Andrew is always the calm in the storm, and when Milo needs it, he always puts his arms around him or lets Milo lean against him, and never complains about the time he takes up when Andrew surely has better things to do.

"I used to do this when I was little," Milo says. It's dark and Andrew's body is warm—too warm. He's sweating in the closet because of the stifling air and the heat of his own breakdown seeping through his skin. But it's good.

"I remember; you told me once," Andrew whispers. Milo cries, silently, and shakes with his face buried against Andrew's shoulder. Andrew's all bony angles and smaller than Milo, but makes room for him anyway.

They never talk about how bad things are getting, partly because they both know it's hopeless to think there is help other than Milo getting away in two years when he goes to college.

o

"You haven't complained about this in, like, thirty whole minutes," Milo says one afternoon. "Are you gonna puke? You'll waste away."

"Oh, look, a comedian gracing my presence." Andrew punches Milo's arm lightly.

"You both need to shut up and focus," Ted says. He's using his whole body, moving the controller and his arms and torso as he navigates the game they're playing. Milo's naturally competitive nature kicks in and he turns back to the game. Andrew holds on as long as he can before throwing the controller down.

"Weak man," Ted says. His eyes never leave the screen.

"Whatever." Andrew closes his eyes. "Do you guys wanna go out? Movies? Coffee?"

Ted swears when he dies again.

"But this is a tournament!" Milo says. "We can't walk away."

"Well," Ted says as he hits the pause button, "we are getting our asses kicked."

"Fuck." Milo puts down his own controller. "Maybe Andrew has a point."

Andrew's already texting and checking times on his phone. "Sarah wants to come, and Lindsey."

Ted moans. "Oh god, not Lindsey."

"You totally want to get into her pants," Milo says. "You can't pretend you don't."

"No," Ted says. He shudders. "She's so annoying."

"But you think she's hot, right?" Andrew says, raising an eyebrow and sharing a look with Milo.

"What movie do they want to see?" Ted stands, changing the subject effectively, but Andrew doesn't miss the way he blushes. Sometimes he's grateful that his skin is not nearly as fair as his friends', because blushing rarely gives him away.

o

They end up watching the sort of slapstick comedy Andrew cannot stand. Thankfully, he's next to Milo, who also hates this kind of crap. Majority rules have forced them here. They banter

35

in whispers, commenting on the clothes, the awkwardness of cheap jokes and poorly choreographed physical comedy. More than once they're shushed by other audience members. When a guy, obviously on a date, turns around and tells them to shut the fuck up, Milo sinks down in his seat, shaking with laughter. It sets Andrew off, who is susceptible to the giggles.

"What does he care?" Milo leans in to whisper in Andrew's ear, setting off a cascade of delicious, nervy shivers. "He's totally going in for the super awkward, probably sweaty hand hold."

Andrew leans forward and peeks. He looks over and, in the bright wash of the screen light, half smiles in agreement. Milo's lips are full and tempting and completely off limits. It's very, very hard not to imagine him brushing them against Andrew's neck. He gulps down a breath and leans into Milo's space. If he inhales again to catch Milo's scent, he really can't be blamed. He hopes it's subtle.

"What would you know? Whose hand have you been holding?" Milo smiles, but it's a little weird. Andrew's wondered about him recently, because Milo never says *anything* about girls or crushes or wanting.

They all eat at a diner after the movie. Sarah's dressed normally—just jeans and a shirt that would work anywhere. She's the kind of classic-pretty with sleek brown hair and beautiful clear skin that doesn't need extra work. Lindsey, on the other hand, tries. She tries very hard. She's dressed up more than any of them, wearing a glittery, slithery tank top that dips a little too low. She reapplies her lipstick while they wait to be seated, and Andrew wonders if that kind of thing works on Ted. Ted's hardly said a word to her all night, but that hasn't stopped him from looking.

At dinner Milo cracks jokes the whole time, poking fun at the movie and actors. He's in a rare carefree mood, and when he's on like this, he's witty and easily funny. Sarah, a notorious food thief, tries to snatch fries from everyone's plates when they're distracted, and when Milo catches her, he swiftly smacks her hand away with a fork. Everyone bursts into loud laughter, drawing attention from other patrons. The line cook, visible behind the counter along the left wall of the diner, shrugs at a couple seated on stools. Andrew loves their town, where people know them and make room for rowdy teenagers.

"Okay, okay," Sarah says, wiping her hand and still laughing. "Ted'll share."

"Maybe Lindsey—"

"No, shhhh," Andrew interrupts Milo in a stage whisper, "don't ruin the romance."

"Oh, fuck off," Ted says over the giddy laughter of the table. He balls up his napkin and throws it at Andrew, but it sails over his head and onto the booth behind them. Next to him, Milo laughs. His hair is a mess, the way it gets by nighttime, after hours of Milo running his hands through it and tugging on it. His freckles are faded as fall has eclipsed the bright rays of summer. When he turns to Andrew, his smile is bright in a way that's very rare, and this moment of happiness settles into Andrew's heart with a strong, cramping, longing weight. He wants this boy, but more, he wants this, to see his face creased with youth and happiness.

o

One Tuesday, mid-November, Milo comes home unusually wrung out from swim practice. All he can think about is how hungry he is, and his guard is completely down. His father is at the kitchen table with a stack of papers while his mother hovers at the stove. Whatever she's making smells so amazing that he misses the lines of worry around her pursed lips and her posture of anxiety: shoulders drawn up and back ramrod straight.

Jude Sierra

It's been well over a month since he's done anything wrong—long enough that he's stopped tiptoeing around, relaxing carelessly into the calm before a storm he should have sensed gearing up. Being caught defenseless and off guard makes everything worse.

"Are you prepared to explain yourself?" James speaks in the cold, controlled tone Milo knows means trouble. He has a split second to cast back for what he could have done today, before his father's fist hits the table with a thump that rattles the matched set of salt and pepper shakers Milo's always thought are hideous.

His father holds up the papers. Though they're almost the same height, he looms menacingly, always bigger in Milo's mind than he really is. His father stops shaking the papers long enough for Milo to see what they are: the history exam he hid in his room. How turned over is his room this time? He has to stop fooling himself into thinking he can hide things there.

"I promise to work harder," Milo says, automatic words he doesn't have to struggle for.

"That's what you always say," his father counters, sneering so his lips peel back. The papers scatter on the floor. Milo's body goes cold, the way it does when he's blessedly shutting down, when he's suddenly not present in his body. It's a thing that has started happening in the last year. He doesn't do it on purpose, doesn't know how it happens. Sometimes it doesn't happen at all and those times are the worst, because there is nothing to protect him then.

After, Milo doesn't remember what was said next. What he does remember is how it felt to come back to his numb body with a jolt; the throbbing sting where his father's big palm slapped him is all the more painful for its unexpectedness.

He doesn't tell Andrew about that. He doesn't call him that night, but texts, managing to fake a light tone that won't tip

Andrew off. After his father retreats to his study to make phone calls, his mother brings him an ice pack. She kisses him with regret and apology deep in her eyes. Milo closes his eyes and swallows his anger, because the most she can protect him from is developing marks that will show.

○   ○   ○

By Friday Milo has managed make what happened into a distant memory. His face didn't bruise, and after a day his father's tightlipped anger faded a little. But after being given notice of an exam Monday in his pre-calculus class, he follows Andrew home to study, cracks open his textbook and, out of nowhere, begins to hyperventilate.

"Hey, hey." Andrew's voice pulls him back. "Here, squeeze." He picks up Milo's hand, and that's both grounding and soothing. Milo closes his eyes, but when he does, he sees his father's face, and he feels the fear he feels every day when coming home. He's breathing so fast he's starting to feel lightheaded.

"Come here." Andrew pulls him up, shoves aside hanging clothes and closes them into the quiet dark of his closet. There's room on the floor; Andrew's taken to keeping it clear so that they have comfortable space. Andrew keeps coaching Milo to breathe slowly and calmly. He squeezes Milo's hand very gently and keeps his tone soothing. It takes a while, but Milo finds himself squeezing back and breathing the way Andrew coaches him.

"Fuck," he says after a while. "God, this is so lame."

"Milo, it's fine," Andrew says, his hand still around his. Milo's not gripping it anymore, but he hasn't let go. Even with it, he feels lost, without moorings. Andrew is cross-legged in front of him and he scoots next to him and tucks his face into Andrew's neck. Andrew always smells the same: clean and light and familiar.

Although Milo is much wider through the shoulders—almost too wide for Andrew to hug him at this angle—Andrew pulls him closer and combs his fingers through Milo's hair. Milo smiles against Andrew's skin.

"God, you're obsessed with my hair."

"It's great hair," Andrew replies easily. "If only you'd let me do it for you..."

"Good luck with that."

Andrew tugs lightly at his hair and Milo sighs into the touch "Eh, a boy can dream."

Milo laughs lightly and keeps his eyes closed and tries not to feel anything, because everything is really close to the surface and it's huge and crazy and too much, even Andrew holding him. He pulls away and looks right into his eyes, because he owes him at least this.

"Thank you."

"Dork," Andrew says, something fond and sweet sweeping across his features. "Anytime. That's what friends are for, right?"

"You know..." Milo swallows and smiles. "I kind of love you."

There's a hanging pause, loaded and heavy. Andrew's eyes widen and then, suddenly, he's kissing Milo. *Kissing.* Milo's shocked enough that his head tilts instinctively. Andrew's fingers are still in his hair; Andrew's mouth is on his and his breath and lips are too much. He gasps in a breath, then... well, he's not sure. Not sure how he goes from shock and panic to kissing back. The kiss is tentative and scared until, in the space of one tiny moment, it increases in confidence; both of their mouths open by fractions and Andrew's hand comes up to cup Milo's check. They stay like this for a long minute, barely breathing and kissing with the newness of youth. But then Andrew moves, deepening the kiss, and panic and confusion surge through Milo's body.

o

Andrew has energy that naturally calms Milo. Maybe it's just the ease of growing up together over the last eight years. In his presence, everything feels right. Milo can be just himself. Milo knows Andrew loves him, just as he loves Andrew.

Except maybe not the same way.

That's the most coherent explanation Milo can land on, once he's in his room, sitting on the edge of his bed, white knuckles gripping the edge of the mattress. His heart is still racing—mostly because he ran home, but also because *holy fuck, what the fucking fuck?*

God, he just ran away. Didn't say a word. He fucked up, big time.

He kissed Andrew *back*. For this one crystal-bright moment, Andrew's lips weren't a surprise, but a revelation, soft and full and sweet. And when he kissed back, Milo let his lips open a little, felt the brush of Andrew's tongue. One of them inhaled, sharp and shocked, and when Andrew surged into the kiss, Milo broke away and covered his lips with a hand and gasped out a broken *I'm sorry* while stumbling away from him with coltish jerks and averted eyes.

The *I'm sorry* was like a slap that slammed Milo's whole body into a too aware and terrified state. So of course he did what any dumbstruck, completely blindsided teenager would do.

He ran away.

I kind of love you, Milo remembers saying. And then Andrew kissed him. *What the fucking fuck?*

Milo groans and flops over on his bed, covering his face with his pillow. What is he supposed to do with this? How is he supposed to face Andrew? Is Andrew like... in love with him? Was that kiss completely random, or some sort of experiment? Why did he like it so much? It felt nice—well, better than nice—but it was *Andrew*. No. Just...no.

o

Andrew hides in his bedroom for as long as humanly possible. He turned off his phone and washed his face and then showered and changed his clothes, as if any of that could possibly erase the whole afternoon. Now he's huddled under the covers watching reruns of *Cara Says*, trying to forget.

He's divided, deep inside: one part of him lingers on the shape and texture of Milo's lips. For more than three years he's wished in wistful longing to kiss Milo. He knew it would never happen though. Just because Andrew is a dreamer doesn't mean he's stupid. He has no idea at all what possessed him to kiss his best friend while he was in the midst of a breakdown. In his *closet*, which is a hideous and hilarious irony.

Here the other half of him jumps in, over and over, a cacophonous force roiling with anger because *why?* Life without Milo would be incredibly bleak. Perhaps if Andrew had never met him things would be different. But somehow, loving Milo— caring for him, entertaining him, laughing hysterically at his jokes—is the center of his world. Milo easily takes Andrew's playful whims and makes them real, like the amazing fort they built near their pond in the clearing, a secret hideout they've taken advantage of so often. From the outside, it's always looked like a tree house sitting on the ground. Inside, it's Andrew's expressive playground, a place where he can draw and paint and decorate over and over.

Only Milo understands how much Andrew needs secret outlets. And yet Milo underestimates how important he is to Andrew. So often when he's coming down from a panic attack or has escaped his home to just be in a calmer place, he apologizes profusely. Nothing between them is unbalanced, not to Andrew, despite the knowledge that he's been in love, hopelessly, for a long time.

Well... until he lost his mind and stupidly kissed Milo.

o

I... don't know how to Doris, Andrew texts late that night. It's too late, but he can't sleep for thinking and rethinking and agonizing over how on earth he is supposed to fix this. Texting seemed the easiest way to reach out. Andrew frowns when he notices the typo.

Do this, I mean, he texts, mentally facepalming. *Autocorrect wins again.*

As always, Milo replies instantly.

This is good, right? Easy banter. The usual kind. As if it never happened. Maybe it's an out. Maybe it's Milo saying they don't ever have to talk about it.

The thing is, Andrew doesn't want to cop out. He's not ready to confess that he's maybe been in love with Milo for years, because that would make things weird, and he's definitely not taking the risk of ruining their friendship over a one-sided crush, even if it's more than a crush. He's gay, and Milo is... Milo. Truth is, he has no idea. They've never talked about Milo's sexuality, and Andrew had never questioned it, but then there's *the thing.*

The kiss back.

Andrew, in re-reel number seventy-five, finally remembered that Milo pressed in, opened his lips and kissed him back before he pulled away. What was that about?

So but seriously, Andrew finally types, *we should talk about this.*

He's met with silence, which is torture.

At least to agree to never speak of it again, if that's what's best.

Still nothing.

Please promise we're okay, or that we can be?

Andrew's stomach tightens as the silence plays out. He pulls his covers over his head, lays the silent phone on the pillow next to his head. The little cocoon he's made is sweltering and suffocating. When the phone finally chimes, he flips the covers off and gasps in cold air.

Sorry, Dad got up, room checked. I had to pretend to be asleep.
Everything okay? Andrew asks.
Yeah, he thought I was up. I should be careful though.

Andrew tries to formulate another text, fishing for an out or an okay. Milo texts again before he can.

Listen. We're still best friends, nothing will change that.

Oh thank god. His relief is huge, exhaled in one gust, leaving him limp. *Go to sleep, don't get in trouble. I'll see you tomorrow?*

Absolutely. Wanna meet at the fort after breakfast? Ten?

Andrew sighs. *Milo it's Saturday, that's torture.*

You'll survive. Plus Ted wants to have that movie/game marathon later, so we should hang out before that.

Oh crap, I forgot, Andrew texts. He's getting sleepy. Now that he has Milo's assurance that everything will be fine, all the adrenaline has seeped away, leaving him a wrung out mess. *All right, ten it is. Bring food, I'll bring drinks.*

Aye aye cap'n.

o

Phone still in hand, Milo wakes up at six from a deep, dreamless sleep, he'd fallen into like a stone. He surfaces grateful for the calm, forgetful dark of such rest.

Milo untwists his shirt from his torso, kicks off his too hot covers, then plugs his phone in. When the text screen pops up with the history of their texts from the night before, he groans. What's he going to do? What is he going to say? He needs to find a way to assure Andrew—who is probably freaking the fuck out—while finding a way to navigate this situation. He doesn't want to think of it as letting him down gently, but the truth is that's what it amounts to. Assuming Andrew wants—well, he shouldn't assume that. He can't assume anything, other than that it happened and it seems neither of them saw it coming.

"Milo, you'd better be up," his father's voice comes through the door, making Milo jolt. He looks at the clock: six-thirty. Fuck, he's running late.

"I am; I'm almost ready," he calls. His swim bag is already packed, so all he has to do is throw on the loose basketball shorts and a gray T-shirt he set out the night before.

His mother has breakfast out for them, complete with fresh-squeezed orange juice. She'll have been up for a while now, because his father expects the usual picture-perfect breakfast. The juice is what kills Milo. He's tried telling her he doesn't care where it comes from, that he'd rather she have some minutes to herself.

"I don't mind, honey," she always assures him. "I like taking care of my men."

Milo hates being put in the same category as his father and hopes she knows that he's a different person, that he'll never be the man his father is. But he understands—in this house, only one energy, one presence, one person orders their lives. She might as well be blind to Milo most days. He understands the nature of survival, the single-minded faith and grit it takes to keep moving each day. Compassion for her grows from the knowledge that there's an end date for his sentence, whereas hers bears no such promise.

College. Two years and he'll be off and away, and she never will, not as long as she won't leave his father. And Shelby Graham will never leave. His father has trained her so well to think she can't survive without him. She's said it gently and indirectly so often: "I have no skills but taking care of my boys. It's where I do my best." The words sink into him; they sit with him whenever he fantasizes about leaving, whenever he imagines himself getting away, because he knows that means leaving her behind. Survival that means abandoning someone is the guiltiest fantasy of all.

"Come on, Milo, time to go." James stands, shaking Milo from his thoughts. He folds his newspaper and tucks it under his plate for Shelby to clear. His father is in a good mood today, which is more unnerving than his anger or punishments. Good moods tempt Milo to hope; they tease out lapses in vigilance; they always, at some point, end badly.

"What are we doing today?" Milo asks, buckling himself into his father's car. James hands over a folded sheet of paper. He's been researching swim sets, trying to find a way to tailor them to Milo's skill beyond what their coach can do. His father is of the opinion that Coach Dave is too small-town to know how to foster Milo's talent. He's been pushing Milo to consider swimming competitively in college. It's exhausting, now that his father has him training seven days a week, but worth it. He doesn't see himself swimming competitively in his future, but he loves swimming just the same.

Time in the water is one of the things that keep Milo sane. He only has to stare at the blue line along the bottom of the pool, count his breaths and let the white noise of the pool fill his ears. Sure, the peace is interrupted by his father's shouts, but for the most part, swimming is all his own, and when he's in the water, Milo feels without borders. Occasionally those shouts are encouragement or praise. When he swims, he gets the best of his father.

His dad is in a good enough mood that today is one for positive words. It grosses Milo out sometimes, how much he feeds on the rare praise—how much he craves it, even knowing how easily that desire can be used as a weapon against him, knowing how quickly the tides can shift and what was praise can become damnation. He'll never measure up, but the dream he had as a boy—if he was good enough, his father might love him and this would all be over—lingers, no matter how hard he tries to shake it out.

Once in the pool, the clean, cold slice of water furling away from his body as he strokes makes him feel as if he's shedding old skin. The gurgle and shush of water with the metronome beat of his heart and tempered breathing set the background for some good thinking. Today, Milo gets a chance to mull over the kiss without distractions. Last night he was emotional, broken down, and Andrew has never been able to see him stay in pain. They were caught up in the moment, right? Milo's own reaction—how nice it had been—is something to contemplate later, if ever, because it brings up shades of something he's been ignoring for a while. Right now, for the next fifty-six minutes and fifteen seconds, all he has to do is swim and think of a plan to fix whatever needs fixing between him and Andrew.

It takes forty-seven minutes before he hones in on the truth that he has only one solution: They can pretend it never happened, and he can assure Andrew that nothing has to change. Because it can't.

o

By the time Milo is finished, he feels like a limp rag. It's only nine, so he has enough time to pull together a brunch—early lunch for him, breakfast for Andrew—and to gather himself together for the rest of the day Ted has planned for them. His body has been changing as he's begun working harder in the pool and added resistance training; his mother took him to Boston for new clothes, a reward doled out by his father: longer pants because of his growth spurt, but mostly new shirts as he's grown too broad for what he had. The reward was his father affirming that he knows best, and Milo is a tool of that proof, but at least he had a rare lunch with his mom.

Milo picks a green and gray plaid button down and worn jeans. He throws on a thick sweater and the scarf Andrew gave him for his last birthday. God only knows how late Andrew will be. Ten is early for him, and if Milo knows Andrew at all, he'll be fussing for a good half hour trying to figure out what to wear.

In the pit of his stomach is an ice cold fear that Andrew might want more, or be hoping for—for a relationship. Or something. Milo hates the thought of hurting Andrew, but being with him like that—it's not something he could ever do. Even if he did feel like that toward him, it would be reckless to risk what they have, when he knows he'd eventually hurt Andrew somehow.

○

In the light of day, Andrew still has no idea what he's supposed to say or how he's supposed to act. He takes special care with how he looks—neither an obviously over the top attempt to impress, nor so sloppy he'll look like as if he's trying to act as if he doesn't care. As a result, he's fifteen minutes late.

"As usual," Milo says as his head pops out of the fort, "last one to the party."

"Beauty sleep and all that," Andrew says, their usual exchange going off without a hitch. It's what they do: banter, understand each other's flaws.

Milo disappears into the fort. Is his smile strained? It's hard to tell, because Andrew is too nervous to get a good read on him.

Inside, Milo has food set out: sandwiches and fruit and a bag of cookies.

"Wow, you really went all out." Andrew shuffles things around to make room for himself.

"Dad insisted I get up early for morning practice," Milo says, already tearing into one sandwich. "So I had more time than I thought."

"Fuck, Milo it's the weekend!"

"Yeah well, he thinks I could improve my times by a few seconds in the next month if I 'really commit.'"

Andrew's jaw drops. "Are you kidding? Milo, you practice like two hours a day."

"'Half-assed attempts,'" Milo quotes, his mouth full of what looks like a bite of tuna fish. Andrew hates tuna. Milo swallows and wipes his mouth with the back of his hand and pushes over Andrew's peanut butter and jelly sandwich. Sure, it's the favored sandwich of eight-year-olds, but that's because it's delicious and eight-year-olds are geniuses. Milo has three sandwiches set out for himself; he always eats at least twice as many as Andrew does, making up calories he burns swimming.

"He's going to tire you into an early grave." Andrew hands Milo a napkin and a Coke and gives an eye roll. Milo's eyes are dark-ringed.

"Might not be so bad," Milo jokes. "I'd finally get a break."

"Milo," Andrew says softly. "Don't—"

"Oh, it's okay," Milo interrupts. "Don't worry. I'm just tired. I'm sure Ted's gonna pick at least one awful movie. I'll catch a nap."

Silence falls over them, pushing in through the window and door. It's ridiculously cold to be out today, and it's dumb for them to be here. Milo is exhausted, Andrew is unsure, and the spaces between them feel wrong. As if this isn't the right time to talk about this. Maybe it never will be. He hopes that's the case.

"Listen..."

"So..."

"Look, I don't want things to be weird," Andrew says when it's obvious Milo isn't going to speak.

"They don't have to be." Despite the silence that's fallen, Milo's voice is so soft it's almost lost.

"I just...I don't know what came over me. We—we can do the thing where it's erased." Andrew makes the familiar gesture, pretending to swipe away writing on a board. He does this often when Milo's stuck on something his father has said to him, or when people throw insults at school.

"Andrew," Milo says softly.

"No, no," Andrew says, rushing and not looking at him and blushing. "As long as everything is really okay, can we call that a lapse in judgment?" He stresses the end. Milo doesn't say anything, and Andrew refuses to look up.

"If that's what you want," Milo says after what seems like ten million years.

"Promise we're still friends?"

"Come on, asshole." Milo punches his shoulder lightly. "Of course."

chapter four

ONE DAY, OUT OF THE BLUE, MILO SAYS, "LET'S GO UP TO P-town."

Andrew's head pops up from where he's been writing with his notebook on the floor. "Why P-town? Pity-the-Lonely-Gay night?"

Milo gives him a look, one of those looks Andrew can't read. It's one of Milo's few ticks Andrew still hasn't cracked.

"For *fun*," Milo says as if Andrew's being the densest person on the planet. "I'm sick of this place." Face set in a frown, he kicks at Andrew's table.

"You had me at fun." Andrew pulls himself off the floor, ungainly and awkward from lying in an uncomfortable position. Milo's shoulders have been set for trouble since he came over. Andrew asked what was up and only got one of those cold blue looks that mean Milo's trying to bank something big and ugly. Sitting around Andrew's house doing nothing isn't going to burn that off. "When is this happening?"

"No time like the present?"

"I'm not showered, Milo! Are we asking other people to go? Isn't it too late? What's gotten into you? This is all wrong; I do the stupid things, you plan the details. You'll—"

"Shhh, don't ruin the romance," Milo says and smiles when Andrew laughs helplessly, remembering that night at the diner when they were all slap-happy and dumb. Milo throws a pencil at him to get him moving. "I told my dad I had study group with Ted and got the coveted permission to stay over at his house. See? Plan." Milo sticks his tongue out and crosses his arms.

Milo's not really "allowed" to stay at Andrew's any more. He's been strongly discouraged from coming over or associating with him at all. Selfishly, Andrew appreciates that this is one of the few things Milo rebels against, although he's sure he suffers for it sometimes.

"Go shower." Milo flips through Andrew's clothes. "I'll find you something hot to wear."

"God, you'd almost think you turned eighteen and became about fifty percent gay," Andrew kids.

Milo's hands pause.

"Har har."

o

"I didn't mean to offend you." Andrew lingers by the door, so Milo makes a show of rolling his eyes and smiling.

"Go shower already," he says, still flipping through Andrew's shirts as if he's really searching. Milo knows every shirt Andrew owns, and which look best on him. Unless Andrew has any other secrets hidden in here, flipping through shirts is serving only to calm Milo's nerves. Tonight he wants to tell Andrew one of the secrets he's been keeping, and while he knows it's right, it's still scary as hell.

"What about you?" Andrew collects underwear and an undershirt. "Are you going dressed in that?"

Milo looks down. He's wearing a sort of ratty polo shirt and faded jeans. "No, I brought something. But I showered today. It's a thing people do."

"You're such an asshole," Andrews says, laughing and scrunching up his nose. "You know I'm a night showerer."

"Go, go." Milo pushes Andrew. Impatience twitches through him. He needs something new; he needs some fun, he needs to get away from himself and this oppressive town.

Besides, tonight is the night. He's ninety percent sure he's almost convinced that tonight he's going to come out. Milo's wondered how long he can keep this a secret from Andrew; their time in Santuit is almost at an end, and he could walk away without ever having to come out. He doesn't have any desire to tell anyone else. He can't rock any of the boats he's trying to balance. In a few months, he'll be out of here. He got his acceptance letter from the University of Southern California and he's fully prepared to finally learn how to be *him*, and free and not scared any more, the minute he walks off the plane. Andrew isn't wrong about Milo's nature—Milo plans everything he can, because everything builds the scaffold to that ever-closer escape hatch.

That doesn't mean he doesn't occasionally want to be surprising, or that he doesn't need to burn out the itching in his skin that comes from holding everything ugly coiled so tightly in his body. He has many secrets, many barbs digging into him from all sides, and only one safe space where he can lessen the torture a little.

Milo wants Andrew to know because Andrew will always be a part of him, even when he's across the country starting a new life. Milo was the first person Andrew came out to five years ago, and the trust he demonstrated was a dear gift—to know Andrew in a way no one else ever had. Milo wants to give this to Andrew, too. While Milo tries not to think about it and succeeds most of the time, he worries that Andrew might still have feelings for him. Despite their agreement to erase that one day over a year and a half ago—that one brilliant, stunning kiss—from their lives, its shape lingers inside the lines of Milo's lips, a burning *what if* that frightens as much as beguiles. Sometimes he catches a glimpse of Andrew—the way his hair is butter-colored in the sunlight or how his limbs take on a fleeting grace that hints at the potential of Andrew's future body—it can be anything— and *yearns*, wondering if Andrew's lips taste like unanswered questions too.

Neither of them has ever pressured the other to think through what happened, because they've operated with the tacit understanding that Milo is straight. The truth is that he's not unsure; there's no maybe. He has passed the phase of denial he coasted on for years, and he's traveled that road without ever hinting to Andrew, because it was Andrew's kiss that truly began to erode the lies Milo had been telling himself. It woke him up, made it impossible for Milo to continue to ignore his own physical desire. Andrew's kiss popped that numb little bubble, and in its wake fantasies of desire and love and sex all sharpened, until ignoring the truth became impossible.

He wants to share this with his best friend, but knows he's walking a tightrope—on all sides he risks hurting Andrew. Somehow he has to fit in a smooth, non-hurtful or self-centered, "I'm gay, but hey, not for you," sort of vibe. It's not that he doesn't think Andrew is attractive: he is really very much attractive. Not pretty, or classically good looking. But there's something slinky and sensual to his movements, a delicate openness to his face when he's at rest and something light and playful, most of the time.

Milo loves Andrew, too—maybe too much, and definitely in ways he doesn't understand. Andrew is his ballast, and the thought of entertaining longing or desire for more seems like a spark too reckless. One wrong breath and Milo will have burned everything down.

○

"This is what you picked?" Andrew frowns at the outfit laid out on the bed.

"What?" Milo pulls on his own shirt. "Those jeans look really good on you." Andrew flits a look at him, assesses Milo's own outfit.

"Wow, that shirt is tight," he says, swallows and turns away. Milo's always been a bigger guy, naturally built like an athlete. But his muscles... *fuck*. "Have you stepped up training or something?"

Milo tugs at his shirt. "Yeah. New system I read about online, tailored for swimmers. Seems to be working."

"Tell me about it," Andrew whispers under his breath.

"Is it too tight?"

"Depends on how you feel about being hit on tonight," Andrew jokes. He's absorbed in his reflection, fiddling with his hair in the mirror. "Ugh, I can never get this to do what I want it to do under stress."

"It looks great, you look great, come *on*," Milo whines, spraying Andrew with cologne while he's not looking, earning himself a yelp and a smacked arm.

Andrew gladly lets Milo drive his car; he hates driving, especially when he can play radio DJ and watch the scenery go by. He looks at Milo: the way the fading light before dusk changes the tone of his skin; the way the muscles of his arms stand out and his lips curl as he sings along, awfully, to the radio. Milo smiles at him, and Andrew flashes a brief one back, wonders how obvious he's being, and looks back out the window at the slipping sand that spills onto the road and the ramshackle businesses along the road.

"So what got this bee in your bonnet?" he asks suddenly.

Milo shrugs. "You sound like my grandma."

"Awesome; I like her. Let's focus."

"So... okay." Milo clears his throat and his fingers tighten on the wheel. "I um, think I have something to tell you. But I'm—"

"Is everything okay?" Andrew interrupts, scanning his memory for any signs of additional distress Milo might have displayed in the last few months.

"Yeah. Well. I mean, um... whatever. But I—"

"What? You're worrying me."

Milo sighs and pulls into the parking lot of a restaurant with a giant crab on the roof. "I can't do this and drive."

"Okay," Andrew says slowly, then unbuckles his belt and turns to face him. Milo's face is a little drawn.

"So, I think I might be gay," Milo blurts. "I mean, I know. I know I am."

There's a full minute of silence in the car while Andrew tries to work the words out. Static screeches in his ears, fleetingly numbing his reaction. *Focus.* He has a few seconds to control his face, to tamp down that sprout of irrational hope seeding despite the chaos, and be ultimately supportive.

"Um." Andrew licks his lips and tries to pull himself together. That seedling wants to grow into something bigger, and he *can't* let it. He looks at Milo's face, which has morphed into something more vulnerable and worried. Hope is a hollow bell in his chest, ringing loud and dissonant; he wants to vibrate out of his skin with the inappropriateness of his own reactions. This is about Milo, not him. "You aren't worried that I'm mad or something, are you?" he manages to say.

"I don't know. Um, your face is doing... a thing," Milo replies.

Reflexively Andrew puts his hands to his cheeks. His fingers are cold. Okay, so he definitely doesn't have his face under control. "No, I... wasn't expecting it, that's all." Andrew's brain, sometimes faster than his mouth, is careening backward. "Maybe I should have had a clue."

"Oh?"

"Well, for starters, you kissed me back."

As soon as the words are out, Andrew slaps a hand over his traitor mouth. Talk about mouth working faster than brain, *fuck*.

"Calm down." Milo takes his hand. "Breathe."

"Shut up," Andrew says weakly, then closes his eyes and sternly orders himself to pull himself together. "Right. So, wrong thing to say. I wasn't expecting you to come out to me on the road on an impromptu trip to gay Mecca." His eyes widen. "Oh my god, is that why we're going? Are you, like, on the prowl?" His volume seems to be working up and not down. He takes another breath. There is definitely a good and bad way to react, and blind jealousy when he's confronted with huge news that doesn't actually change the way Milo feels about him is most definitely a bad reaction. Whatever might be growing in his chest, Andrew can't pin its survival or growth on a few glances shared with a boy in so much trouble.

Milo laughs. "Oh god, no. I was just curious. And I wanted to go somewhere fun with you."

"Okay." Andrew orders his face to smile and thankfully, it obeys. He pulls himself together and takes a good long look at Milo. He still looks unsure, and so Andrew does what comes most naturally to him: swallows whatever feelings he's having and focuses on Milo's. "Hey, come here." He pulls Milo into a hug. It's comforting, if not precisely comfortable over the console and with Milo still buckled in.

"So," Milo says, taking a breath and clearing his throat, "I know this is dumb, because it's a given..."

Andrew shudders. Where is Milo going with this?

"But you promise we're still friends?"

It's through incredible strength that Andrew keeps his eyes open, smile on and resentment boiling invisibly inside. In five minutes Milo has turned everything around, and, silly dreamer that Andrew is, he gave himself three minutes to hope against all hope. It's not Milo's fault Andrew is so hopelessly in love. And that sharp, ugly spike slicing Andrew's insides isn't Milo's fault either.

"*Duh.*" Andrew takes a breath and offers Milo a genuine smile. They're still a ways from their destination, and it's quiet in the car, mostly. It doesn't take long for Andrew to realize the barbs spreading inside are a combination of jealousy, bitterness and anger. *Why?* Why does this have to happen? The biggest reason he's used to comfort the ache of being in love with Milo was Milo's inability to reciprocate his feelings. Only now that's a barrier removed and still Andrew is no closer to getting what he most wants.

So now Andrew has to recalibrate. In this version of his life, Milo is gay, but *still* only wants to be friends. Milo's friendship might leave him longing for something more, but not with anyone else. Andrew doesn't want that love with anyone else. It's not that he's settling for only friendship. Andrew's always thought that loving someone involved longing for something more. At least with Milo, Andrew will always want more from the person he loves the most.

o

"So I did my research," Milo says as they approach the city. "What do you feel like? Dancing? Sitting around? A drag show?"

Andrew snorts in a laugh and shoots him a look. "What do you want?"

"I don't know. I'm here for the ride. Just wanna take it in."

"Okay." Andrew thinks. "Dancing."

Milo feels his eyebrow jump up, but doesn't say anything. He bites his lip and when he glances over at Andrew he sees a small vibration in his shoulders. "Well, you are a natural, just ask that poor lamp—"

Andrew bursts out laughing, smacking the back of his hand against Milo's arm. "We swore we'd never speak of it again."

"No, *you* did. I did no such thing."

Andrew gasps. "Oh my god, you liar! You're the one who broke the lamp, not me! You made me swear never to say anything so my mom wouldn't know."

"But realistically—" Milo says through laughter, then stops laughing for a moment to breathe. "Can we talk about the fact that your mom had *just* been in the room, laughed at us and gone downstairs? I am *sure* she heard that lamp break as soon as she left."

"This is not the point." Andrew crosses his legs. "The point is it is a thing we don't speak of for fear of hurting your delicate feelings about your complete, furniture destroying, inability to dance—"

"Mine! Oh my go—"

"You've always been so shy about your skills," Andrew says, gasping for breath. "Oh god, you have to stop; I might cry."

They trip over each other's words and laughter. Milo's smile is face-splitting—not just from one of his favorite memories, but because this moment is shimmering; it's perfect. It's them: Andrew catching the giggles the way he does, and Milo holding back his own laughter over a memory of a day no one else would see the humor in.

"Given your unfortunate skills, dancing was not what I expected. Ow!" Milo rubs his arm where Andrew poked it. "You are a menace!" He grabs Andrew's knee and squeezes hard, making Andrew squeal and flail.

"Stop! *Stop, stop.* I'll pee." Andrew laughs. Milo stops, finally. "Oh my god, Milo, you can't tickle someone while driving; we'll end up dead!" Andrew says, catching his breath.

"Not my fault," Milo singsongs.

"Uh..."

"Well, maybe it would be a little my fault."

Andrew opens the car window, letting cool air rattle in suddenly, then closes it just as quickly. "I wanted some air," he explains when he sees Milo's look. His cheeks are red from laughing.

"All-righty then," Milo says, shrugging. They drive quietly with the low hum of the radio in the background.

"How are we getting in anywhere?" Andrew asks.

"Fake IDs!"

"How old did you make me? I have a baby face."

"Twenty-one," Milo replies. "I'm hoping they won't be too picky, though."

"If you say so." Andrew shrugs.

The quiet in the car lingers, and Milo gets the strangest feeling that the laughter and ease of a moment ago is unspooling behind them along the highway. It's overcast, the sun has set and the quiet in the car has become too still. When he looks at Andrew, he's doing that thing he does, where his thumb picks at the nail of his index finger. It's his thinking tell. No, not thinking. Mulling. Milo resists the urge to sigh. He knew Andrew would support him, but he also knew it would be hard for him.

o

Provincetown is... not what Milo expected, mostly because it's so busy. The streets are full of people walking the sidewalks and down the middle of the road, laughing and weaving their way through traffic. It's almost insane, trying to navigate and find a place to park.

"There, there—" Andrew points to a meter. "Wait, I don't know if I have change for a meter."

"I brought money, no worries."

"Wow, you really planned ahead."

"Well, you know me—"

"Cross your t's and dot your i's," Andrew finishes for him, and they share a smile.

Milo fishes the IDs he's had made for them out of his wallet as soon as they're parked. "Here."

"How did you get these? I had no idea you were such a deviant," Andrew teases. The truth is Andrew might be the only person in the world who really knows how deeply rebellious Milo wants to be, and when the timing is right, is.

"Secret's in the sauce," Milo says and winks. He's feeding coins into the meter.

"This is a prime example of how I should have known you were gay," Andrew says with an eye roll.

"What?"

"You can quote from *Fried Green Tomatoes* without blinking an eye."

Milo laughs and bumps against him.

"We'll have to come back and feed the meter in two hours if we aren't ready to go."

"Cool." Andrew sets a reminder on his phone and nags Milo to do the same.

o

Milo gives him the names of a few places they can go, but Andrew tells him to pick; he's not paying much attention. Instead, he absorbs it all, the myriad faces and the noise. There is a festival atmosphere, without the garish lights or the fried sweet smell. He watches a drag queen handing out fliers and a girl in a *Rocky Horror* costume teasing a group of guys gathered with arms slung over shoulders and hands slipped into back pockets. The air is buoyant. Andrew feels he could fit in perfectly. It's a place for adventure, so far from his life that he feels as if he could slip out of his skin at any moment and become something new, brilliant and unfettered. The thought makes him hungry. *I want to do it all.*

"I think we need to go this way," Milo says, pointing past a row of shops: crafts and sex toys and a hamburger joint. Several pride flags flutter in the breeze. Two gorgeous men pass by, holding hands. Andrew laughs for no reason.

"I'm just happy," he says, when Milo gives him a curious glance. Milo smiles in return; not his fullest, but a real one— the proud one that appears when he knows he's made Andrew happy. It's a look Andrew knows is only for him; it's a scrap he holds around his heart. It's hope without hope. It's enough, mostly.

"Come on." Andrew looks up at him and links their arms. "Let's go do something wildly uncharacteristic."

"You're gonna do your homework?" Milo jokes.

"Oh, aren't we the comedian." Andrew follows when Milo tugs him along. The streets are haphazard and crowded enough that it's a little confusing. In a store window Andrew sees the most neon orange T-shirt he's ever encountered with the words DICK DOCK emblazoned on it. "What is that about?"

Milo glances up and twitches and looks away. "I have no clue."

"I'll ask someone. Maybe. Get a drink in me and we'll see." Andrew winks, and Milo offers him a shy smile. They're both doing a marvelous job avoiding any undercurrents from their conversation. Definitely. Thinking about it doesn't count as not avoiding, does it?

The club is moderately busy. Andrew can only imagine what it must be like at peak season. As it is, it's crowded, hot and full of men in all states of attire. There's a five-second period when he suffers the extreme self-consciousness that comes from wanting to look at something and thinking he shouldn't. He has the sense that he's been dropped into a really bizarre episode of *Queer as Folk*.

Unless it's Milo-related, Andrew's never been the martyr type. Fleeting seconds of doubt skitter into the dense air, and then he looks. He follows Milo to the bar and looks. He makes eye contact with some men. Not with others. He looks again. The whole goddamned place is a fucking feast for his eyes. It's the land of honey. The floor is literally vibrating with the force of the music, through Andrew's boots and body and coming out in a primal, unconscious movement that he thinks might soon end in a disastrous attempt at dancing.

At the bar, Andrew lets Milo order him a drink. Everything is sticky and glittering and fabulous, except for maybe Milo. He's beautiful, yes. He's beautiful everywhere. In the strobe lighting his hair could be any color, a dark, empty palate, and his skin is a series of shadows, beautifully stretched over perfect bone structure. But he's obviously uncomfortable.

Andrew leans to shout into his ear. "You wanna leave?"

Milo is sweating a little: Andrew can't see it, but it is a scent he knows by memory: visceral, scorching memory. Heat rises through Andrew's face.

"No, no." Milo shakes his head. "Getting my bearings. I'm feel a little zero-to-sixty right now."

I bet, Andrew thinks, not as kindly as he should, maybe. Milo hands him his shot glass and they clink them. "To dick docks," Milo says, making Andrew almost choke on his shot.

"What?" he finally says, wiping tequila residue from his lips and shuddering through his laughter.

"I don't know, it felt like it needed a toast." Milo giggles. It's a *thing*, for Andrew, seeing Milo like this. Robust, publicly stoic and possessor of classic good looks, he looks both completely out of place and totally natural, laughing boyishly, nose scrunched and eyes squinting.

"Another?" Milo holds up his empty shot glass with its desiccated lime wedge.

"No, let's give it a second."

Milo leans back against the bar and watches the crowd; he seems to be thawing to the environment by degrees. His leg bounces in time to the bass-heavy club mix.

"You gonna dance?" Andrew shouts, shoulder-bumping him.

"No. You know what that looks like. Disaster."

"Ohh, honey you definitely have it in you," Andrew says, low and flirting and joking. Only he's not, a little bit. Sometimes, there's a tiny thread of honesty to his interactions with Milo that he can easily convince himself doesn't mean what he pretends it means.

"You sure know how to make a man feel good," Milo plays back and then laughs when Andrew does. "At what point in our lives will it not be weird to call ourselves men instead of boys?"

"I don't know. Maybe you need someone to make a man of you," Andrew lobs easily, eyes still on Milo's. It's this crazy discordant note, the way they are carrying their usual banter, only now it feels thicker because. *Because*. Because of the car and that hug, because of the shots and the press of beautiful, queer, sensual men around them. Milo doesn't say anything, just looks, looks at Andrew, and he could swear his skin throbs.

"Excuse me," a voice shouts directly behind Andrew, scaring him out of whatever the fuck that moment was. "I'm Mike." He holds his hand out for Andrew to shake, and, caught off guard, Andrew does. Mike squeezes it for a beat too long; his lips are quirked as if he's got the best secret. As if he knows Andrew's secrets.

"Uh, um. Andrew," he finally says. He gestures to Milo. "Milo."

Milo waves awkwardly; Mike barely spares him a glance. There's a long moment when nothing happens.

"So you wanna dance or what?" Mike finally says.

"Oh." Andrew bites his lip, unsure. "I don't—"

Andrew looks at Milo for a clue; other than looking Mike over carefully, he betrays nothing. What might have been a thread stretching between them, maybe too taut and sudden, starts to shred.

"Unless your boyfriend minds?" Mike slides a smile toward Milo that's not entirely kind.

"*Not* his boyfriend," Milo says. "Go ahead; have fun."

Milo gives a one-shouldered shrug that reads indifferent and dismissive. It's not. Andrew knows it's not and for a second he's really quite blindingly furious. That shrug is all he needs to confirm that Milo felt exactly what was happening between them a moment ago. That's his pretend *I don't give a fuck* shrug. That's a shrug for everyone else. That's the shrug that sheds his father's words and hurt, dismisses expectations, gives the finger to things Milo might have to care about but isn't up to coping with.

Andrew isn't sure if Milo was toying with him, if he's being jerked around, or if Milo's fears are speaking louder than the undercurrents Andrew is sure he felt. But that other undercurrent Andrew's been dismissing since Milo came out to him and friend-zoned him clumsily flares up, too. Fine. *Fine.* Milo can fuck off. Andrew sends him the bitchiest, most obviously annoyed smile he can. Milo's not stupid. It's incredible, the two-gesture conversation they've had that no one else in the world would understand.

Andrew turns to Mike, puts on the most innocent air he can, bites his lip in a totally different way, and nods. "I've never done this before," he says into his ear. "You'll be gentle, right?"

Mike laughs, a shocked little noise, and pulls Andrew onto the dance floor with two hands around his waist. "Only if you really want me to be, honey."

○

Milo tries not to watch, but for the first torturous thirty minutes, he does anyway. Andrew dances with Mike, and with another man, although still with them both; he's boyish and awkward angles, but also so much pent up sensuality Milo hadn't expected that it's impossible to tear his eyes away. Every now and then their eyes meet and Andrew's lips press into that little *fuck you* smile he gets, and it twists hard into Milo's gut.

He comes back with Mike and they all do another round of shots. Milo and Andrew do a marvelous and simultaneously shitty job of ignoring every bit of subtext. Milo sets his glass down on the damp table and breathes through the burn. Mike and Andrew do another, despite the look Milo gives Andrew, and then Andrew's face flashes into a falsely, dazzlingly coy smile, looking right at Mike, letting himself be led back onto the floor. It's definitely more crowded now, and they're quickly swallowed by the throng of bodies. Milo tries to track them over the heads of the crowd, but it's hard in this light. He checks his phone. The bar closes in an hour or so. He'll check in on Andrew in twenty minutes.

"Not having a good time, honey?" A tiny slip of man sidles up next to him. There's no doubt he's old enough to have earned that *man* title, despite being about two-thirds of Milo's size. He doesn't seem to be hitting on him—not that Milo would know if he were. At the very least, it didn't look a thing like that guy Mike's blatant approach.

"Not especially," he admits.

"Saw you with that boy," the man says. "I'm Roger, by the way."

"Milo." He does that awkward hand wave thing again. He has *got* to stop doing that.

"So what's your story?" Roger gestures to the dance floor and Milo understands he's referring to him and Andrew.

Milo shrugs. "Best friend."

"Oh, it's *that* thing," Roger says, laughing. Milo feels a surge of annoyance.

"No, not that thing."

"Oh honey." Roger pats his shoulder. "Who do you think you're fooling?" Milo feels himself turn a furious red. "I'm not trying to pry or anything. Just saying, one old queer to... well, you're so fresh." He smiles. "It's gonna be okay."

Milo looks down at the sticky table, then up into the blinding lights. "I don't know about that." He doesn't just mean Andrew.

"Sad puppy." Roger pats his shoulder. "Come dance. Nothing funny. Have some fun."

"I don't—" Milo hangs back, feeling uncomfortable. Andrew is still somewhere out there, invisible and lithe and sweetly caustic. Milo's made his bed, and it's for the best. The alcohol and buzz of tonight's confession, and how he's fucking everything up, is messing with his thoughts enough that it doesn't sound like the worst idea. "Okay. But I'll suck."

"Babe, you're in a room full of gay men; you'll fit right in," Roger quips, startling a laugh out of him.

Ten laughing minutes later, feeling awkward but lighter and looser, he stumbles off the floor, waving at Roger and his friends and going back to his place at the bar. Andrew is nowhere to be seen, and the club is packed. Milo takes a second to gather his breath and then looks around, winding through the dancers to try to find him.

It takes three looks for his brain to process that the guys making out in the corner are Andrew and Mike. Andrew is pressed against the wall, nearly invisible in the throbbing lights and the palpable energy of sex and uninhibited bodies. It's a punch in the gut to see Andrew like that.

Milo makes his way over. "Andrew," he says loudly, poking his arm and trying very hard not to notice that Andrew is not just kissing this completely strange guy—he's being kissed senseless.

"What?" Andrew's head lolls against the wall and turns toward him lazily. His lips are swollen, and he's breathing hard and smiling.

"We have to go soon," he says. Andrew starts to giggle, then turns his face into Mike's neck and laughs harder.

"Relax, Milo. We have some time. Go have fun." He wiggles his eyebrows and, without trying, manages to dismiss him completely. "I'll meet you at the bar or text you when the shop starts to close, okay?"

"Fine." Milo is still for a second, unsure of his footing. Andrew gives him a kinder smile and then grabs his hand.

"Let's go dance, guys," he sing-songs, pulling Mike and Milo behind him.

Milo loses Andrew again not ten minutes later. He's not surprised, considering how quickly dancing devolved into something more intense between Andrew and Mike; Milo turned around to smile and fake it when one of Roger's buddies came up, and when he turned back around, Andrew was gone.

"Don't worry so much; you'll get wrinkles," one of them shouts. Milo fakes a smile and keeps moving in his disjointed marionette way and counts down the minutes until this whole thing is over.

He waits by the bar for ten minutes. He texts Andrew, grows increasingly worried when he can't find him, then blessedly upset: Upset is always easier than worried. He fires off a string of texts until finally he gets a response.

Calm down. At the car.

Milo stares at his phone. "You have got to be kidding me," he mutters, then takes a breath. By the time he's made his way out of the club, he's talked himself calmer. Andrew's not being the most thoughtful he could be, but he was pretty clearly pissed earlier, even if Milo doesn't want to think about why. It was sweltering in the club, and he can understand if Andrew wanted some air.

He finds Andrew draped against the side of the car, eyes on the stars, disheveled in a thoroughly sexy way Milo absolutely does not want to let himself acknowledge.

"I was worried," Miles says, unlocking the doors. Andrew folds his arms on the top of the car and looks at him, sleepy and mischievous. The streets are raucous with the purge of bars onto the uneven cobblestones.

"I was having fun, weren't you?" Andrew says so quietly it's almost lost in the waves of voices laughing and singing and cat-calling.

Taking deep breaths, Milo slides into the car and starts the engine. It's his fault everything went down the way it did, really. Andrew opens his door and manages to get in. He's had more to drink, Milo can tell; he's all colt limbs and tequila smell. The quiet they make once Andrew closes the door seems louder than the bar.

"Not really," Milo admits.

Andrew looks out the window. His hair is a riot. He shakes his head. "I'm sorry."

"It's not your fault. Well. I don't know. I did have some fun." Milo thinks of Roger and his friends and how they encouraged him to be foolish and dance and, for a tiny bit, push away what else was happening. Maybe he imagined having that with Andrew—a celebration of sorts, a kind of fun they never have at home. He can't blame how the night went on Andrew. "Maybe next time I should come out to my best friend and let my feelings settle for at least a few hours before I go to a gay bar."

"Mulligan," Andrew says wisely, then cracks up. His laughter has always been irresistible, and Milo finds himself chuckling too.

They drive in silence. Milo's had a while to sober up in the bar and is quite a bit bigger than Andrew; he's hoping the drive will sober Andrew up, because sneaking into Andrew's house will be one thing, but a drunk Andrew is a liability.

Out of nowhere, Andrew starts to laugh. "Dick dock." He wheezes between giggles.

"What?"

"I found out what it is," Andrew says, slurring a little. "Under the dock where they have the Tea Dance, it's where guys go cruising."

"Oh, did Mike tell you that?" Milo tries to erase any bitterness from his voice and ignore the tug in his stomach. He can't tell if it's interest or anxiety or both. Andrew laughs harder.

"After a fashion."

"What does that mean?"

"It means that hand jobs are the best; *god,* who knew it would be so much better than when you do it alone," Andrew murmurs, then sighs. Milo almost swerves off the road.

"*What?* You went and had—you did—I mean—*Andrew!*"

"Oh, calm down, Mom." Andrew shoots him a look.

"You went under a dark dock, alone, with a complete stranger, *to have sex?*" Milo's tries and fails not to shout.

"Are you kidding? I'm not a little kid. You don't get to judge me, or what I do." Andrew's voice is getting louder. He rarely shouts. His hand is wrapped around the handle of the door.

"Leaving aside the fact that you are underage, drunk, in a strange place, not telling the *only other person you were with* where you were, you go off with a stranger and—"

"What? Gave it away? *Did it?*" Andrew says in a dangerously sweet, taunting tone. "What am I supposed to do, Milo, save it for someone special?" The last is said so venomously it reverberates through the car like an electric storm, shocking through Milo. His whole body burns with anger and understanding and shame, because he knows exactly what Andrew is saying. It's not only about acknowledging tonight, but also everything else, the things they don't talk about, the thing Milo never lets himself feel. Andrew's breath has picked up and his face is the sort of angry he almost never gets, the kind that Milo knows often degenerates into tears because Andrew is an angry crier. He feels a little sick, because he's never been the one to do that to him.

He turns off the headlights and coasts into Andrew's drive, and they sit in the two o'clock in the morning darkness for a while, not moving.

When he hears the hitch in breath that signals Andrew's tears, Milo says, "Andrew—"

"Don't," Andrew whispers, his voice broken and wet. He pulls himself out of the car and closes the door slowly. Milo does too. "Go home, Milo."

"What?" Milo feels more than a little sick before Andrew says that. "Andrew, wait; come on."

Andrew wobbles, then steadies himself. "I don't want to see you right now."

"Andrew, you know I can't go home. Please don't—" It's on the tip of his tongue; he's scared because he can't go home and because Andrew has never kicked him out, ever. He doesn't want to admit he's been keeping more secrets, not with Andrew white and tearstained and vibrating like this. But if he risks going home right now, he's risking far more than the consequences Andrew knows about.

"Go to Ted's; isn't that your lie?"

"Andrew, I can't and you know it. Please," he says, trying to keep the begging fear out of his tone. "You don't understand, it's—" His voice breaks. "Worse."

The cicadas sing around them, and Andrew is unsteady in the moonlight.

"Wait, what do you—?" Andrew swallows and closes his eyes. Milo can actually see him processing his words. "Oh, god," he said finally. "*Fuck.* Milo—"

"Please, Andrew," he says, softly now. "I'm sorry I said those things, I'm sorry about tonight."

"You've been lying, haven't you? About your dad?"

"I—" Milo looks down.

"All right, come on," Andrew says. He's definitely still angry, but seems willing to help Milo. "We are definitely talking about *this* in the morning."

Milo doesn't respond, but takes Andrew's arm when he trips over the gravel of the drive, and carefully helps make their way to Andrew's back door.

○

Andrew wakes up wanting to throw up. His skin feels thin and sandpapered. He stumbles out of bed and trips over Milo, who is burrowed under a pile of blankets on the floor. "Wha—" he starts, then lurches toward the bathroom so he can empty acid from his stomach.

"Hey." Milo comes in quietly, gets him a cup of water with the small paper cups Andrew's mom still stocks the bathroom with. Andrew doesn't say anything; he sips his water carefully and closes his eyes. Milo wets a washcloth and wipes Andrew's face. Everything hits his memory like a truck, and Andrew throws up the water.

"Don't be so nice to me," he says hoarsely.

"Stop it," Milo says mildly, wiping his face again and pushing Andrew's hair off his sweating forehead. "Are you going to stop being nice to me?"

"No." Andrew pushes Milo's hand away. "But I think I'm still angry about some things."

Milo glances down and bites his lip and looks so young and vulnerable that Andrew has to breathe the anger out.

"No—hey, no; I take it back." He takes Milo's hand, which is wet from the washcloth. He can never really be mad at Milo, not for long. Milo is so sensitive to anger directed at him, and god knows he's so beautifully fucked up it's hard for Andrew to blame him for his actions.

"It's okay if you are," Milo says. "You should be."

"Hey—"

"No, it's okay. I wasn't really that happy with you last night either."

Andrew looks into Milo's eyes for a second before he has to look away. There are things they should talk about, and things he never wants to address again.

"Do you want me to get you some crackers?" Milo asks. It's a reprieve, for which Andrew is grateful.

"No, I want to get into the shower because I'm gross, and maybe take some Advil and then go back to bed and then we'll both talk some of this out."

"Okay."

Milo leaves and closes the door behind him. Andrew strips wearily and gets into a lukewarm shower. He remembers all of last night while washing gingerly, and tries unsuccessfully to sort a pile of data he's not really prepared for. Some things he knows he has to shelve because the most important part is talking to Milo about his admission last night. His own behavior is last on his list of worries.

o

He finds Milo on the floor again, a blanket around his shoulders, flipping through Andrew's copy of *The Gunslinger* that's been left on his night stand.

"Get off the floor and get into bed," Andrew commands. He's too tired for this shit.

"Are you sure?"

"You always sleep in my bed. It's a fucking king; don't be a martyr."

"That's not... you made me sleep on the floor last night!"

"I know, come on, I'm too hung over for this; let's lie down. How are you feeling?"

"I didn't drink that much and I had a lot of water before bed," Milo says with a shrug. "I got you some more." There's a glass on the night stand, too.

"Thank you." Andrew drinks slowly. "For taking care of me."

"It's hardly a repayment for all the taking care of me you do."

"Don't do that, Milo. We are never, ever going to do that I-owe-you thing. *Ever.*"

Milo looks at the blinds, which are glowing with midmorning sunlight.

"Don't open them, please," Andrew says as he settles back into his bed and snuggles under the covers. "My head is pounding. Lie down."

"Do you want to talk or go back to sleep?" Milo asks.

"Talk."

"All right." Milo squashes his face into the pillow.

"What's going on at home, Milo?"

"It's worse, is all."

"Worse how? How can he possibly treat you worse?" Andrew swallows down a rising nausea. "He's hitting now, isn't he?"

"I mean, not like—it's not exactly like that," Milo hedges.

"How is it like?"

"Not all the time. A few slaps, or once or twice a little... worse. Mostly it's... so hard to keep track of where I am in arguments when he's angry. He has this way..."

"This way?" Andrew prompts.

"Of making me doubt what's really happening. He'll say or do something, or I will, and somehow in the argument or punishment he twists things and it's like... I don't know what really happened."

"Milo," Andrew says softly, then roots around under the covers for Milo's hand. His eyes burn. "Why didn't you tell me?"

"There's nothing to be done. High school is as good as over. I'm almost out of here. I just want to get out; I can handle a little more of this."

"No," Andrew says, steel in his voice, "I won't let you."

"Andrew, you can't. This isn't like when we were kids. Nothing good will come from it. What can they do? It's not a secret that things are shit. No one talks about it because it's my *Dad*. He's fucking *Council Member James Graham*. He owns half the town."

"Milo, he does *not* own half the town."

"You know what I mean, Drew."

Andrew closes his eyes for a minute. Living in a town with secrets that are badly kept because so many people are cowed by the presence of one influential man is the one thing about Santuit that disgusts him. When he opens his eyes, Milo's are direct and pleading.

"I've already gotten into USC. We have a summer left. Please help me get through this; that's what I need."

"You didn't tell because you didn't trust me to keep it a secret," Andrew whispers.

"No. Not really. It's just. I don't know. A part of my brain knows he's fucked up, he's fucking me up, that this isn't my fault. But another also knows that everything he's done has pushed me to be a hard worker and to be determined. And he does love me, in his way, and sometimes that's the worst because I want that and I hate that and hating someone you love makes you a terrible person."

"Milo, no. No, please don't. You're—you're amazing and strong and it's okay to feel like that."

"Just help me get through this, *please*."

"I will." Andrew pulls Milo closer. "But if it gets worse, or... I don't want you hurting."

"You know that's not realistic right now."

"God, I'm so sorry," Andrew says against Milo's hair.

"For what? This isn't your fault."

"That you felt like you couldn't trust me. For trying to kick you out last night. For last night."

"Stop, no. You didn't... let's forget last night," Milo says. "And it's not that I didn't trust you. It's hard not to feel ashamed."

Andrew's fingers tighten around Milo's bicep. "Ashamed of what?"

"Look at me, Andrew. I'm strong; I lift weights and I train and I'm the best swimmer on our shitty team. I'm a big guy, and I let my father make me feel like the smallest, worst thing."

"Milo, you don't *let* him. He's worked your whole life to break you. You're incredible; look at you. You are going to get out, you *are* surviving, you are a beautiful person and he's never going to break you. You won't let him. *I* won't let him," Andrew promises.

Milo sighs against him and Andrew can feel the weight of his long bones and dense muscles begin to relax fully. He matches his breaths to Milo's, and after a while they slip into an uneasy sleep.

○

Milo struggles for the remainder of the summer—not with sharing his secret with Andrew, but with everything else.

Trapped in that seething cage of a home, sometimes he wakes up at night, heart throbbing and chest tight from dreams where he hits back, where his voice reaches that vicious, breaking tone his father specializes in. Where he gets on top of him and hits and hits and hits until there's nothing but blood and crunching bone. The worst is waking up and knowing utter futility and helplessness.

He wakes up and lives his life, but there are days when he doesn't think he'll ever get through without Andrew helping him breathe with light touches and easy smiles. If he ever let himself, if he ever gave in to the sweet, silver thread of longing he has for Andrew, he knows he would somehow end up breaking everything. There'd be no happy ending. He's so scared he could lose his very best friend that he manages to settle them both into friendship, and tries so very hard to give everything he is capable of to Andrew, who deserves so much more.

One Wednesday, Milo can't find Andrew. It's overcast and cold for mid-July. Andrew isn't answering his phone and he's not home. Milo has no reason to seek him other than wanting to be with him, but not finding him makes him feel colder.

Andrew's mother lets him in, and he settles at Andrew's desk and tries to read a book, but Andrew is still going through a horror novel phase and Milo isn't into that. Although something of Andrew lingers intangibly, he's not here.

It strikes Milo that in a few short weeks, they'll be across the country from each other. Until this moment, that understanding hasn't really imprinted in his bones. A fear so big he sees gray covers him.

It's suddenly clear that somehow Milo needs to learn to stand on his own. He throws Andrew's book on the nightstand, grabs his shoes and runs all the way home. He locks himself into his room and prays his father won't do a room check tonight.

He's gotten much too big for it, but Milo needs the close, dark shape of the closet around him. Losing Andrew is going to kill him unless he learns how to live with it. He turns off the closet light and puts his head against the wall and uses the memory of Andrew's voice to help him breathe and tells himself that that's good enough, that he doesn't need his hands in Andrew's and the comfort of his shoulder when he comes down, shaking and broken.

chapter five

MILO HAS A HUNCH FROM THE FIRST EMAIL EXCHANGED that his roommate is a douchebag. If he's reading the subtle undertones right (if, *dude we're gonna be wasted all the time, it'll be awesome* can be considered an undertone), it's going to be... interesting, to say the least.

Milo isn't interested in partying. He's never been huge on it, dislikes the out of control feeling that comes with being drunk. Even with friends, down at the bonfire or up in P-Town, it's rarely been as fun as others seem to think. Maybe it's the fear— fear of his father finding out, of being caught, of having an anxiety attack—whatever it is, Milo has never found a way to completely let go.

His roommate really is a douchebag. By the time Milo arrives, two big suitcases in tow, seventy-five percent of the wall space is covered in posters of mostly-naked women, and the room reeks of beer. Two other guys are hanging out and there are beer cans lined up on the windowsill. Thank god his father is downstairs commandeering the rest of his belongings.

"You have to put those away," he hisses, slamming the door shut with his bags still in the hall.

"Dude, hey, you must be Milo!" Shane holds his hand out, a too wide smile on his face.

"My dad is downstairs." Milo speaks in a low tone in case he's somehow managed to get up here that fast. "He will *kill* me, you have no idea. Could you guys clear out until he leaves?"

"Whoa, what?" Shane, to his credit, has the presence of mind to pass the can he's holding off to the shaggy blond-headed guy who had been leaning against the desk. He high-fives both guys on their way out. Shane roots around in a desk drawer and finds some gum. "Want some?" He holds it out, and Milo shakes his head. Shane already has a box fan set up in a propped window, so Milo turns it around and turns it on, trying to get the air out. He tosses all the cans into the garbage can and the can into the closet. Then, before his dad can come up, he opens the door and props it with his bag.

"I'll tell him it's for cross-ventilation if he asks," he mutters, mostly to himself.

"Are you okay?" Shane looks at him.

"I'll explain later." Milo hauls a bag onto his bed, and tries to ignore the poster of a vintage *Playboy* bunny spread above his bed. "If this works, he'll be thrilled," he says to himself. Not that he's ever so much as hinted to his dad, but the fact that Milo is gay is starting to become the secret everyone suspects but is kept, like all secrets, tucked into the deep silence of their home. The fan is loud enough that Shane doesn't hear him. God only knows how he'd take that; the last thing Milo needs is a homophobic roommate.

"Miles?" James thumps in with a large box and another suitcase in tow.

"Here, let me get that." Milo takes the load easily. Sometime in the last two years he's grown bigger than his dad. His father doesn't like looking up at him, and Milo will always feel smaller. "A lot more?"

"Just a few boxes; your mother is watching over them." James brushes his hands off.

"I'll grab them, then," Milo says.

"Hi, um, sir," he hears Shane begin, "I'm Shane Abernathy."

"Huh," is all James says. Milo winces and then sprints down the stairs to find his mother.

o

"Shane seems nice enough," his mom says over dinner.

"I suppose." Milo is busy with his food. It's a surefire way to stay under the radar. If there's anything his father approves of, it's Milo eating. So long as he eats healthily, Milo's big appetite is a sign that Milo is training well.

"Room smelled like beer," his dad says tightly. Milo's stomach falls. They're at a nice restaurant, pretty far from campus. His mother wanted one last nice dinner to top off the whole horrible moving-to-college experience. Milo wanted to do it on his own—not only because the specter of his father on such a day was enough to swallow, but because this is the start of a whole new part of Milo's life, one he hopes his father won't be a part of in any way.

It's a pipe dream, but a nice one. He takes a careful bite of his broiled chicken and wonders if he should fess up to Shane having alcohol.

"Now, honey, it's college. Some kids are going to get up to trouble," Shelby says.

"Not Miles though, right?" James turns pale eyes in his direction. "You're a good kid; I know you're smarter than that."

"Thanks, Dad," Milo says. "Nothing to risk my education, right?" It's true, too, but his father has a way of looking at everything he says as if it's a lie.

"Don't be dumb while you're here," James warns, then quicksilver-transforms his face into a genial one for the waitress.

81

"Trust me Dad, that is not the plan," Milo says under his breath. Nothing is bringing him back home, not if he can help it.

"Good." His father closes the black leather book with a signed card receipt and stands. "Shelby, it's time to head out. Want to get back in time to turn in the rental and get to the airport."

"Thanks for dinner, Dad." Milo smiles. So what if it's aimed at his mother? His father takes everything he sees as his due.

o

"So your dad seemed..." Shane looks up from where he's kicked back at his desk, watching Milo unpack. Shane moved in earlier in the week, so everything of his is stuffed or strewn in some sort of order. Milo refolds all his clothes carefully before stacking them in his drawers.

"Yeah," is all Milo says. There aren't really words to cover his father. Sometimes his father is an excellent actor. Others, not so much. He had no reason to impress Milo's roommate; many, in fact, to intimidate him, if he thinks Shane is in any way a detriment to Milo's future. Not that he is going to be one on his second day of college. But still. "He expects Great Things," he explains.

"So..." Shane watches him fold for another minute. "Wanna get hammered?"

Milo laughs. "No, not really. Not my thing."

Shane shrugs. At least he's not coercive. Milo tucks his last stack of laundry away, then sets about making the bed. All around him are mostly-naked breasts. It's so disconcerting.

My roommate has naked girls all over the walls, he shoots a quick text to Andrew.

gross
like literally. he hung one over my bed.
hopefully not an actual girl
well at least she'd make interesting conversation

ohhh, I see this is going well already
kill me now. Even his closet doors have girls
shut up, go have fun, stop acting like an eighty year old man.
And tell him you like dick. Put a picture up of a giant cock. Come
out of the closet on your closet.
you shut up you ass :D

"Girlfriend?" Shane asks innocently. Fishing. Milo tosses a smile back over his shoulder. It's too soon in the year for this.

"My best friend, Andrew," Milo says, dropping his phone on the nightstand.

"Where's he?" Shane is texting someone, too.

"Brandeis."

A knock at the door startles him.

A close-cut brown head pops in. "Hey guys." Whoever this is has a hard, well-defined face, an interesting face with deep brown eyes. "Shane," the guy waves. "You must be Miles?"

"That's me." Milo takes the proffered hand and shakes it. "You can call me Milo."

"Cool. I'm Josh, your RA. You're the last one here, just in time for the weekly hall meeting. Come on out to the commons by, like," he checks his phone, "eight thirty?"

"Sure." Milo smiles. Hall meetings. It's a college thing. This is a college thing. He looks around again. The room is small, and he's living practically on top of a messy, potentially gay-hating, party-loving stranger, but his father is on a flight back to Boston. For the first time, Milo can be anyone he wants. And what he wants most of all is not to be James Graham's son.

o

From: Miles Graham [milodgraham@---]
To: Andrew Witherell [drewithit7@---]
Subject: this sucks

I still haven't come out to Shane. It's been a week and so far he's brought two girls over. I see boobs everywhere I turn (not the girls, on my walls I mean). I have run out of ways to say no to parties. Do people do anything constructive here?
Tell me more about your roommates. How did you settle on room arrangement?

o

From: Andrew Witherell [drewithit7@---]
To: Miles Graham [milodgraham@---]
Subject: RE: this sucks
stop whining and go have fun like any hot blooded 18 year old. Go find an alliance. I looked a few up for you, I'll email them later. Find a little haven. Go for a swim, it calms you down. I know you decided not to do the swim thing there and focus, but you can do Masters Swim (I looked that up, BTW, you can use the internet to find things, did you know?)
Go get laid, stop being the oldest virgin this side of the Pecos. I like them ok. For now we're testing out having all the beds in one room and the other for study. But we're all open to changing that if one person is too annoying :D It's hard to tell now, but Damien and I get along great. Levi is hard to read.
-a

o

From: Miles Graham [milodgraham@---]
To: Andrew Witherell [drewithit7@---]
Subject: RE: this sucks
asshole, I don't even know that there are Pecos between us. Thanks for the other links. I'm on the fence. I guess at some point I have to "officially" come out. Will I ever feel ready? How the fuck do you do this?

I might do that master club thingy (idk I need to figure out how that works). My course load is pretty heavy. There is a workout room in Marks Hall I can use too. I'm glad you get along with your roommates. I'd feel so confined with three people in one room. Send pictures.
p.s. You go get laid....
-m

o o o

THE FIRST week of college is hard for Andrew: harder than he admits to Milo, because he knows Milo is out of his depth in a way Andrew isn't. Andrew misses so many things about home: the sound of the water at night; the pinpricks of starlight he mapped into constellations of his own making; his friends and parents; and, terribly, achingly, Milo. But he knows it's not nearly as hard as it could be.

On the sixth day of his new life, Andrew starts a blog. Not only to commemorate his new life, but as a blank space in which to document it. No one he knows will read it, which is freeing. Although he promises himself he won't use it to pine over Milo, Andrew's lying to himself.

Brandeis isn't a party school. That doesn't stop people on his floor from celebrating new freedom from parents by getting to know one another with the ease provided by alcohol. The sounds of drunk people slamming in and out of their rooms, raucous laughter and music keep Andrew up at night, irritated and longing. He wants new friends, too.

On the seventh day he admits his homesickness to Milo.

"I didn't realize you were having difficulties too," Milo says.

"You're having such a hard time—"

"Andrew, don't do that. You don't have to hold my hand like a child. I want to be here for you too."

Andrew swallows. The bright campus lights flood his room. "It's hard. I live on the first floor and it feels really exposed. I just—three is such a crowd, the bed is tiny and, god, this comforter my mom got me, it's so lame—" Andrew stops at Milo's soft laughter. "See," he says, but with a smile, "I told you it was dumb. I know I'm being dramatic."

"No, it's not dumb. I'm laughing because you're funny. It's nice to hear your voice like this. I miss it."

Andrew squeezes his eyes shut and pushes down the longing cramping in his heart. "I think you're the thing I'm most homesick for," he admits.

"Me too," Milo says. They breathe into the quiet, and despite twenty-five hundred miles between them, Andrew feels so connected to him.

After they hang up, his room is quiet until someone in the hall turns on a throbbing, room-vibrating song. Andrew's been staring at his computer, debating the wisdom of devoting himself to another dramatic monologue, this time for a faceless audience, about how viscerally he needs Milo. He misses Milo's smell; he smells so keenly of boy and home. He recalls the way Milo's head fits perfectly in the curve of his neck, and the beautiful face he's watched grow for years, pressing into new skin from a round, adorable, pouting, tragic boy into a strong-boned, handsome, at times silly young man.

The blog isn't meant to be devoted to confessions of missing a lover. No matter what he wants, Milo is not his lover, and never will be. Andrew is in love with a boy who can't love him back in the same way, who is thousands of miles away, trying to escape the life he had. If Milo can work to escape his old life, maybe it's time for Andrew to try to move past a childish, unrequited and impossible love.

"Come out here and have some fun." Kent, a boy who lives three rooms down, stumbles through the open door of his room.

Damien left it open since he's floating in and out. God only knows where Levi went. He comes and goes like a ghost.

Andrew bites his lip and shuts down the empty blog post. Enough sitting around and moping. Maybe it's time for him to act his age, find some trouble. Grow new skin.

o o o

WHEN MILO tries to sleep, he can't stop thinking about Andrew. And when he wakes up, it's Andrew. He misses him. He longs viscerally for the nearness of his body in a deep, cutting way Milo didn't expect.

Once he got past that first week, Andrew took to college like a duck to water. Milo's received late-night drunk texts twice; has had the dubious honor of hearing Andrew rave about that scorching hot guy down the hall he's got his eye on. He knows Andrew is already fast friends with a group of kids in his dorm. He has plans for the weekend and the one after.

Milo has a roommate he avoids talking to for fear of saying the wrong thing and has the constant, itching feeling that he has no idea how to function like everyone else around him. As the days crawl by, he finds anxiety lurking behind corners, waiting to catch him unawares. He wonders how long he can live in a box with someone else and not have an anxiety attack. Or worse, have one in front of him.

Maybe it would be for the best, though. Milo thinks maybe hiding things is making it worse.

Halfway through September he massively tanks a weekly exam in his calculus course.

Milo sits in the unusual quiet of his room—Shane must be out—before eventually dialing Andrew's number.

"Hey you," Andrew's voice sings through the receiver. That alone is enough to calm Milo from all-out panic to merely roiling fear.

"You sound happy," he manages. There's noise in the background.

"You don't. What's up?" The noise fades.

"You're busy, aren't you? I'm sorry, I can call you later—" Milo checks the time. It's already ten; later would be a bigger imposition. Or, knowing Andrew's habits, an impossibility, because he'll be partying.

"No, I'm not. What's going on?"

"Nothing. It's dumb." Milo looks down when he feels a sharp prick against his finger. It's his own nail, digging in.

"Milo—" Andrew says, in that soft, homey way of his.

"Look, don't worry about me. I'm having a bad day." Milo bites his lip. It's occurred to him more and more how incredibly dependent on Andrew he is. How little he gives back to him, how pathetic it makes him to need Andrew so much. How unhealthy it is.

"So talk to me about it," Andrew says.

"No, you tell me about your day."

"Well, hm. It's Friday, so nothing much to tell. The usual."

"Only two orgies so far?" Milo jokes.

"Nah, only one. Getting a mite bit old for those shenanigans." Andrew's laughter is like bells. Milo's stomach unwinds.

"I didn't pass a quiz," he says after a moment, when it's clear Andrew is waiting for him to speak again.

"How much is it worth?" Andrew asks.

"Um..." Milo looks over the syllabus again. "Ten quizzes in the semester worth twenty-five percent of the grade."

"What score did you get?"

"A seventy-one."

"Okay now," Andrew say slowly, in that asshole tone he uses when he's teasing a smile out of Milo, "you're the numbers guy; I'm the pretty face. So I might have it wrong, but I think you'll be fine."

"You do have it wrong. I'm the pretty face."

"Keep telling yourself that," Andrew says. Shane slams the door open suddenly, then shut again, making Milo startle.

"Shit." He breathes shakily, trying very hard not to glare at Shane.

"What was that? Did an elephant break out of the zoo and collide with your room?"

"No, if only."

"Oh, the roommate," Andrew says.

"Yeah."

"I'm sorry things are hard. You never sound like you're having fun out there." Andrew's voice is soft.

"I'm not sure I know how to do that," Milo confesses.

"Sure you do; I've seen you do it lots of times. I'm going to find some fun things for you to do, and you're going to go do them and make a new friend."

"Drew, you don't have to mother me."

"I'm not. I'm being your best friend. I know what's best for you."

"Shut up," Milo says. Then takes a breath and lowers his voice, turning away from Shane so he won't hear. "Is it wrong that I can't do this without you?"

"You shut up. No. We're supposed to support each other. Expect an email. I expect a full report tomorrow that involves you attempting something other than sleeping, exercising or reading that horrible book."

"You don't know what I'm reading!"

"I know your taste in books. It's horrible," Andrew says. He hangs up without saying goodbye.

89

"So," Shane says from behind him.

Milo winces and forces himself not to startle again. "So?"

"You look like you're having a bad day."

Every day is a bad day, Milo thinks. "I didn't do well on that quiz."

"Is that my bad?" Shane asks. He flops onto his bed, still wearing his shoes. His blanket is on the floor and the fitted sheet has pulled off the bottom corner of the bed.

"No, I'm just getting used to things here," Milo lies. Shane was distracting him to no end last night. It's not his fault, though, that Milo didn't want to leave the room to find a more peaceful place to study.

"You should come out this weekend. I get that it's not your thing. But you could meet people. Relax."

Milo looks at the red crescent-shaped mark at the base of his thumb. "Yeah, maybe," he says without meaning it. A ping from his computer notifies him he has an email. It's from Andrew, holding his hand yet again. Milo's bed looks much too comfortable, and next to it his book beckons. He's been re-reading the *Game of Thrones* books. It would be so easy to turn everything off, to tune out. But he can't keep expecting Andrew to hold him up, not when they're supposed to be living separate lives. Not when his friendship is a weight around Andrew's ankle.

He looks over the information Andrew sent. It's easy to hide and buckle down on his studies and push and push himself the way his father trained. But this was supposed to be his escape and his new life, and he's done nothing to break free. Fear is an ever-present weight that drags him down constantly. Andrew has a point. If Milo can't do this, he'll drown.

○ ○ ○

WHAT IT TAKES

By October, Andrew has a whole new group of friends. It wasn't as hard as he thought it might be; all it took was a resolve to open himself to new things and let go of small-town Andrew. One girl in their hall, Nat, has become a fast friend.

It's sweltering in the small house they've jammed themselves into. Andrew lost sight of Damien an hour ago, and Nat's in the corner with two girls he doesn't know, laughing and whispering over something he's sure he doesn't care to know. Next to him on the sagging couch is a gorgeous boy whose eyes haven't left Andrew's for at least fifteen minutes. It only took five minutes of strained conversation for him to turn his body toward Andrew: invitation for a night of flirting. Testing the waters. Andrew's not averse—when the boy is cute enough and appreciative like this one, he's always game for a good time.

Andrew didn't catch his name. He hopes that won't be a problem.

"What's your major?" the boy asks. He has engaging green eyes. Andrew shrugs and smiles in a way he's practiced in the mirror. It's acting, but it has a wonderful success rate.

"I'm not sure yet. Maybe something creative, or something responsible, like journalism."

"Are you a responsible guy?" The boy's hand is on Andrew's knee, sending heat through Andrew's body. Invitation. Andrew's eyes linger on his lips, which are full and pink and shining. He's had enough beer to feel a wonderful buzzing that loosens him, but not too much.

"Not always." He lifts a shoulder, and when the boy kisses him, he lets himself be swayed back against the arm of the couch. "Hold on—" He breaks out of the kiss when he feels a hand creeping along the inside seam of his jeans. "I'm definitely not into public shows, though."

"Upstairs?"

"You live here?"

The boy laughs. "I told you that a few minutes ago."

"Oh." Andrew's eyes are still on his lips.

"It's like that?"

"Is that all right?"

"Definitely." Andrew takes his hand and follows where he's led. He passes Nat on their way to the stairs and winks, ignoring her frown. He's remembered the lesson of disappearing without telling Milo where he was going in P-Town. Someone knows where he is, and he doesn't much care what that frown means.

The room is dark; Andrew likes it, and between the breathless and sloppy kisses of new mouths adjusting to each other, he whispers that.

"Whatever you like. You should know, my name is Rob."

"Oh?"

"I want you to say my name," Rob says, then presses Andrew into the mattress, and the words send a flashing heat of arousal through Andrew's skin.

"I can do that," he says before pulling him back into another kiss.

°

"You know you're kind of slutty, right? How many boys have you slept with since you got here?" Nat asks. She's sitting cross-legged on his bed.

"Are you kidding?" Andrew looks up from the floor he's sprawled on. He mutes the TV. Anger stains his cheeks. Damien spins his chair away from the TV and focuses too hard on his computer screen.

"No. I worry about you," she says.

"No, you're judging me. And you're doing it in front of someone else. What I do with my body isn't yours to judge and it's not your business."

"Come on, Andrew—"

"Nope. I think you need to leave." Andrew says. He pushes himself up, tossing the pillows he's been cushioned on back onto the bed. Nat stands, not looking at him, and he tries very hard not to slam the door behind her. The silence is incredibly heavy and awkward. Damien doesn't look at Andrew. Damien sleeps around more than he does, but no one gives a shit how many girls' names he's notched into his headboard. A het Lothario is granted an invisibility built into the idea of masculinity. That's a lesson he doesn't have the energy to teach small minds.

He slams into the bathroom and starts the shower. Andrew stares at himself as he undresses. By the time he's naked, the mirror is mostly steamed. His body isn't perfect, but it's desired—the hands and mouths of boys on it tells him that story. He's never bothered that it's just sex, and regardless of Nat's word—slutty—Andrew isn't. He is choosy and knows what he wants. He doesn't want arms around him in the after and he doesn't want sweet kisses or words. He craves touch, and he gets it. Anything else he craves he knows comes from a longing he can't fill right now. But he saves it, keeps it close to his heart.

o

To: Andrew Witherell [drewithit7@---]
From: Miles Graham [milodgraham@---]
Subject: I cave
All right, you sort of win. I've been following the QuASA fb and am gonna take the plunge. They're having a thai and movie thing at URC. It sounds low key enough that I might be able to handle it. If I can handle being the weirdest moose amongst strangers.

o

To: Miles Graham [milodgraham@---]
From: Andrew Witherell [drewithit7@---]

Subject: RE: I cave
I am so proud of you! Call me after and tell me everything.
I'm not sure I get the moose thing?
-A

o

Andrew answers on the first ring. "So how was it?"

"It was okay." Milo hunches his shoulders. It's not cold out, but it is dark and he feels very alone.

"Just okay?"

"No, well, I don't know. They seemed nice. The food was good."

"Oh well, I'm *so* glad you expanded your culinary horizons. I was really worried you weren't liking the food out there."

"Okay, okay." Milo laughs and switches ears. "I'm..." Andrew waits him out. "I'm so weird. With people I don't know. It's like my mouth freezes and I have no idea how to talk normally."

"You do fine. You always over-analyze."

"How do people *do* small talk? I can never think of what I'm supposed to say next."

"Some people are just gifted."

"Oh, you're gifted, all right," Milo says, and Andrew's laugh is delighted. It loosens him a little, after an uncomfortable night.

"Did you meet any nice people?" Andrew asks.

"Yeah, they all seemed nice. And I got the feeling..."

"That?"

"It's probably not shocking, meeting freshmen who are lost or strange."

"Yeah," Andrew says slowly. "You're not strange, Milo."

"Not with you." Andrew waits him out again. "They invited me to a get-together next weekend."

"Are you going to go?"

"I don't know." Milo shoulders the front door open. "A part of me feels like it would be easier to stay home and read. Less stressful."

"Maybe in a way, it will be. But it's lonely. I know you're lonely. And I know you're far away. But change isn't always easy, or everyone would do it. You went to USC for big changes, Milo."

Milo leans against the closed door to his room. Andrew's not wrong.

"You have to make those happen, Milo. All that awkwardness and anxiety when you meet new people... they don't have to cripple you. They can be growing pains, and you'll outgrow them soon."

"Drew, do you really think I can do that?"

"I know," Andrew says. His certainty roots inside Milo. Maybe he can do this. "I know you can."

chapter six

ANDREW CAN'T MEET MILO AT THE AIRPORT WHEN HE COMES home for Christmas. Milo's parents will, and he knows that Andrew's presence, something his father frowns upon, won't help what is already going to be a hard enough trip. They text from the moment Milo lands until they can finally see each other. Milo manages to sneak out two days later with the excuse of meeting with Ted and the group.

At the door to Andrew's home, Milo has to take a deep breath and calm himself. When Andrew throws the door open, Milo catches him in a crushing hug that lifts him from the ground.

"You're covered in snow," Andrew says. The scent of winter follows Milo in, but it's Andrew's cologne that permeates his senses. Andrew's lips barely brush the skin of Milo's neck and Milo has to suppress the shudder that runs through him.

"Well, then let me in," Milo jokes. They disentangle and Milo stomps excess snow from his boots and brushes the fine dusting from his coat—outside lovely, fat clumps of snow obscure their view, blanketing everything in the calm a winter snowfall brings.

"Milo, honey," Andrew's mom says, coming in from the kitchen. "It's so nice to see you; we've missed you." She winks at

Andrew. Her hair is darker than when he left in September, the natural highlights she passed on to her son are now almost brown and, for the first time, threaded with silvery grey. But her eyes are the same steady dark brown as always, and right now they look familiar and welcome. "Probably not as much as this guy."

Andrew rolls his eyes and hangs Milo's coat. "I've made snickerdoodles and hot chocolate," Caroline continues.

"We're not ten—"

"That sounds amazing," Milo interrupts. Andrew's face splits with a smile because even if he's protesting, Milo knows he can't resist snickerdoodles. Milo fits into the fabric of their home seamlessly; after more than ten years of friendship, Andrew's home feels more his to Milo than his real home. Over the cookies, Milo fills them in on what he's been up to in school. Most of it Andrew's heard, but it's cozy in the kitchen, and Caroline is so interested.

Once they've eaten their fill of cookies, Andrew leads Milo to his room. The first thing Milo does is flop onto his bed and sigh.

"God, I've missed this. Your bed has to be the most comfortable place in the world."

Andrew hesitates, and Milo pushes past the moment of uncertainty. What he wants is to have Andrew crawl onto the bed with him as they've done a million times.

"Come here, you asshole; let's talk," he says. He props himself on the pillows and arranges himself, creating a careful space between them, and then turns to Andrew. His face is beautiful, with a wide smile and bright eyes. His hair has remained bright, with unpredictable strands of lemon yellow and warm brown woven throughout. His eyes, in the dim room and against the green of his comforter, are almost hazel. Milo hopes they can find time to go down to the beach, even if it's freezing, because the way the sun teases out the flecks of green in Andrew's eyes always makes it seem as if his whole face has transformed.

"God, I've missed you," Andrew says without thinking. Milo takes his hand and threads their fingers together.

"Me too." Milo shifts down and rests his head on Andrew's shoulder, and they both squirm until it works comfortably. He tries hard not to feel the nearness of Andrew's body in a way he shouldn't.

"How's home?" Andrew asks.

"Harder than I thought." Their voices are little more than whispers, as if the topic and admission would be too much spoken any louder. "I've been so lonely and lost at school, I thought there wasn't a difference—"

"What? It can't possibly be the same, Milo."

"It's not. But being unhappy..."

"God, that sucks." Andrew pulls Milo closer.

"It's nothing like being here. Being lonely and unhappy are so much easier. I guess I didn't realize that independence really meant something, even though I hate it there. What is it about him that makes me feel like this when he hasn't even really started in on me?"

"I don't know. Because he's been fucking with your head for years?"

"I'd rather he do it from afar."

"Yeah."

Milo closes his eyes and tries so hard to put the longing in his heart, which is flooding his body, into a box. "But it's worth it," he says. He twists the material of Andrew's shirt in his fist. "To see you."

"I wish you didn't have to be hurt to do so."

Milo doesn't reply. The early dark of winter begins to dim the room. After a while, Andrew's breath begins to deepen and slow, a rhythm Milo hasn't heard in months, but knows means he's slipping into sleep. He moves away and they settle side by side on the bed, and the last thing Milo remembers is how their hands draw together like magnets between their bodies.

○

When Andrew wakes, Milo isn't in bed with him. Andrew tries to blink the gritty leftovers of sleep from his eyes. The clock on his nightstand reads late—almost midnight. There's a note on his desk.

Had to go. Didn't want to wake you. Call me later.

Milo's jagged and nearly unreadable handwriting covers the slip of torn paper he must have gotten from Andrew's journal. For a gut-churning moment, Andrew's stress levels spike. There's a whole lot in that journal he doesn't need Milo reading. The things they don't say are spilled with brutal honesty in those pages.

Milo wouldn't violate that privacy though.

Despite the late hour, he texts Milo.

Should have woken me. I'll never get to sleep now.

You looked way too peaceful

When did you leave?

About eight? Early enough not to get the third degree. Helped mom with pies.

Thrilling. When are we hanging next?

I think after Christmas ☹, dad being a jerk

Andrew bites his lip and pulls back a frown. He was hoping to see more of Milo over break. He understands, but it still hurts.

Remember to delete that before he checks your phone.

All right. Later.

Night.

Sleep won't be coming soon. Andrew feels too alert for it, too buzzed on Milo's nearness and his smell, which lingers on the pillow. Andrew buries his face in it and inhales. He doesn't feel guilty; needing Milo is visceral. He's enjoying college, but missing Milo is a constant, like the star-strewn sky. Even with a blanket of clouds obscuring it, it's always there.

Milo is the same as always. Andrew knows he himself has changed—his body finally seems to be letting him grow into it, and what was left of his gangly, coltish and too thin body has stretched into something slim and filled out in good ways. Andrew wonders if Milo noticed that, then shakes his head. Why would he?

It's dark out, and, when Andrew touches the pane of the window, cold. Too cold for a walk, and cloudy too, so that the night sky blinds his view of the stars. Andrew picks up his journal, rolls off his bed, away from the tempting smell on his pillow, and goes downstairs. The fire his parents built is nothing but glowing embers, but he enjoys them nonetheless. His journal falls open to his last entry, and he takes a few moments to clear his mind before starting the next.

o o o

WALTHAM FEELS less familiar after Christmas than Andrew expected. He has to work harder to lose himself in the moment. The nights he walks back to his dorm alone, so late sometimes it's really morning, the air is so stifling, despite the cold, that he imagines the press of the full campus closing in on him. In his bed, skin still painted with the scent and buzz of whatever party he's left, he'll ease into sleep, not with the memories of a few hours ago, but of the way the moon paints itself, distorted and quivering in endless motion, on the water of Chickopee, his favorite beach. His heart is always the most open there. Home whispers in a language of familiar longing. Here, in this school skin, he is a different person.

o

Milo is on his way home one night in February, thinking of the email he'll compose to Andrew, reporting what he's done and sharing semi-good news, when he decides he'd rather call. It's late, so he knows the call will be hit-or-miss, but he misses Andrew's voice.

"Hey," he says when Andrew picks up. "Is this an okay time?"

"It's always a good time to call me."

"Well, no, not really," Milo says, thinking of the nights Andrew answers drunk, or nights when he doesn't text back until hours later. Sometimes he over-shares why he's taken so long. Milo doesn't much like that, but he can't tell Andrew what to do, or even *why* he's uncomfortable. He isn't sure why he is, which makes articulating it impossible.

"What's up?" Andrew asks. He yawns.

"I went to another thing."

"Oh, awesome! Another movie night?"

"No, more like a mixer thing?"

"That sounds like something straight out of the fifties," Andrew says, laughing. Milo looks up at his dorm building. It's so nice out; he's still getting used to the mildness when he could be home, mired in winter. He doesn't want to go inside. It's dark; early nightfalls still press on them.

"Yes, but it wasn't," Milo says. "The kids told me about this thing called the Rainbow Floor. A few of them live there."

"Oh yeah! I remember seeing that on the website. Didn't I tell you about it?"

"Maybe? I don't remember, but if it was early last semester, you might have and I forgot. I wasn't absorbing much."

"Yeah," Andrew says softly. "Do you want to live there? Would your father know?"

"No, this is the great part," Milo says. "They, like, disguise the floor for parent and family weekends as a multicultural floor. Housing Contracts won't say anything. It's in the Century dorm, which is nice. There are four-person apartments, a pool, volleyball courts and all sorts of stuff."

"Wow, that's swanky. I'm planning on shitty student apartments, houses or crowded dorms. Can I come live with you?"

"Please," Milo says with feeling, "That would be great."

"If only."

Neither speaks for a long moment.

"So do you think you'll do it?"

"I'm definitely going to check it out."

"Good," Andrew says. "Milo?"

"Yeah?"

"I'm really proud of you. For going out tonight and everything else."

Milo watches the stars and treasures the warmth in his stomach and the familiarity of Andrew's voice. "Thank you."

o o o

ANDREW'S SUMMER break ends sooner than Milo's. Andrew's worried over it, and tells Milo he hates the thought of leaving him even for a little bit. The months at home have worn Milo by degrees until the carriage and confidence he brought from school have been stripped by his father's control and words. Occasionally, his father grants Milo nights away from home, no curfew or rules, as a reward for doing so well during his first year of college.

The night before Andrew has to leave, Milo is granted one of these stays. He asked his father with a gut-churning worry over the lie he was telling—a night with other friends—and also because he so badly needed to be with Andrew before he left. His father smiled and clapped him on the back.

They watch movies late into the night. Andrew's bought all of Milo's guilty pleasure snacks and planned the order of movies. Milo laughs at some of his choices, but goes along when he sees *Juno*, which is his favorite.

"How do you possibly think we'll stay awake for all this? Or that your attention will last that long?"

"Hope springs eternal," Andrew replies, voice dry, rolling his eyes.

○

Halfway through *The Order of the Phoenix*, Andrew turns to Milo. "What's your plan when you go back?"

Milo turns the volume down and looks up to the ceiling. "Deprogram?"

"How?"

"I don't know." Andrew turns toward him, head flat on the pillow. His face is sad. The flickering lights of the movie cast strange shadows. "I still suck at making good friends."

"God, I wish we weren't so far from each other," Andrew says.

Milo takes his hands and folds their arms together until Andrew is on his side, close enough to his body to feel the heat radiating from him. He's always been so much warmer than Andrew's near-permanent cold state. They're both comfortable in silence. It speaks to them and for them.

But there aren't words for the look in Milo's eyes when Andrew meets them. It's too dark to see the color, but bright enough for the intensity of his gaze to spark an electric connection they've only shared once, when they kissed.

Neither of them move, and Andrew holds that look, and his breath, for too long. Milo presses his lips together and then licks them and Andrew *knows*, knows that if he wanted, he could tip into the last layer of space between them and kiss him.

Instead, he closes his eyes and tries to breathe and force his mind into a rational frame. Milo is vulnerable now, and so softly open, and he wants, *oh*, Andrew wants too badly what he knows he can't have.

"Drew." Milo's whisper is barely audible and so different from his usual voice. Andrew feels the breath of the words and opens his eyes to see Milo closing that space between them; everything else slips away then, when Milo's damp lips and hot breath touch him. He kisses back by instinct, pushing closer, as close as he can, and when the tenor of the kiss changes —when Milo's lips tremble from hesitant to passionate—Andrew opens his mouth, sucks lightly at Milo's bottom lip and then welcomes his tongue. He scarcely dares to breathe, terrified to break whatever spell has been cast on this moment.

It's only when hunger comes over them, when Milo pushes in roughly and Andrew rolls easily onto his back to accept it, that Milo pulls back. He tightens his hold on Andrew's hands, but when Andrew opens his eyes, Milo's eyes are closed and his breathing is rough and uneven. "I can't," he says in a graveled voice. His eyelids tremble, and he radiates fear and aching longing.

o

When disappointment sags through Andrew's body, Milo's disgust with himself swamps every muscle and bone. His body, so close to Andrew's, and his lips still savoring the taste of that kiss, wants and wants to keep Andrew on his back, roll over him and surround him with the call of his heart and body.

But it would be impossible. Andrew doesn't need sex from him—he's not shy about getting it where and when he wants. And while Milo knows he wants it, and that it would be different between the two of them, the thought of letting this friendship with it's too-much intimacy slide into something else terrifies him. Milo isn't the one Andrew deserves, someone clean and capable of healthy love.

"I'm sorry," he whispers, because Andrew deserves to know. He tries to tell himself he can't feel the pain radiating from Andrew. "All I do is drag you down. You deserve better."

"I wish you wouldn't say that." Andrew's voice breaks, and, deep inside, something breaks in Milo as well.

"I wish I could give you what you want," Milo whispers. "I'm going away in a few weeks. I can't make promises, and I don't want to break *this*. You're my best friend, Drew."

Andrew tips his forehead against his. Everything they should say to each other smothers them both. They don't speak again.

o o o

FALL COMES with a new room, one not wallpapered with breasts or heavy with the weight either of homophobia, or of the stifling loneliness that plagued him the first year. It will take a few weeks to begin to feel like himself—the new him—again. Milo's new roommate, Paul, and suitemates, Dave and Will, are a welcome change from Shane. The whole floor is, of course. Milo's never experienced this level of automatic understanding and community. He doesn't expect to be best friends or close to anyone just because they all live on Rainbow Floor, but his room is laid out well, and he loves that it's in an apartment. He shares the space with three other men he doesn't know, but he likes them all immediately. His first instinct upon moving in is not to try to hide a panic attack. That's progress.

Once he's settled in, he organizes his desk, memorizes his schedule and plans a trip to the bookstore. He knows he'll have to explore the new building soon. For now, though, what he wants is to stretch out on his bed and call Andrew. He rolls onto his bed and thumbs over Andrew's number, but doesn't call.

Milo's first summer home from school passed in a dizzying blur and ended on such a bittersweet note; he wonders how long it will take him to integrate it all and digest it. He plays the best of his summer on a loop, rifling through memories like snapshots—not to find the spaces where he let his father break him down, but to find things to hold on to so far from home.

Lucy and Ted in June, bold in the yellow light of a too-bright bonfire, cajoling everyone out of their clothes and into the water in a blur of Cuervo and laughter. He tries not to remember the long line of Andrew's spine or the way his skin glowed, because he wasn't meant to look.

In July Andrew promised to make up for their awkward trip to Provincetown. This time they went with friends. Ted laughed from the backseat at every song Andrew picked as Milo drove. In the rearview mirror he could see Sarah and Lucy squashed next to Ted, one blonde and the other brunette, heads bobbing in time to the music. As they went from one club to club to another, they'd all loosened up, and through the whole night, Andrew stayed with him. By the time they got to the last club, they were all raucous and sweat-dewed from dancing. Milo's hair began to fall from its hold, and Andrew's hands were blazing hot, urging him to dance when "Shut up and Dance" came blaring on. A long time ago, when they were kids, Andrew was obsessed with that song with its catching loops and lyrics he couldn't help but dance to. He remembers the lamp they broke when Andrew turned the music up and forced him to his feet, and laughing the whole time. It was little more than jumping around gracelessly, bumping into each other and laughing loud enough to draw Andrew's mom up to see what the racket was. She turned the music up louder, kissed them both and went downstairs.

Provincetown that night was like that. Laughing and brave. He danced with Andrew, with his friends and strangers, as if the strings that tied him in his father's grip, a helpless marionette caught in webs of pain, had been cut. That night he pretended they had.

In August, when even the trees seemed to sweat, he forced Andrew into the woods with planks of plywood and a bag of nails and screws, and a tool belt Andrew cracked up at immediately, to go fix up the old fort. In the winter he'd seen what a wreck the snow and a year of neglect had made of it. Seeing something so important falling apart settled, aching, in his chest and nagged at him until he had to fix it. And fixing it wouldn't have been the same without Andrew there to complain and swear at him. When the sun dappled between the shifting leaves, trailing shadows over Andrew with his lightened hair and his skin an unbroken smooth tan from days in the sun and in the water, Milo knew he loved this boy so deeply that it seemed impossible to hold it back.

When September called them both away, he mourned his discretion. It hurt them both, but it was better than the hurt he'd inevitably inflict if he took Andrew's face in rough hands and kept kissing him as sweetly and helplessly as he loves him. When he woke the next morning after that ill-advised kiss, Andrew was boneless and tangled with him, warm and soft and heartbreaking. Staring at the ceiling and feeling too much roiling in his stupid body, he wished for once that Andrew would get mad at him. Because he deserved it, and Andrew's unwavering forgiveness and understanding seemed like pity for the broken boy he'll always be.

o o o

"I KNOW I promised not to judge," Nat says late one night, "but you've been extra..." She's on Andrew's beanbag chair with a hand mirror, plucking her eyebrows. The tips of her black hair are white, styled in crazy spiked tufts. Her lips are still stained from the blood red lipstick she wears whenever she leaves her room.

"Extra?" Andrew tries to control the edge in his voice.

"Active? Sad?"

Andrew stops tapping his fingers against her desk and looks at her carefully. She's watching him with unusual kindness. Nat's a fun friend, but not a soft person by nature. He sighs. The weight of what passed between him and Milo sits so heavily, crouching at all times, ready to steal his breath with its strength.

"Maybe I am." He lifts a shoulder and wills a familiar sting from his eyes. "Maybe it's okay for me to do whatever I have to do to forget some things."

"Andrew..." She puts down the mirror and moves as if to come closer, but he shakes his head. "What happened? What's going on?"

"I don't really want to talk about it."

"Can you tell me why you think what you're doing is going to make you feel better?"

He stares at the assortment of pens and paper and sticky-notes littered on her desk. Studies the laces of his shoes and the rough texture of the cheap carpet she's covered the linoleum dorm floors with.

"Are you getting what you need?" Nat asks.

"Maybe one thing." A door opens and slams shut in the corridor, and the sound of chatter and laughter slinks in from the hall. It's almost dinner time.

"You're in love with him, and he's not in love with you, so you sleep around?"

"No," Andrew snaps.

"No, you're not in love with him?" Disbelief is clear in her voice.

"No." His voice cracks with tears. "He *is* in love with me. I told myself for a really long time that he wasn't, even when I thought maybe he was."

"So what's the problem?"

"He won't," he says. It's simple to him because, intellectually, he understands. He understands Milo's fear, yes. But also he knows, even when it makes him feel helpless and angry and resentful, that Milo doesn't trust it will work, that either of them is capable of making a relationship last.

"So this—" She waves her hand. "Is what, sloppy seconds?"

He winces at her words. "No, not exactly. When I'm with him, there's something I don't want from anyone else. A way we're close, and how comfortable it is to be with him, or next to him or holding him."

"So let me get this straight. What you're saying is you get your cuddle on with him, but fuck other people because you can't get that from him?"

Andrew lets her words sink in, because so baldly put they are like a hit to his stomach.

"I never would have put it that way. It's... the thought of being really intimate, like that, with anyone else, is—" He bites his lip and searches for the words. "It makes my skin crawl."

"But you're a horny nineteen-year-old who has to hump like a rabbit?" Nat jokes. She's trying to lighten the mood, but he doesn't appreciate it.

"You make it sound gross. And it doesn't feel that way to me."

"Explain."

"I mean, the sex. I don't know. It doesn't feel like anything wrong, and I don't like the way you judge me for it. Or anyone else. Sex is sex to me. I enjoy it. I don't need or want extra strings attached."

"You don't want those together one day? If he really can't love you like you want him to?"

Andrew realizes suddenly he's clenched his fists hard enough to hurt. "It's fucked up when you put it that way," he admits. She doesn't say anything, but stands and pulls him into a hug. "I can't stop hoping that one day..." He sighs. "Why can't I make my heart behave and understand and be patient or kind or realistic?"

"Because we can't make our hearts do everything we want."

chapter seven

HIS MOTHER'S VOICE IS WAVERING OVER THE PHONE LINE and Milo has to duck his head and cover his ear to hear her. It's loud in Claire's apartment; the blare of TV and shouted conversation overpower the sound of his mom's voice.

"Milo..."

"Mom, is everything okay?" Milo half shouts. His mother calls him once a week, dutifully, Wednesday evenings at seven. Gives him boring town gossip and pretends her calls will keep him tethered to her.

Love can't save someone who won't be saved, and it's taken Milo a while to figure out that no matter what he says, she'll never leave his father. The crushing guilt of leaving her alone with him almost killed him that first year at USC. It's easier to forget that her acquiescent silence was as damaging as his father's special brand of abuse. His summer at home made so many things clear to him. With the bond between him and Andrew slackened, Milo feels less and less responsibility to care about the place that used to be home. California might never feel like home either, but it certainly doesn't hurt the way Santuit does.

"Your father is in the hospital," she says. "He had a massive heart attack; he's been on life support, but they don't think he's going to make it." Tears; he definitely hears them now. He doesn't feel anything.

"Okay." For a moment he's completely blank, and all the noise of the room falls away. He should offer condolences? Offer to come home? Feel bad?

"Will you come home?" She makes it easy, because he doesn't have to make an empty offer. "Help me say goodbye?"

Milo closes his eyes. He's made his way out of the room and into the hall. He pinches the bridge of his nose and swallows shouts of frustration. Her persistent invention of a life where he'd *want* to say goodbye frustrates the shit out of him. The pretense that must have sustained her through years of enabling his father in demeaning and abusing him with words and sometimes hands makes him sick. Loving her makes him sick too because, like everything else, he can't help it.

He doesn't yell though, because that won't change anything. "Sure, Mom. I'll find a flight."

None of his dorm mates are home, which is fantastic news, because Milo is on a single mission: Book a flight and then get shit-faced alone.

It doesn't take him long to do either, and soon enough everything is a surreal, nauseating blur that begins to sit on him heavily, while his thoughts careen beyond his control. He isn't numb at all; he's brought on helplessness. The specter of his father, a man much bigger in Milo's memory than in real life, nags him. The secrets he keeps locked away begin to rise.

He throws up once and then puts his too-hot forehead on the floor and tries to breathe, but he can't slow his brain and his lungs. Despite the unspooling of the tie that's bound him to Andrew, there's only one person Milo depends on when panic and fear hit him like this. His face is wet with tears he hasn't registered, whose origin—panic or fear or grief—he can't name. They leave wet splotches on his shirt when he wipes them away, but the screen of his phone still blurs when he calls Andrew.

"I'm sorry," is the first thing he says when Andrew's concerned voice prickles through the line. Shit, it's one a.m. "I always call when I'm a mess."

Since the summer, this is what they've reduced themselves to. Texts, sometimes, because longing and frustration are easier to handle like that, and phone calls when he's in a panic. Milo realizes more and more that he should erase himself from Andrew's life, because Andrew's hurt is so clear. Although he tries to hold out, whenever things are at their worst, he can never stop himself from calling Andrew to help him get through it.

"Milo, what's going on, you sound awful, are you drun—okay, Milo, you need to take a long, slow breath." Andrew's voice immediately goes into calming mode. That sound is enough to slam Milo into that ugly, scared and weak place, which is also that space that's so safe.

"M-my dad..." He hiccups. "My mom called and he's in the hospital. He's dying."

"Oh my god."

"She needs me to go back. To help. Or something. She said she wants me to say goodbye." He ends the sentence feeling a bitter anger that burns up his throat and into his mouth.

"You don't have to, you know," Andrew says. "You don't have to go back, you *don't*."

"You know I do. Of course I do."

"No, no." There's a rustling in the background and Milo can hear Andrew whispering something.

"God, fuck, have I interrupted something?"

"Nothing more than my sleep, dummy."

"Sorry," Milo says lamely. He knows Andrew isn't alone. The only time he ever experiences Andrew's anger is through texts he gets late some nights. It's not vicious, but it's bitter, because they both know Milo doesn't need to know about the boys Andrew sleeps with.

"Stop apologizing."

"I don't mean to only call you when I'm like this."

"I know," Andrew says softly.

"I do have to go home." Milo is lying on the floor now with the fuzz of the bathroom throw rug scratching against his hand. "I can't not. She needs me."

Andrew breathes. It's calming, and Milo can feel himself slipping into a near sleep.

"Well, I'll see you there, then."

"Andrew—" Milo whispers, wanting to protest because he should.

"Sleep it off. Call me in the morning to give me your flight details."

o

"Everything okay?" Emery rolls over, eyes still mostly shut, hair a fucked-out mess, eyeliner smudged.

"No, I have to—you have to go." Andrew trips over his own discarded pants, then pulls them up over his bare ass.

"Andrew, it's one in the morning." Emery sits up with the sheet pooling in his lap.

"I'm know, but I have to pack and find flights." Andrew tosses Emery his shirt. The frown starting to build on Emery's face clears.

"What's happened?" Emery asks, hopping into his clothes. He's still half drunk, too, so he almost falls over. "Fuck, I hope you aren't planning on going anywhere right now."

"No, I need to shower and get myself pulled together. My friend's father is dying."

"Who?"

"No one you know, from back home." Andrew shakes his head as if that will clear it. He's still tipsy, but also a little hungover, some sort of sick post-party twilight he's never visited before. "God, fuck, what did we do?"

"You and I, or the party?"

"Har, har." Andrew shoots Emery a smirk. "I remember what we did quite clearly, thank you very much."

"You are so welcome." Emery, dressed at last, leans forward to peck Andrew's lips. "Can I do anything for you here, then?"

"No, I'm going to shower first and finish the sobering process."

"Well then, until next time, and all that—"

"All that?" Andrew follows Emery to the door.

"You know, the next time you tell me you really aren't going to sleep with me this time."

Andrew laughs and pushes him lightly out the door. "I mean it this time."

"I'll believe that when I see it," Emery calls out.

The laughter dies on Andrew's lips as soon as the door is locked. His head throbs a little, and his body is layered in sweat and the scent of sex and smoke; his bed is a wreck, and his mouth tastes like garbage.

First things first: Andrew drinks enough water for three people, pops three Advil, and sets the shower to lukewarm. While he's in the water, edging it a little cooler, he begins to feel clearheaded enough to plan the next few steps.

○ ○ ○

MILO WANDERS upstairs feeling as if his insides are expanding beyond the borders of his skin, as if the stifling gray he's been swimming in since his mother called might roll out of him and spill throughout the house. The sound of people speaking in hushed tones—as if they care, as if no one knew what kind of man James Graham was—follows him all the way to his room.

He barely remembers the last week: the redeye flight home; holding his mother in the hospital after she signed off on terminating support; pulling together a funeral whose details had already been planned. Of course James Graham would not trust anyone else with this. Even dead, he's exerting his control.

The funeral reception is in full swing, if such a thing can be said of such a somber gathering. Downstairs, people tell stories that portray his father in much kinder light than he deserves. Milo spares a few moments to wonder what it is about death that makes people want to sanctify the person who passed. Milo stood with them as long as he could, biting back every wave of anger and urge to tell all the truths hidden in this house for so long.

His room is a refuge. Milo sits for a long time in a floating, almost unbearable space. He forces himself to breathe as Andrew coached him time after time. His eyes trace a scuffed mark along the baseboard of the far wall. He can't for the life of him remember how that had happened. If his father ever saw it, Milo is sure he would remember, because there would have been hell to pay. The sight of a coffin being lowered slowly into the hard ground echoes in his head. His heart is cramping and he isn't sure why—why it insists on feeling grief when what he should be feeling is freedom. No. *Nonono*, he cannot not afford to let his father's memory in, not for a second. If it does, if he tears that thin membrane protecting the world from that turmoil inside, nothing will ever be put to rights again. For anyone. *He* will never be put to rights again.

The door slides open a few inches; Andrew slips in and closes it behind him. No noise follows—Milo supposes enough time has passed that everyone has left. Andrew is all soft eyes and familiar smile; the collar of his soft lilac dress shirt is unbuttoned, his tie has been abandoned and his sleek black pants are losing their crease. From the moment he met Milo at the airport with a hug and a hand to hold, but offered silently, Andrew has been, as always, exactly what he needs.

"Hey," Andrew says. Milo's room is as it has been since he left for USC—mostly stripped, a sad shell of what was always pretty sad space. Andrew takes it in with a cursory glance. "Everyone is gone."

"Thanks," Milo says. He doesn't look up. "Sorry, I just—"

"It's fine." Andrew sits next to him carefully. "Your mom went to lie down, so my mom and I put the food away."

"God, I'm sorry. I didn't eve—"

"Stop." Andrew puts a hand on Milo's knee and squeezes hard. "You don't need to think about that stuff right now. That's what I'm here for. What we're all here for."

"What you're here for," Milo repeats. His voice lifts a little and when he looks up at Andrew, his eyes are intense and bright. Andrew bites his lip and exhales through his nose. Milo could spend every moment of these few days together looking at Andrew and relearning every detail he's missed in the last months, as well as the new ones. Andrew here today is both the same boy he's known and altogether someone new.

The distance between them, like two sailboats slipped farther and farther from their moorings in the last few months, has never seemed so real or so scary. He regrets every time he wanted to call Andrew and didn't, every new thing they've done and haven't talked about and all the space they've pushed between them to avoid something he knows won't ever change.

"What do I do now?" Milo whispers.

Andrew frowns. "What do you mean?"

Milo sighs and closes his eyes, then turns himself toward Andrew's body. He pulls him in tightly; Andrew's breath is hot against his skin.

"Who am I even, like this?"

"You're you."

"Andrew," Milo says as he pulls back, his voice scratchy with tears, "my whole life, he's been there. Sometimes, it felt like all my life *was* him."

"But that's not true." Andrew kneels on the bed and puts his hands on Milo's shoulders. "You're so much more."

"Drew, I'm not talking about how you see me or how you want me to believe in a greater future or anything like that. I mean that my whole life feels like it was centered on being scared of him. Of wishing," he says, dashing tears away, "*fuck*, that I could fucking make him happy for once. Of working for his love and wondering how I could love him."

"Milo," Andrew says, but it sounds hopeless.

"He was the only thing, the only thing." Milo moans, bent over and crying against Andrew's knees. "I thought it would be over when I went away. I thought I'd break away from him."

"I know," Andrew whispers. "We both thought that."

"I'll always be stuck here, won't I?"

"No, *no*," Andrew says fiercely, fingers digging into Milo's shoulders and pulling him up. "No, that's not true." He uses his thumbs to swipe at the moisture on Milo's face.

"I'm sorry."

"Oh my god," Andrew says with a watery laugh. "Stop apologizing—"

"Ugh." Milo covers his eyes. "I was barely holding it together, and then you came in. You're always my emotional overload victim."

"Well, I'd hardly say victim," Andrew says with an eye roll. "Like I said, that's what best friends are for." He presses his lips together as soon as the words are out.

"I know you said not to apologize, but I *am* sorry things have been off for the last few months."

"Well, that's on both of us."

Milo pulls Andrew's hand from his shoulder and holds it between his own. "I've really missed you, though."

Andrew's fingers are warm. His face glows. "Good. Because I've missed you too."

"Do you ever miss the way things were?" Milo pulls away and lies on the bed, pulling Andrew with him.

"What, before college?"

"Yeah," Milo says.

Andrew shrugs. Their knees bump together. On his side and so close, Milo can see that the tan Andrew sported over the summer has faded. His face is beautiful: familiar and sweet and open and so missed. Milo hasn't named his longing, but it's a subterranean ache he's carried around as he's gone off into his new life. It's not a best friend kind of longing, what he's lived with since September. It's a love longing: the one he's talked himself out of for a ridiculously long time.

"I miss some things. I miss my mom's cooking," Andrew says, glossing over the silence.

"Yeah, me too."

"Obviously, I miss you," Andrew says more quietly. He shifts a little closer; the heat from his body and the sound of his voice are comforting. "But I don't miss you being here, because that was hard for you. I'll never miss you being in pain."

Milo closes his eyes when they start to burn. "Andrew," he says helplessly.

"That's why I'll always be okay with missing you," Andrew whispers. "Because it's better than the alternative."

"He's gone."

"Is he?" Andrew asks. "Here?" His hand covers Milo's chest and his thumb moves rhythmically back and forth. Milo covers it with his hand. Andrew, *oh god*, how is he always just right?

"Maybe one day," Milo says. "God, I h-hope—" Milo's face crumples and he starts to cry, thinking of all the years he's struggled, and how he feels as if it's all still inside, a poison he doesn't have an antidote for . Andrew is right; he's not free yet.

"Milo." Andrew shifts forward, closing the space between them. "I'm sorry about the texts." For all their quiet, Andrew's words pierce Milo more sharply than anything he's felt in the last week.

"I'm—" Milo bites his lip and takes a breath and rushes through the confession. "I'm sorry about that night. I'm sorry I've always been so scared. You deserve so much more."

Andrew holds him tighter, his smell overpowers Milo, and against his cheek Andrew's skin is a soft welcome. Home is here, wrapped up with this man. He can't help but press a small kiss to the skin of his neck, then the jut of his jaw where stubble has started to roughen it, before taking Andrew's parted lips with his own. Milo's kissing him for the love they've been in, for the desire and longing he's denied himself. Even the idea of letting another person this close has scared Milo for as long as he can remember. Andrew is the safest person in his whole world, the only one he can ever imagine himself really wanting.

He kisses Andrew's cheeks and nose and mouth, all slippery with his tears. But by the time he works his way back to Andrew's mouth, all he hears is Andrew whispering his name, shocked and gasping. Milo works his lips over that gasp, captures Andrew's mouth in a kiss that's familiar despite the fact that they've only done this twice in four years.

"Milo, what—" Andrew breaks away. His fingers are twisted into the fabric of his shirt.

"I love you," Milo says, knowing no words can really express what's happening inside him right now. "I love you and I've missed you and I want you." He looks away and takes a breath before meeting Andrew's eyes. "I've never done this. I want to give you this."

"God, *oh*—" Andrew kisses him then, quick, light kisses Milo wants to chase. "I love you too. Please say this isn't just for me, though."

"No, no." Milo shakes his head. "I didn't mean it like that—I'm so—"

"Don't apologize." Andrew winds his leg between Milo's and rolls them over. "Just kiss me right now, please."

Andrew kisses him so hard, desperate and a little dirty, and all heat and passion. Milo races to catch up but can't and so submits, gives what Andrew is seeking, lets Andrew's mouth and touch take him somewhere safe and new and full of feelings he's never let himself have.

"Do you have—"

"Here," Milo says, fumbling for the half forgotten lube in his bedside drawer.

It's very dark and very quiet. Milo isn't sure what impulse makes Andrew shut off the tiny light, but he doesn't say anything. In the dark, everything can be Andrew. In the dark, Milo can let Andrew erase the last of his borders.

Andrew settles them so that Milo is on top of him. His fingers find the buttons of Milo's shirt so easily, as if this is a dance they've done a thousand times before. Milo's fingers feel clumsy and unsure, but Andrew catches them, kisses them and helps guide them. The only sound in the room is the whisk of cloth as they pull shirts off, and the near silent flump as they hit the floor. Andrew toes his shoes off, and they clatter to the floor. Milo breathes carefully and helps Andrew with his pants. Andrew handles the lube with ease, and then his hands squeeze Milo's hips hard when he pulls them together. His skin against Milo's feels heartbreakingly intimate. He wonders if his door is locked, and then Andrew's lips brush his again, and again, and Milo stops thinking.

o

Andrew tries to let himself be carried on the wave of frantic need that carried them into this moment, so he won't have to stop and think. But as soon as his skin is on Milo's, with their shirts off and Milo sweat-damp and dream-spun under his hands, guilt crests faster than desire.

"Is this—? Milo—"

"Don't ask." Milo opens his mouth over Andrew's and draws a wicked kiss, needful and dark, from him, then gasps when Andrew runs his hands down his back to cup him closer. Andrew knows the tone. It's the no-nonsense tone. It's the one he never questions, the one that never needs questioning.

Milo's fingers skim Andrew's body. His touch is tentative and curious and thrilling. It's also laced with pain. Not at his father's loss, exactly, but because it's an ending that means many things will change, most of all Milo. Milo has been gray mist since Andrew picked him up at the airport. He's been fog, empty and lonely echoes.

"You know I'll always take care of you, right?" Andrew asks. He slides his foot up Milo's calf and opens his legs so he can cradle Milo between them. The vulnerability of the words and his body set off an ache in Andrew's core.

"Andrew—" Milo's words cut off when Andrew rolls up against him, one long line of sweet, hot skin and desire clearly transmitted through the state of his body. Andrew's lips open over his again, dragging Milo into their heat and into the waves of devastating desire they let crash between them.

o o o

MILO WAKES alone, deep in the night. There's a note on the pillow next to his head.

Milo, meet me there

Milo sighs and lies back, feeling the air, too cool, slipping over his naked torso. The barest light emanates from the small bedside lamp, he recognizes Andrew's words written in his most careful handwriting: the lovely curled M a remnant of Andrew's calligraphy-learning phase, the tiny dotted star trailing the end of the E. He used a ballpoint pen; when Milo traces his fingers over the words he can feel the barest edge where the tip dug into the thick paper of the note card.

He checks his phone. It's well past midnight, and, while he has no idea what time he fell into sleep, he has a pretty good idea that Andrew's been gone for a while now. The sheets in the bed next to him carry no lingering warmth.

Milo dresses carefully, rooting through his suitcase for something other than the suit currently wrinkling on the floor by the bed. He throws on a ratty hooded sweater unearthed from the catacombs of his closet, a maroon and yellow college sweater with a crackled logo and tattered hems. It's worn through in spots, and he'll be cold almost before he's halfway there. He stops by the couch downstairs and grabs a throw blanket and a coat. The flashlight his father kept for power emergencies is where it always was, where it probably always will be.

Milo will leave, but his mom never will, not as long as she can stay. And even without James in their house—or in the world—she'll maintain everything as she's been trained.

Milo flicks on the buttery light of the flashlight as soon as he's slipped out the back door. Frost-brittle leaves crunch under his feet, and from far off the ocean shushes the night. In the slight heat that rises through the neck of the sweatshirt is a scent—Andrew's smell—one he hasn't smelled on himself in years.

Andrew's woken him; his touch ripped Milo painfully into his body when he most needed the numbness. And it's not the pain of his father's death, but another pain, a deep-rooted pain he anticipates will strengthen and become more complex before he's found his way back home.

Light filters between the ill-fitted boards cobbling their fort together; it filters through the trees from afar, registering as a small twinkle until he comes close enough to see clearly. There's a blanket over the open square that was the lookout window. Milo can't help but think that nothing has changed, yet nothing is the same because he's not the same boy who built this sanctuary and walked through the framed door into a world of make-believe Andrew could always craft so easily and vividly.

Milo clears his throat before stepping in. Andrew is sitting with his legs curled in the far corner, huddled into a fleece blanket. A lantern casts light and shadows around the small room. It's small enough that there's not enough room to sit without bumping knees or feet.

Andrew's sleepy-eyed and mussed; he looks small under the blanket that envelops him.

"How long have you been here?" Milo asks, keeping his voice low.

"I don't know," Andrew whispers back. His lips tremble in the cold. Milo moves to get closer, but Andrew gestures him back. Milo settles back with a sigh.

"It's not that I don't—" Andrew tips up a shoulder, and his face is rueful. "I thought we should talk."

Milo wraps himself in his own blanket, covers the lantern and knocks it over. Once he's untangled and righted it, he's temporarily blinded by the direct glare. He blinks; when he looks around he notices how much darker the walls are than he remembers.

"Hey," he says softly, nudging Andrew's knee. "You painted."

Andrew looks up, and Milo can see him swallowing. "Yeah, I did."

"When?"

"When I came home for the long weekend in October." Andrew's fingers trail down the wall. In the night, the walls look black except where the lantern reveals a deep blue. Above his head are scatters of light pricks and moons and planets.

"Finding your way?" Milo jokes lightly. Andrew has always found his way by the stars, not using standard constellation maps, but his own visions.

"Searching for Cygnus," Andrew says. Milo's not sure which one that is, only that the irony in his tone means something.

They don't say anything, letting the night settle over their tiny retreat like its own blanket. Milo lets this place, a place that was always theirs—one that they've outgrown—settle him. He dropped out of sleep heavily; that *something's missing* feeling startled him until he realized it was Andrew. That disoriented him even more.

He takes time, now, to look him over. That uneasy sense that they've both changed irrevocably in the months since September has dissipated. Andrew doesn't look any different—he's the boy Milo has always known. Well, man. They're supposed to be men now, forging into adult lives away from school and their parents.

"I can't tell what I'm feeling," Andrew says.

"Yeah, I'm sort of there myself."

"It's cold. This is dumb," Andrew opens his blanket and arranges himself, inviting Milo to share his body heat. They shuffle and tangle until they're perfectly fitted in a space a shade too small. *This is the shape of my childhood, too tight around me.* But Andrew makes it okay.

"Are you okay?" Milo asks.

"Of course I am." There's a tiny thread suggesting otherwise in the words, though.

"How is this going to work?"

Andrew's fingers slide between Milo's, tracing the beds of his fingernails and the palm of his hand. "I think you have to say goodbye."

"I didn't mean home. I meant us."

Andrew's shoulder shrugs under his head.

"*Andrew.*" Milo presses his forehead into Andrew's shoulder.

"I've thought of this for so long, you know," Andrew says.

Milo nods. "Do you feel like I took advantage of that? Because I promise it wasn't like that—"

"I know," Andrew says. Milo looks up and Andrew's cheeks are wet, too. "I hope you don't think I took advantage either?"

"Of course not."

They are quiet. The dark presses against the walls outside the fort. The helplessness of thinking he'll only ever amount to the shell his father made of him has lifted. Whether thanks to Andrew's touch, or his unwavering support, he now dares to hope he'll move on this time, from this life and his father.

"I've been so afraid to love you," Milo admits.

"I've never been able to do anything else. That's why I've never stayed with anyone else," Andrew says. "And that's fine. That's just the way it was."

"You've loved me for years. Have you waited?"

"Yes. But not like you think. Waited might not be the right word." Andrew's fingers curl and tighten around his. "Hoped without hoping."

"You have always deserved more."

"Oh, I don't know about that."

"Don't play this off, Andrew. I want you to have love, you know?" He doesn't mean it to sound the way it does—he wants nothing more in the world than to be able to give him that love. He thinks of Andrew's last words before their bodies took them beyond speech, promising to always take care of Milo. "Will

I always only be the broken boy you worked so hard to keep together?"

Andrew stiffens, and Milo searches for the right words. Andrew kisses his temple so softly it's a whisper of touch.

"I don't know that I can love you best," Milo says finally. "You deserve more than someone who has always been scared of letting himself be loved, or believing he's worthy. I want so badly to be a different man."

"Nothing will ever feel like this for me," Andrew says, voice so thick with tears it's hard to understand him. "That was the best one-night stand of my life." Andrew's tone is playful, regardless of the tears. Despite the kiss, there's a deep tension in Andrew's body.

"Is that what this is?"

"I'll always be Andrew from your past, won't I? I'll always be a part of that life, Milo."

"Why is that so bad? You were always the best part—"

"Because you can go now. He's gone. I want you to be better, Milo."

Milo swallows, because he wants to deny all of that, deny it as if he hasn't been thinking something similar. After a silence they fill with shuddering breaths, Andrew speaks. Despite his own confusion, it's clear what Andrew is saying, and it's goodbye.

"Will you make me a promise?" Andrew says, words thick with tears.

"Yes, of course." Milo turns so they are face to face.

"Learn to believe it. Do everything you wanted to do that you were scared of before."

"Andrew." Milo kisses him, inhales him and tucks this moment into his heart. "I wish I could have this with you."

"Do me a favor?" Andrew pulls back and takes a deep breath. He closes his eyes, nuzzles into Milo's hands and wipes his face clear of tears. "Write them down. Every dream you have for the future. The things you always wanted to do. Bring them to the bonfire, tonight."

Milo searches Andrew's eyes. "Only if you will, too." He has no idea why Andrew wants this, but he'd do anything right now for him.

o o o

EVEN FOR Andrew, who loves winter, it's colder than usual this December. Perhaps the coldest part is the mood that lingers in the air, in the planned goodbye to a father who never deserved such ceremony.

They planned a bonfire for Milo's last night, something they used to do as teenagers that was just for them, a special group of friends bonding. Tonight it's to say goodbye. These friends and their families—Sarah and Ted and Lucy, over time, had come to know the secrets the Grahams hid. They all understood the rigid care James took to ensure no harm was great enough to bring trouble to his door, and that the only support they could offer was harbor and complicity, giving Milo as many spaces and moments as possible in which to be a teenager. This bonfire is worlds away from the false front of the wake.

The only one to say that out loud is Ted, of course: This bonfire is meant as a *fuck you*. Milo would never say the words, but the idea was liberating.

Now only Andrew and Milo know what kind of goodbye it really is. And Andrew was so strong when they said it before parting, going different directions in the deep dark of the forest. He holds himself together with the knowledge that it will be best for both of them. Milo can only love Andrew with shadows from the past shaping them. The conversation with Nat lingers in Andrew's memory: The truth is he does want a future with someone, one in which he can have complete intimacy.

He can't imagine that with anyone but Milo, and despite the synchronicity of vulnerability, love and comfort they shared hours before in Milo's room, he's not sure he can picture that ever happening between them again. Too much stands between them.

In this moment, with the shape of Milo's body remembered in his fingertips, Milo's heart finally so open for him, Andrew cannot fathom how he'll ever move on. In his own bed, sheets bitter cool and neutral cup his body, curled tight around a too-huge grief. All the boys in this last year, flings and one-night stands, sweet ones who only lasted a few weeks, others easy to walk away from because they never matched his expectations—now, when he goes back to Brandeis, he'll have to try for something else.

He wakes the day of the bonfire, heads to the hardware store and buys a gallon of the most neutral paint he can find, a light taupe, and a wide brush.

It's almost impossible to see while he paints, he's crying so hard, but he does it. He spends the day in the tiny space they once made to hide in. It takes three coats to cover the stars he painted with the hope that one day Milo would come back and find his way to him. He never thought it would be for goodbye, least of all a goodbye just as Milo woke up to him. Andrew knows his constellations, the names and colors of stars, but what he'd imagined for them was unique. He'd come here in October, picturing his body curled around Milo's, and painted a map that might be all their own.

When he's finished there's paint in his hair, his eyes are swollen and his body still feels nothing but pain. But it's good. It's the start. A start toward a new reality where he isn't going to love Milo like this, as if Milo's his Earth and he a lonely, constant satellite, cold and hopeless.

o o o

SARAH AND her new boyfriend, whose name Milo can't remember, bring most of the firewood. She's grown up in a way he completely missed in the last few years. When he came home, all he noticed was Andrew. Tonight Sarah's hair is curled in tight corkscrews, shining in the firelight, and she wears makeup with a cat's-eye effect.

He hasn't noticed and can't remember so many things. How much is simple distance from this old life, and how much the impenetrable skin he brought back to Santuit with him in a naive attempt to get through without feeling anything? Going through the motions today, he's had time to reflect and reject his foolish idea that he'll go back to USC, take off his travel clothes and wash everything down a shower drain. Because here's Andrew, doling out coffee and hot chocolate, doctoring it, with a smile and laugh, with liquor from a brown paper bag.

Milo watches as Ted sets the wood alight. When the wind whips over the deserted chiaroscuro landscape of late dusk, he flips up the collar of his cashmere coat and huddles over a mug of Bailey's-laced hot chocolate. The fire catches, burning oranges and yellows that mesmerize, and a glow spills onto the faces of his friends who had been fading into the dark. Milo lays the last of the wood himself and looks up across the pyramid—into the eyes of the man who has known him best his whole life. Who has loved him best, and whose love has kept him afloat in the years he thought he would drown in the big house his father kept.

Andrew looks tired, and his eyes look the way they do when he's been crying but is trying to hide it. No one else seems to notice, or at least they're not saying anything. Milo has known Andrew in so many ways, but never so intimately as now. Andrew: slip-gentle skin over long bones, his thin but soft flesh giving easily under Milo's fingers. Andrew, who was open and unashamed, comfortable with taking pleasure and with giving comfort and pleasure to him.

"Here," Andrew says when Milo comes to him. His hand holds a cream-colored piece of paper, folded in quarters.

"Your list?" Milo asks. Andrew nods. His eyes are painfully direct on Milo's. He searches his pocket and finds his own list, considerably more crumpled. "Are we reading them?"

"If you want?" Andrew strays closer to the fire. "I'll always remember mine. Will you?"

"Mine or yours?"

"Either," Andrew says plainly. "I will. Both." Andrew tries to smile; it's an utter failure, but paints his lovely face so heartbreakingly that it's nearly impossible not to reach out and touch his cheek. Andrew takes a small step away from Milo when he moves closer. With shaking fingers, he reads Milo's list. The only change his face makes is a raised brow. When he's finished, he looks at Milo. Milo opens Andrew's list. He's right. Even through the cramping panic in his chest, and the tears in his eyes, he knows he won't forget Andrew's dreams.

They could be *it* for each other, in a perfect place. Milo couldn't put Andrew's name on his list, no matter how he ached for it. His name isn't on Andrew's. Andrew loves Milo *who was* and Milo strains so for the Milo *to be*; neither would chain him to the past through a list of wishes. Milo understands, although it hurts, that he'll only hurt Andrew if they don't walk away, because there's nothing Milo won't damage, given time.

Andrew slots their fingers together and steps closer to the fire. "Please remember—"

"I'll never forget, Andrew," Milo promises. Andrew's head on his shoulder is a brief comfort; the scratch of his hair and his scent are wisps of sensation. Andrew carefully feeds Milo's list to the fire, letting one corner catch before the flames and heat suck it into the vortex as black ash curls inward. Milo does the same and understands that they're not walking away from dreams. They're forging promises to make this choice the right one.

o

Long past nightfall, the logs burn themselves into collapse. Milo feels sunburned from the heat, but also cold. He's had enough to drink to feel hazy, but not too much. He's spent the night watching Andrew, watching sparks fly into the night, mentally cutting open the shell he's been living in. Everything is starting to hurt, and when Milo thinks of how long it will hurt, and how much it will take to grow out of this, he wants nothing more than to close that shell again.

He could walk to Andrew and take his hand, lead him home and beg him to put him back together. But then a part of him would always be here, only half alive.

Andrew's face is tipped up to the stars, and Milo takes a picture in his mind. Then he gets up and walks away.

part Two

chapter eight

MILO GETS OFF THE PLANE AT LOGAN AIRPORT WITH A clipped step and a determined mind. He doesn't know how long he'll be back in Santuit. He's not sure what his mother's real state is—her voice has grown increasingly soft, losing the vibrancy she gained slowly in the years since his father's death. Opening their old home as a bed and breakfast had revived her spirits.

Milo hasn't been home in seven years. He's seen pictures of her transformation of the old house. Inviting as it looks now, for Milo it will always be an ugly reminder of the past he's worked to come to terms with. Once he acquired his job at Miller Green Developers in Denver, he had extra money to send her. The first few years, she slowly rebuilt herself, then confessed her desire to run a B&B. She sent emails with dozens of pictures attached: dreams and then transformations, until one day Graham's Bed and Breakfast was born. She offered to ship what possessions he'd left behind. Milo barely bit back the hard response that she could burn them for all he cared.

He didn't want a single thing from that home or his youth. He still doesn't.

But she needs him now. She held off on asking; once she did, it came with an admission that she needed help. Milo's not sure what's going on—she was circumspect on the phone. There are few things in the world Milo wants less than to return to Santuit, but one of them is abandoning his mother when she needs him.

At the car rental place, he requests something cheap and small.

"How long will you need it?" the clerk asks, cheerfully tapping away at a keyboard with only a brief glance at him. His name tag reads "Rob." He's very good looking, with startling green eyes that stand out in contrast with his beautiful dark skin. Milo knows it's polite to use the names of customer service representatives, but he wants to be in and out, not chat with a stranger, even if he is hot.

"I'm not sure, a few days?" He'll figure something out, should he need to stay for any length of time.

"All right, we'll write you up for a week for now?" Rob says.

"Sure." He's barely paying attention. He signs what he needs to sign, swallows down impatience, because none of this is Rob's fault and yet Milo's being an ass, and stuffs his bags into the car. Milo takes a moment to familiarize himself with the car, then sits a while with his eyes closed as the air conditioner runs to battle the humidity already settling over the city.

o

The drive is as ugly as he remembers. He never understood how people found this beautiful. He passes a windmill that makes his stomach clench for no good reason, other than that it's so big it's a little unsettling. Once he's over the bridge and coasting down highway 28, the tension eases a little. He reminds himself that, while this is familiar, he's not the same. It's been a long time since he's had a panic attack; he's damned if he's going to regress because he's visiting a place full of painful ghosts.

o

"Hey, Mom." Milo hops up the moss-covered rock steps to the lawn, then pulls his mother into a tight hug, lifting her tiny body off the ground. She's thinner.

"Oh, it's good to see you, honey." Shelby squeezes him back. Although he flies her out to his house in Denver when he can, it's not often she finds time to get away from her business. Even in the off season, she's constantly busy.

"Mom, you look thinner," he says right off the bat.

"Oh, let's not talk about serious things right now." She swats him playfully. Her smile is real and open.

He kisses her forehead. "Let me grab my bags."

o

"So where do you want me?" Milo stacks his bag and carry-on in the foyer.

"I assumed you wouldn't want your old room," she says. *Observant, sweet Mom,* he thinks. They don't talk about it much, but it's always a surprise, a comforting one, when she acknowledges the reality of their past subtly.

"Do you want the front room or the attic room?"

"Attic."

"Are you sure? It's so small!"

"I'll be fine, Mom. All I need is to be able to sleep. You still have the big bed in there?" Milo lifts his bag.

"Yep. Pretty much all that fits in there." Shelby grabs his carry-on, which he gently takes away from her.

"Don't. We can't both manage on those steps."

Milo heads upstairs, then opens the door to the narrow, steep steps that lead to the attic. As a kid, this was an alluring but sacred space: his mother's sewing room, her retreat. Respecting her need for a getaway, he'd rarely gone up there without invitation. He's always loved picturing her in there, the warm Cape light falling through steep skylights, the sloped ceiling and rich blue of the walls, the braided rag rugs in kaleidoscope colors she'd learned to make from her grandmother. His mother loved homemaking, even when James sucked its joys out of both of them.

He wrestles his suitcase up the stairs, ducks his head through the doorway, then goes back for his carry-on. The ceiling is almost low enough to touch his head at its peak; the room occupies the A-frame top of the house. But the bed is a four-poster with his grandmother's quilt on it, and tucked against the wall is a dresser he'll have to stoop to use. It is too small, but it feels perfect: close and redolent of the only soft memories he has of the place.

"Milo, honey," Shelby calls up the stairs.

"Coming." He sets the stack of shirts on the bed and maneuvers his way down. It's definitely going to take some getting used to, the steps are so steep, but he hopes he won't be here long.

She's at the table in the kitchen with a warm mug of tea in front of her. "I didn't know if you'd like coffee or tea or water?"

"I'm fine. Mom, you look tired." He sits across from her.

"Oh, I'm a little worn; I didn't sleep well last night."

"What's up?"

"Lots on my mind. Excited to see you. Don't worry so much. We have time to talk," she says, dismissing his question.

"Mom—"

"Would you mind running to Winslow's and grabbing some stuff for dinner, honey? I forgot to make time for it."

"Winslow's?" He remembers the tiny market too well.

"You know I like to support the local businesses," she says patiently. "Is that okay?"

"Yeah, of course. Do you have a list?"

"Yes." She looks around vaguely. "I can't remember where it is." She laughs, an almost lost sound, it's so quiet. His anxiety spikes. "Milo, sweetie, it's okay," she says, reading him perfectly. "I really am just tired. I worried, asking you to come here, if it would be too much for you."

"Mom, I'm fine. I want to help you. I think we need to talk, though."

"We will, I promise. Let's have a nice night with some good food, and enjoy each other, please?"

"Of course," he concedes, hand over hers.

o

Winslow's isn't quite what he remembers, even when he was a teenager. It's all haphazard shelves, hit-and-miss stock, overpriced produce and the same old retired folks gossiping over poorly kept checkout counters. But it's not as crappy as he remembers. Or it is, and his adult perception is different. Santuit has its own pace, its own flavor, the special energy of the full-time residents who know the waters and winds and ever-shifting sand. He's always thought of it as a little big town.

"Hey," the woman checking him out exclaims. She has poofy white hair that's curled in the regimented style most Santuit women over sixty wear. Her face is weathered but familiar. "Miles Graham? Oh lord, oh we haven't seen you in years!"

"Mrs. Shoon," he manages after casting around in his memory for her name. "I can't believe you recognized me."

"Oh hush, you." She begins bagging his selections at a snail's pace. He recognizes the rhythm. It's small talk and catch-up.

"As if I wouldn't; didn't I watch you grow up, always at the candy aisle wishing for more quarters with that, that friend of yours—Andrew?"

"You make it sounds like an episode of *Leave it to Beaver*," he jokes. *Andrew*. Andrew, a name and a memory, but so crucial to his childhood history that those with long memories will always connect them.

"That's life here, darlin'," she jokes. "So, here to help your mom?"

"Yeah," he pulls out his wallet. "She needs help, then?" He winces. "Obviously. I mean, you know—I mean—" He really doesn't want to gossip about his own mother, but he's dying to know what's going on.

"Oh, I don't know about that. I assumed a boy like you would come back to a place like this for his mother."

"Good call," he says with forced cheer. "Well, I guess I'll be seeing you again, then," he adds, all awkward phrasing and unsure conduct, because he's not sure how to cut short the curious and gossipy town rhythm.

"All right then, hon. Enjoy your day."

"You too, Mrs. Shoon." He hefts his two paper bags and heads out along Main to his car. On the opposite corner is Ashe's: one of the nicer restaurants in town, the special-occasion place his father would patronize when he wanted to perform "perfect family" for the big moments. The last dinner Milo remembers there was to celebrate his departure for USC.

o

His mom manages to talk around and under the topic for three days. After pressing on the second day and seeing her get upset, Milo resigns himself to not pushing until she's ready. He hates feeling itchy but doesn't want to demand answers, especially because some of that itch is the simple desire to get the hell out of Dodge.

"You know, honey," Shelby says over breakfast the third day, "Ted still lives here. Married a sweet girl; they have a little boy. Oh, and your friend Sarah, she's up at Norwalk. You should give them a call."

"Oh, I don't know, Mom," he hedges, disguising it with an over-enthusiastic application of strawberry preserves on his toast. He doesn't want to revisit his past more than necessary. There's little he could say to friends he'd let drift away when Andrew cut ties with him. For a long moment they avoid looking at each other, because they know things must be said.

"You know, honey..." She pauses, then looks out the window. The sky is gunmetal gray. "I suppose we do need to talk."

He puts his knife and soggy toast down carefully. "Yes, that might be good."

"I'm not sure where to start." She laughs. It sounds rueful and sad.

"You don't have any guests this week?" Milo asks. He's been wondering.

"Um, no. I had a last minute cancellation."

Milo's not sure if he can read the truth on her face. Even in the years they've both allowed themselves to flourish, it seems they both remember how to conjure the blank faces that often saved them from someone's anger.

"Milo, I'm not going to pretend I don't know how hard this is on you, being here. I know you know I know, we all here know," she jokes, "but it had to be said. I thought a lot about what the right thing to do was, because I feel I owe it to you to spare you everything I can, after not having—"

"Mom, no, please don't."

"Like I said, it has to be said. But I wouldn't have called you here if I didn't need you."

He takes her in, the streaks of gray that startle through her once mahogany hair, the creeping lines around her dark-circled eyes. Her skin looks thin, almost papery. He finally asks.

"You're sick, aren't you?"

Her eyes go back to the window, again and again. He wonders what they're drawn to, when all they can see is the peek-a-boo, colorless sky between the leaves of the oak tree in the side yard.

"I'm sorry, honey," is all she says. Milo stares out the window with her, then clears his throat, trying to force the tension out.

"Don't be; it's okay." He squeezes her hand. "It'll be okay."

She gives him a sweet, mother-shaped smile and seems to think through her next words.

"All right."

○

Milo settles her on the couch and himself in an armchair and gets to the business of fact-collecting so he can construct a plan.

"Please don't panic," she starts, ominously. "It *is* breast cancer—" She leans forward and shakes his knee when he inhales sharply. "The doctors think we have excellent odds. It's stage two, so it needs treatments and surgery, but also has excellent odds for survival with the plan we've decided on."

"Wait, have you already—how could you not—?"

"Milo," she says softly.

"You wouldn't have told me?" Incredulity sharpens his voice.

"No, no, I would have. Just maybe... with better news?" she says.

"Oh!" Now it's sarcasm. "'Better news,' she says."

"Milo, I wanted to spare you—"

"How is keeping secret your *cancer* sparing me? What if—"

"Milo, please understand. As a mom, it's my job to try to spare you. And I have so much to make up for."

"Mom, please stop. *Stop.* You don't, okay? We were both there. He did it to us both."

For a long time after his father's death, he blamed her, and anger and resentment simmered. He always managed to tamp down those feelings when he spoke to her. It took therapy and effort to forgive and understand. But he has forgiven, and does understand, now.

She takes a shaking breath and makes an abortive motion with her hand that he knows means she's dismissing it for the moment. *Fine, we'll come back to that later.*

"There didn't seem to be a clear best choice. Ask you to come back here when I knew it would be painful, and you've worked so hard to start somewhere new, or keep this a secret from you when I knew you should know."

"But only because you need surgery you've decided to tell me?" Milo says. A hot wave of resentment he doesn't want to acknowledge stirs.

"No. Now that I've started chemo, I don't think the surgery itself is going to be the hardest part. I was going to tell you anyway," she says, sitting up straighter. "I promise. I just wanted to wait it out."

He evaluates her face, her posture, tries to read if this is true.

"You don't have to believe me. You can be angry at me if you want, honey. If you want to leave, I'll understand, too," she says.

"Christ, Mom, if I want to leave? When you're sick and need chemo and surgery and whatever else and *need* me?"

She blinks back tears, and he sighs, runs fingers through already messy hair and tries to channel some calm.

"I shouldn't have yelled. This is just a lot."

"I know, I know. I'm so sorry, baby."

He closes his eyes. She hasn't called him that since he practically *was* a baby. He's not sure when she stopped. When his father started pulling them apart, he supposes.

It's a long time before he speaks up again. His voice bumps into the jagged silence, against his own hesitation and her expectant breaths.

"When do you need surgery?"

"In about two months? I haven't scheduled it yet; I thought I'd wait to talk to you. I feel awful, because calling you now means I'm asking you to stay for so long."

"And what are you having done? How long is it, how long will you be in the hospital?"

"It's called a lumpectomy. The surgery is outpatient, thankfully. The doctor can explain all of the treatments better than I can."

Milo closes his eyes again. Her hand on his knee is meant as a comforting weight, but he's not sure he knows how to handle it. Of course, Milo's first instinct is to push it away, to let the automatic irritation he feels when he's at his most overwhelmed and scared wash him away. But she needs him right now.

"All right. Then let's make our plans. We'll schedule it, and figure out the car rental situation so I can plan to stay here. Do you see your doctor soon? Can I come and ask questions?"

"Yes," she says. "Of course. I know you'll have a lot of questions. I'll be seeing him for my next round of chemo."

"I'll have to call work and figure out if I should take a sabbatical or work remotely."

"Oh, Milo, I'm sorry—"

"Mom, seriously, don't be; I have leeway."

"All right, honey."

"Now, what about the B&B?" he asks.

"Well, I still have bookings coming up, and I don't want to cancel them if I don't have to. I know there are girls from town who will be willing to help out if I ask."

"I can help, Mom."

"I know you can. I meant with cleaning and cooking stuff. I thought you could handle the business end."

"Mom, you do know I've been living on my own for years. I can cook."

"Bachelor food," she scoffs, but it's friendly.

"How little you know me," he says wryly. "No, really. It's a hobby."

She squints at him. "How did I not know this?"

"I guess we've both been keeping stuff close," he quips, and immediately feels like crap because her face falls. "I was kidding, Mom."

"All right," she says, voice a little softer, a little apologetic.

"I promise, I wasn't being passive aggressive or anything,"

"Okay, okay, I believe you," she says, rolling her eyes. "This is officially enough gloom and doom."

"But we have to plan for the business—"

"Milo, we have a week before the next booking. We have time. I want you to digest. I know how hard that is for you. Go for a walk. Go down to the beach. Clear your head."

"I don't want to leave you alone, though."

"Sweetie, I've had some time to get used to this and think it through."

"Maybe I don't want to leave you," he says.

"Well, it looks like we're in for a long haul. I'm fine. I need to think, too." Milo is pretty sure she's saying that to get him out of the house. But he sees her point, because his stomach feels full of needles.

"I don't want you to think I'm doing the running-away thing."

"I know you're not." Shelby gets up, then puts a soft, cool hand on his cheek and pulls him down to kiss the crown of his head. It's unfamiliar comfort, like a home he never had. He feels a longing for her sometimes when they've not seen each other for months—the need for her affection and love he stored up during years of being too scared to let himself want. "I'll see you in a while. Dinner?"

"I doubt I'll take that long." He stands and stretches.

"We'll see."

Milo goes upstairs to grab a light sweater. He's not sure where he wants to go—town seems too likely to be full of people who might remember him and talk to him. The woods and the beaches feel laden with other memories, but they're a better option. If he does go down to the beach, he'll definitely want a scarf, with the way the wind tends to whip in over the water.

o

In the end, he drives to Pine Beach. It's on the other side of town, a place he didn't much frequent as a kid. Eventually he'll have to face the memory-saturated air in other places, if he's going to be home for any amount of time.

The wind is up, but the beach is deserted. This has always been a quieter one, thanks to a longer walk through the dunes. There are sandbars far into the water at high tide and the sand is mostly exposed at low tide. A line of pebbles sweeps in an arc above the waterline, and below it is a second arc of seaweed. The tide is mostly out. The dunes wear their usual blend of pretty purple and white flowers and sharp grasses.

Milo sits a few feet above the rock line and pulls on his sweater. The sun is blinding off the water, but he wants to be blinded, wants to be forced out of his headspace. It's so quiet, save for the agitated water.

Legs crossed, Milo pulls himself up straight. He closes his eyes and ignores the swirling colors behind his eyelids. He counts a slow breath in, three beats, then exhales for three. Takes a three-beat pause before breathing in. He imagines his breath as a triangle and projects that shape from his body. He lets his senses take in the beach, the quiet, the water, the grit of the sand whipped up by the waves. Tension seeps out of him when he exhales. He lets it go. Nothing is taken from him, nothing is forced. He can count these breaths as he wants. He suspends himself in the pauses: pictures a white canvas, bleeding jumbled images of worry and anxiety, reds and blacks and angry oranges slowly dripping off, as if washed away by rain.

When he opens his eyes again, he's calmer. That buzzing, anxious feeling is gone. The seaweed has been swallowed by the sea. Tide's coming in. Milo watches it. The water begins to run in a slow progressing rivulet in a channel between the rocks. As the water creeps ever closer, it rises over uneven sandbars until it meets in the middle of that small channel, eventually overflowing and overrunning the strip of sand in the middle. Before it's gone, Milo walks into the cold water. The rocks are rough under the soles of his feet. They're thin-skinned against the sand; when he was a kid they'd been callused and used to beach and forest.

He searches out bigger, colorful rocks and tosses them up the beach. He finds a perfect half shell with pinks blending into white in the center. In the middle is a bright blue fleck of sand. He picks that up too.

By the path into the dunes and back toward his car is a wrecked piece of driftwood, hollow and pale from sun-bleaching. He arranges the rocks on top, makes a pattern of colors with the shell on the end, a frangible beautiful thing, and then takes a picture. His mom will like that. The memory of making art of beach flotsam with Andrew haunts him.

o

He and his mother bump around each other without addressing her illness, upcoming doctor appointments, or the logistics of keeping her business going for a few days. He helps with the housework, and they watch TV in companionable silence at night. Milo goes for walks. He walks and walks; the years of his childhood haunt him mercilessly, and it takes a lot of meditation to keep them at bay. The town has changed, but what he feels when he marks paths with his feet is the same. He explores neighborhoods south of the B&B, down to Graylock and takes in the details of the homes. Despite being the closest beach to his home, it's the one least familiar to him. As a kid he'd spent countless hours marching down Chickopee with Andrew, darting into the woods just north of the dunes, and farther still to Andrew's home. Now Milo walks westward along Graylock's length, then down Pine, around the peninsula before turning back. No matter how many walks he takes, he avoids Chickopee.

Eventually, he knows, all things must come to a head. But he's not ready.

○

"Have you called work yet?" his mom asks over breakfast on Wednesday.

"No, I was thinking I would do that today or tomorrow. I took a two-week vacation, so I don't have to rush. Setting up something like this will take a little time and negotiation, though."

"All right. I have an appointment on Monday, so we'll see Dr. Schroeder and you can meet him."

"Great. What time?"

"Ten. I'm sure you'll have questions. You can keep me company for this round."

"I'll have to buy a binder," Milo says. She laughs and taps his foot with hers under the table.

"That's my boy. Ready to organize everything."

Milo smirks. "Speaking of which, we should break out the books soon. Have you found help yet?"

"Yes, Kathy and Emma will be helping. They're gonna come tomorrow and we'll work out pay and hours and everything."

"Then you and I should sit down tonight."

"What's the rush there?"

"Mom, how will you know what to pay them if you don't look at your income? If you don't plan ahead based on bookings?"

"God, honey." She sips her coffee to hide a smile.

"Who are Kathy and Emma anyway? How old are they? Do we trust them?"

"Yes," she says, outright laughter lacing her tone. "Kathleen Jones? She's Ted's wife."

"Oh," Milo says, then winces. "I forgot; crap."

"And Emma is the Kipplings' youngest. I don't know if you've met them."

"Doesn't sound familiar. But we've established that I have a terrible town-related memory."

She picks up his plate, and he puts a hand on her wrist, then takes the plate back. "Go rest. You look tired. I'll do this."

"Milo, you can't baby me all the time."

"Um, wrong. I think you'll find that I can." He puts his hand on her shoulder and gently turns her. Protest abandoned, she acquiesces, lies on the couch and smiles thanks when he brings her the book she's been working through.

The dishes are dispatched quickly. When he comes to check on her she's asleep, head pillowed at an angle against the arm of the couch. They've always been deep sleepers; he arranges her easily—she hardly weighs a thing. Over the back of the couch is a beautiful afghan she made when he was younger; it took her years of putting it aside and pulling it out to complete.

Milo sets up his computer in the kitchen after swinging the door closed, and composes a memo to one of his partners outlining his situation and potential outcomes, as well as a few contingency plans. He'll have to propose a way he can work from home: There is plenty of work he can do remotely. He'd rather not take a sabbatical. He loves his work, loves the meticulous nature of it, the commitment to it that fills the empty spaces in his life.

There's not much to leave behind in Denver. No pets, no current lover, no great attachment to his home. He'll wait for the appointment with the doctor to make bigger plans, but begins to think about renting out his house. A small pain burrows in his stomach. It's a loneliness he feels often when he's making something complex in his state-of-the-art kitchen, when there's only one place setting and only his thoughts to clutter it. It's been a while since he's had a lover or a boyfriend. He's not great at relationships. Years of work and therapy, and he still finds himself always an arm's reach away, on the brink of trust that feels too big, too frightening. Trust—full trust—means giving someone the power to hurt you. He's not good at vulnerability.

o

That night Shelby is pale and drawn. The air around her is thick with depression and weariness. Perhaps the weight of holding a secret is finally working its way out.

Milo pours over her books—mostly hand-written paperwork with little system he can discern. He resists the urge to ask how on earth she's managed a business like this. She's always had a survival magic he couldn't understand.

"I'll have to organize this before we can figure out pay," he points out. He's got his laptop open, QuickBooks at the ready.

"All right." She's breathing in the floral scent of her favorite loose leaf tea. He brought her some when he came home, knowing it wasn't a thing she could get at Winslow's, and that it's an extravagance she'd never mail order for herself. With it he'd carefully packaged a new hand-painted teapot and a single-serve cup with a diffuser and a saucer. Pink-cheeked and lovely eyed, she carefully put them up on the display shelf in the kitchen where she keeps the cup and saucer sets her mother passed to her. Milo took them back down, cleaned them and set about making her a cup of tea.

"You're too good to me," she says, wrapping her arms around him from behind and tucking her face between his shoulders.

"I could never be good enough." He drops the German rock sugar she loves into the cup.

"Oh, honey," she says, voice thick with tears.

"None of that." He turns and kisses her forehead. "Let's watch some *Bar Rescue*. There's a marathon."

"How do you know all of my guilty pleasures?"

"Stealth," he says and carries the tea for her.

o

Too soon Shelby loses interest in even her favorite TV show, wandering back to where Milo is still working through the books. She sets her tea down and hugs him from behind. She's so small; Milo thinks about the care parents give their children that shifts as they grow, until it is the child's time to care of the parent.

"Still burning the midnight oil?"

Milo laughs. "Hardly. It's not even ten."

She pours herself what water remains in the kettle and settles at the table across from him. "What can I do?"

"Go to sleep." He doesn't take his eyes off the computer screen, but can't manage to ignore her sigh. "Seriously, Mom. I have this. In the morning we can go over it again. But you need sleep."

"You're babying me."

"No," he says, and takes her hand. "I'm loving you."

o

Milo insists on stopping before Shelby's appointment to buy a new binder and other organizing tools. He puts up with her teasing with smiles. "You know I can't help it."

"It's adorable. Let's buy you the four-pack of pens. You can color code your notes."

"Shush, you," he says, then picks up the pens with a smile. Some sides to him she's never seen, but some she'll always know because they're second nature. He's a facts-and-figures guy all the way.

Dr. Schroeder turns out to be a tiny, gray haired and naturally gentle man. Milo supposes his bedside manner is excellent comfort to his patients. It doesn't comfort him, though. He imagines what it might take to be an oncologist, constantly delivering bad news. What's the loss rate for an oncologist? He makes a note to look that up later, then crosses it out. Stress he has in spades at this moment. There's no reason to add more by looking at numbers.

"I've checked with Nancy, and it looks like we'll be able to do the surgery by June," Dr. Schroeder says.

"So soon?" his mom says, paling.

"We don't want to put this off, Shelby," he says gently.

"I know, I know." She puts a hand to her forehead. "It seems a lot more real when we're talking about surgery."

"I know." Dr. Schroeder smiles carefully, then turns to Milo. "I see you have a notebook at the ready, young man. I'm assuming you have questions?"

"Actually, yes." Milo flips to the list of questions he's been making all week. His mother laughs softly.

o

They drive home in quiet. She has a classical station that she prefers on low. Milo finds it slipping through him and lulling him into an autopilot haze. The scenery blurs past him; for once he doesn't observe it with resentment.

When they get home he makes her some tea and then laces up his shoes. "I'm going to go for a walk."

"Good." She's burrowed under a blanket.

"I'll turn down the AC," he says when he sees her tuck it over her shoulders.

"No, don't. I'm not cold. Just want some comfort," she says, smiling up at him. He hesitates.

"I'll stay home—"

"Milo, go. This is going to be hard on us both, and I know you need time to yourself. We both need to figure out ways to get through this as best we can."

Milo pushes back the sweep of hair falling over her cheek and tucks it behind her ear.

"I'll stop at Winslow's on my way home. I feel like making a 'spoil Mom' dinner."

"You don't have to spoil me."

"But I want to." He kisses her cheek and turns toward the door.

o

The beach isn't quite deserted. Tide is at its highest, covering the rocks and debris and a good portion of the sand where he usually sits. It's overcast. Far down the beach a couple walks in the shallows, hands clasped.

Ted's wife seems nice, and he's promised to go to their house for dinner soon. They have a little boy, just over a year old. Kathy showed him pictures with that special pride only new parents have. Dylan is adorable, but in the generic way all young kids are. Milo is embarrassed to have put off reconnecting with someone he once knew very well for so long. He's regaining his footing here, slowly, and he has faith he'll be steady enough to renew old friendships as his new self. Ted is a new person now, too—an adult with a wife and a child and a home: all things Milo struggles to picture when the Ted he remembers was a smart-mouthed kid, a rabble rouser and their class clown.

It looks as if Milo will be home for a while, and the truth is he's a little lonely. Back home in Denver, Milo's begun to feel the empty spaces in his life friends can't fill: here, he feels them in every way. Aching for something he can't have is useless, and there's no reason to punish himself by lingering over it. For now, a few friends while he's here will do.

The water quiets him with its rhythmic movement. The tide starts to let out, and the sun peeks through scattering clouds. Milo is startled out of his calm when he hears a laugh peal down the beach. The couple he saw earlier is closer now, kicking water at each other in a playful game. He watches as they come closer, and as the sun makes a sudden brilliant appearance, he recognizes with a shock that he knows one of them.

Because one of them is Andrew.

chapter nine

Milo has to resist the urge to run when he sees Andrew stop stock-still in the water, not moving when his companion splashes him.

Milo closes his eyes and then pushes himself to stand. Sand clings to his pants and he takes a moment to brush it off, internally scrambling to figure out the protocol for this. Excitement mixes with panic. His heart is in his throat like an angry hummingbird, choking his breath. The seven years between them is a chasm he learned not to want to cross, much less approach, and now he's suddenly on its edge.

"Wow," Andrew says once they're close enough to hear each other. His companion trails along, confusion clear on his face. Andrew has changed in the last few years, but subtly. His hair is blonder, long and deliberately tousled. He seems slightly taller, and his once long-limbed, almost too-thin frame has settled into something lithe and devoid of angles. "Um. Wow."

Milo is equally eloquent. "You're here?" He winces and shakes his head. "That was dumb. Of course you're here. I mean, um. *Here.*" He snaps his lips together. Andrew's cheeks are a high pink.

"Same," Andrew says.

"All right," the man next to him kicks in. "We've established that we're all here?"

"Oh, oops." Andrew smiles at him, strained but familiar. "Um, Milo, Dex Howell. Dex, Milo." His hand does a thing, the thing it does when he's nervous. Milo swallows hard. It's a gesture he saw hundreds of times growing up. For a startling moment he feels young again. He gathers himself enough to reach out a hand to shake.

"Milo, huh?" Dex says. His eyebrows lower, then he smiles. He must know who Milo is: that expression was clear. Next to each other they seem night and day; Dex is black haired and brown eyed, stockier than Andrew and shorter than them both. They shake hands, both putting a little too much strength in it. He thinks of the picture they made, silhouettes against the sun, playing on the beach. Andrew's lover? Partner?

"I'm stuck at wow," Andrew says then. Milo shoots him a look. This is probably the most awkward Milo has ever felt. He wonders wildly what happens now. Talking? Sitting in the sand and reminiscing? Walking away and pretending this never happened? Andrew here in Santuit was not a possibility he'd considered. His mom would have told him if she'd known, right?

"Are you visiting your mom?" Andrew says. They all squint against the sun, which bursts through the clouds again.

"Yeah." Milo is not about to go into details. Not when the air is this thick between three people who are two-thirds strangers. Andrew's skin is darker than Milo remembers; it's still tan, even coming out of a long winter and late spring. He still looks younger than his age, but he's no longer boyish.

"I thought you usually had her come out to you?" Andrew says, then looks away. The admission that he knows such a thing is startling.

"Change of pace, I guess," Milo lies. The words stick uneasily.

"Well," Dex butts in, "it's been a while since you guys saw each other. You should catch up sometime."

"Uh—" Milo starts.

"We have plans tonight." Dex rolls right over Milo's interruption. "But we should meet up." Milo doesn't miss the emphasis on the *we*.

"Oh, definitely," Andrew says. Milo can't read the tone. The wind tosses his hair and the sun catches the lighter streaks.

"Great," Milo says, trying for authentic enthusiasm. The panic is starting to tingle and grow. He needs to get away so he can pull himself together.

"You at your mom's?" Andrew asks.

"Yeah."

"We'll call you there, then." Again with the *we*.

"Yeah. Great. Sure." Milo sucks in a breath and balls up one hand. "I have to go; I was about to leave. I'll talk to you soon."

"Looking forward to it," Dex adds. Milo wants to imagine there's bitterness in his tone, but there's not.

Once they've walked away, Andrew shoots one last unreadable glance over his shoulder. Milo stumbles up the path to his car with the deep sand sucking at his feet and making it a slog. By the time he reaches the car, he's out of breath. It's his once-constant companion, anxiety, coming back to run his life, constricting his lungs.

He thinks of the view from his home in Denver, how calming it is, how in that life anxiety and fear are more memory than reality.

Fuck.

o o o

"SO THAT's the famous Milo," Dex says, folding his sweater and putting it onto his shelf. Andrew has to pop his head into the closet to hear him.

"What?"

"I said, so that's the famous Milo."

God, not now, Andrew thinks. Although he supposes it's never going to seem like a good time. "Famous?"

"Well, you've told me all about him," Dex points out. It's true he has. Moving on has never meant forgetting to Andrew. Well, maybe forgetting certain things. But he never planned on deleting his childhood best friend from memory, even when he unfriended him on social media, forbade friends from mentioning him and buried what he'd let go deep inside.

"I don't see how that makes him *the famous Milo,*" Andrew says, air quoting defensively.

"Andrew." Dex takes him by the hand and leads him to their bed, patting the spot next to him. Dex's hair is always neat and orderly, but Andrew smooths it with nervous fingers at his temple where the slightest hints of grey are coming in. "I'm not dumb. I know it has hurt, losing contact with him. I could tell how surprised you were. You can talk to me about it."

"Hm." Andrew puts a hand on Dex's cheek and looks into sweet, steady brown eyes that rarely look at him with anything but genuine care. "I was surprised," he admits. "I'm not sure how I feel about it."

"Seeing him?"

"Yeah," Andrew says and then kisses Dex. "I don't know what brought him back here, but it's probably not a good thing."

"Why is that?"

Andrew shakes his head. "Let's not talk about this tonight." Milo's story isn't his to tell, and their story is more complicated than he could explain to Dex. Telling him only bits over this last year has seemed like a lie. A lie of omission, meant to spare his own heart.

"I don't mean to upset you," Dex says, then kisses him back. Andrew closes his eyes and breathes him in, the steady comfort that's *Dex*. He focuses on feeling his lips track down his neck and the light touch of his hands lifting Andrew's shirt as he lays Andrew down. Dex is the one who has been with him longest, who has loved Andrew despite his initial fears and his long-time inability to commit.

Dex makes love to him as if he's precious tonight. He saturates every one of Andrew's senses until he is senseless, and his pleasure peaks with Dex's name on his lips.

It's only after, when Dex is lax in sleep beside him, that Andrew remembers what it was like to fall asleep with another man he's worked fruitlessly for years to push out of his heart.

o o o

IT TAKES two days for him to contact Milo. He tries to learn what's going on through town gossip, but he's not really able to probe without giving away his hand. It's Dex who makes him call, after Andrew repeats that something awful must be going on. He only tells Dex that Milo had a very difficult life here and had to move on.

"Well then, he'll need a friend," Dex says sensibly. Andrew can tell that Dex's initial sense of unease has bled out. Andrew's done everything he can think of to reassure him without words— touches and thoughtful gestures and open intimacy that he sometimes shies away from. Fucking, he can do; Andrew gets that. Tenderness and vulnerability are incredibly hard for him and something Dex wants more often than Andrew can manage, even after all this time.

Andrew fiddles with a pen while he dials. Dex is at work, so he's alone. He cannot handle an audience for this.

Shelby answers on the fourth ring. "Hello, this is Shelby at Graham's Bed and Breakfast."

"Mrs. Graham. It's Andrew," he says. His voice is shaky. Hers is a little breathless. He hopes he hasn't made her run to the phone.

"Oh my goodness, Andrew honey, it's so good to hear from you."

"It's good to hear your voice, too."

"I'd heard you were back."

"Yes, a few months ago. We're settling in."

"We?" she asks, only curiosity in her tone.

"Uh, yes, my boyfriend Dex and I."

"Oh, wonderful. I should have you both over for dinner sometime. I assume you know Milo is home?"

"Yes, actually we ran into him on the beach a few days ago. We talked about getting together to catch up. That's why I'm calling."

"He went for a walk a bit ago. Do you want me to leave him a message?"

"That," he says as he clears his throat and squints hard at his ottoman, "that would be great." He rattles off his number and promises to come over to see her sometime.

○

He has several articles due in the next few days and he hasn't updated his blog all week. He has a religious schedule of posting somewhere every few days. As far as his personal blog goes, he'll have to figure out what the hell he'll say. He's never held back from talking about his life. There's something about his candor that draws readers. There's something about the distance between his heart and his words and the readers that has always made him feel safer about exposing himself to that world.

Milo's sudden reappearance—or his reaction to it—isn't something he thinks he can share yet.

Milo calls about an hour after Andrew left his message. He's finally managed to make some headway on one of his pieces when the phone wakes him from his work zone trance. That's what Dex calls it, because it's hard to rouse him from it.

"Andrew?" Milo's voice is steady but unsettling. Familiar, but not.

"That's me," he tries for a light tone. "You called me," he says like an idiot.

"You called me first," Milo points out. There's a bantering tone in Milo's voice. He's definitely regained footing since their run-in at the beach, where Andrew could tell he was shaken. Hell, they both were.

"Well, we did promise." Andrew winces at the *we*.

"So what's up?" Milo says after a too-long beat that's incredibly awkward. At least for Andrew.

"I thought we should get together. Catch up," Andrew says.

"Yeah. How about lunch? Unless you have to work—?"

"No, lunch is good, my job is very flexible. I don't know about Dex; I'll see if he wants to come along?"

"Sounds good. Let me give you my cell number and you can text me. I'm free as a bird for the time being."

Andrew is dying to know what's going on, but he can't really ask over the phone.

"Free as a bird?"

"Shut up." Milo laughs. Andrew sighs and absorbs the sound.

"All right, I'll text you after I talk to Dex," Andrew promises.

"Awesome."

Andrew sits, staring at his phone. How should he handle this? The truth is he doesn't want Dex there. Not for this meeting.

He and Milo have a lot sitting between them and he doesn't know how to navigate that with his boyfriend there. Andrew is tempted to search the Internet for some sort of guide, but he doesn't think there is one for *how to juggle a man you loved for years and the one you love now but don't want to know about it or get involved.*

In the end he texts Dex, *Milo is free for lunch, can you get one off this week?*

No I'm swamped. No dinner?

I don't think he can. I don't know what's up.

There's a long pause before the next comes.

Go ahead and meet him for lunch. Maybe we can do something all together another day.

Andrew sighs with relief. It's hard to read tone through text, so he's not certain what Dex really feels. He opens his contacts, adds Milo's number and texts him.

This is Andrew. Lunch is good. What day?

Like I said, any day is good. Even today.

Andrews closes his eyes, thunks his head on his desk and takes a deep breath.

Tribute? Is that good?

Oh, we've become fancy with age have we?

Andrew laughs. *Fancy enough for Tribute. Maybe not ready for Ashe's. Plus they have excellent white wine sangria.*

Well you had me at sangria. Noon?

Sure. See you there.

o

Andrew spends twenty minutes in his closet staring blankly at his clothes before he pulls himself together with a strong chastisement. This isn't a date; it's Milo. He doesn't have to dress to impress.

But he wants to. To show who he's grown into. A small and bitter voice thinks, *to show how I've grown without you.*

In the end he picks a three-quarter sleeved T-shirt in soft, deep purple cotton and shorts. His hair is a too-long disaster; he's overdue for a cut. He does what he can, looks himself over and tucks his wallet and phone into his pocket. He can do this.

o

Milo has to deal with his mom being sappy about his old friendship with Andrew when he tells her where he's going. She always loved Andrew, even when his father wouldn't allow him to visit after Andrew came out. Despite the distance between them, she had to have known Andrew was Milo's refuge.

By the time he's extracted himself from her, he has five minutes to get ready. He changes out of the ratty shirt he was wearing into a deep blue polo, throws on some sneakers and rushes out the door. Wondering what will happen, what he can possibly say, takes up most of his thoughts. Right behind that is an excitement he can't deny. They promised to move on for good reasons. He's a different man; he assumes Andrew is. A trip down memory lane and reconnecting with a childhood friend sounds like something he's more ready for than when he sat on the beach a few days ago, contemplating calling Ted. Meeting Andrew is more fraught in many ways, but oddly, also easier.

Andrew is sitting on the patio, under the arch of the gorgeous old maple that dominates the front of the restaurant.

"Is outside okay with you?" he asks when Milo sits.

"Of course," Milo says. Andrew's already got his sangria. The sun is stippling between the leaves, at times bright and then shading green.

"So this is the famous sangria," Milo says with a smile. Andrew's hand pauses midair, and a strange look crosses his face.

"Yes," Andrew says after a beat. "Do you want to taste?"

"Sure, why not try something new? I'm generally more of a beer guy."

"Not shocking," Andrew says. His eyes travel over Milo's torso in a flutter; if he weren't watching Andrew so intently he might have missed it. Milo's face heats up. He takes a quick sip of Andrew's drink and shakes his head. "Too sweet."

"And here I thought I had you at sangria," Andrew says. Milo smiles in response.

"Well, I tried a new thing; I'll cross that off my bucket list." His smile fades as soon as he says it. "Anyway." Milo sits back, determined to pry his foot out of his mouth. The chair is wrought iron. He feels huge in it.

"So how are you?" Andrew asks. His tone is tempered—offering an out for an easy, unrevealing answer. A waitress comes to take their order; Andrew asks for more time and Milo orders a draft beer. After she leaves they both pretend to peruse the menu. Well, Milo does. He doesn't have many real confidants in his life. He's learned over time to be an island. Reaching out isn't natural for him.

"Well," Milo puts his menu down. "I'm here, aren't I?"

"How bad is it?"

"What?"

"Whatever's forced you here," Andrew says with unnerving directness.

"It could be worse?" Milo thinks of the odds Dr. Schroeder gave them. He looks up at the big, star-shaped leaves above them. He takes a deep breath and doesn't look at Andrew when he speaks. "Mom has breast cancer."

He hears before he sees Andrew's sharp breath. When he looks back at him, he has to swallow something too big and too painful clogging his throat.

"Milo," Andrew says helplessly, "I am so sorry. How bad—I mean, *god*."

"Like I said, it could be worse. She's seen an oncologist at the Cape Cancer Center. He seems good. She's having surgery in a couple of weeks."

Andrew moves his hand, a flutter as if he's going to reach across the table to him, but doesn't.

"He said her chances are really good."

"Okay." Andrew swallows and looks away.

"Hey, it's okay," Milo says, because Andrew's eyes are bright in the way they always got when he was about to cry.

"I feel awful. I've been here for a few months and I should have visited her or something."

"Andrew, you're not a mind reader." Milo doesn't say what he's thinking—that Andrew probably avoided her because of him. Their waitress, Denise, comes to take their order. Milo orders the first thing his eyes land on. Andrew orders carefully. Milo has to hold back laughter.

"Still picky, I see," Milo says. Andrew makes a face at him.

"I see no reason not to enjoy every bite of my food," Andrew says primly, and they both laugh.

"Tell me about you."

"I'm afraid my life is not terribly exciting."

"Well, you said you've been here for a few months?"

"Yeah. I wanted to be home. Turned out that city living wasn't for me."

"What city?" Milo asks.

"We were in Baltimore for a while. Dex had a great job there. He's a CPA. But he had an opportunity to change things up. So we're trying this out, to see if he can manage Cape living."

"It's not for everyone," Milo says.

"He seems good so far." Andrew smiles at Denise when she sets their food down. Apparently everything is right on his order. Milo begins to slather his fries in ketchup.

"Want some fries with that ketchup?" Andrew jokes.

"Nope, just ketchup with ketchup," he quips back, then bites his lip.

"So what do you do?"

"I write," Andrew says as though it's obvious. It's not. Milo remembers that he toyed with the idea of studying writing in college, but never figured he could or would make a living from it.

"Like, books?"

"No, freelance stuff, plus part time at the *Santuit Chronicle*. I have a few blogs." Andrew pokes through his salad delicately. "Maybe one day a book."

"Wow. That's impressive."

"I know. I thought I'd be a starving artist," Andrew jokes. "I still kind of am. On the brink, perhaps." A large group is being seated at the table beside them. They pull more tables together, and their chatter is loud and intrusive.

"Artist?" Milo says over the din. Luckily the group quiets. The open air releases the noise and the muttering of the trees buffers the sound.

"Back when I wrote fiction. Not so much anymore. I double majored in college: journalism and creative writing." Andrew shrugs it off, but Milo wonders how he really feels. They eat in silence. Every now and then Milo darts a look at Andrew. He seems lost in thought, but Milo catches his eyes once.

"So you'll be here for a while?"

"Yeah. We don't really know how long. But I'll help Mom out. She refuses to close her business for a while and let me take care of things financially." Milo pushes back the recurring frustration.

"And you can take a break from your job?"

"No. I toyed with taking a sabbatical, but I spoke to my partners about it and we're fixing things up so I can work remotely after the surgery."

"Where do you work? What are you doing?"

"I work for a company called Miller Green Developers. I've recently become a partner, but more of a junior partner. We rehab and renovate older or run-down homes, make them green-efficient and resell."

"So you're like… home flippers, only hippy style."

Milo laughs. "That's an interesting way to put it."

"They must really like you to give you so much leeway." Andrew pushes his salad plate away. He's on his second sangria.

"I'm doing well there." Milo doesn't want to brag; he doesn't feel that his work is really brag-worthy. He's worked hard for what he has, for where he is. But he isn't sure that makes him any more special than the next hardworking individual.

"That's great to hear. Where is *there* exactly?"

"Oh yeah," Milo says. There's so much they don't know. It seems like an impossible chasm. Are they doing this thing? Is this going to be a lunch and done, or some sort of friendship renewed? "Colorado. Denver."

"I would never have pictured that." Andrew leans back in his chair.

"I like it there. Have you ever been?"

"Nope." Andrew shrugs.

"You always wanted to travel the country," Milo says. He suppresses a wince. One of Andrew's wishes, caught in that bonfire. Is it okay to mention them? They promised to remember, and Milo had.

"I did." Andrew's eyes flitter away, taking in the pedestrian traffic and the shifting leaves above them. His expression is coded. "I travel-blogged for a while. I got to see so many things. Just not Denver. Well, I mean there's lots I also didn't see. You know what I mean."

Milo smiles and feels it in a deep but aching place. The things he hoped for Andrew when he left—it's nice to know he got some of them. "That's excellent."

"And you?" Andrew asks, delicately, as if broaching Milo's personal life might be too much. When they parted, they both believed the work Milo needed to do was harder. It was invisible work, impossible to quantify.

"I have done well, I think." Therapists and medications, pulling through a deep depression he thought would swallow him whole. Traveling too: Prague, the most beautiful place he's ever been. Paris and Athens. Florida and Oregon and so many others. Falling in love, for a lovely time. Even handling the breakup with Patrick had been an achievement. Or it seemed like it. When things fell apart with Patrick, Milo got through it without falling into old habits or another depression. He doesn't say any of that to Andrew, though.

Denise brings them their checks and Milo considers the rest of his day. There's nothing for him to do, really, not until he can work again. He's not felt this aimless in years, and it's getting a little boring.

"What are you doing the rest of the day?" he asks, taking a chance. Extending this, deepening this, is a risk.

"Nothing." Andrew smiles, brilliant and exquisite.

"I'd love to hear more about your work and those blogs," Milo says. "Want to walk?"

Andrew pauses and looks out to Main Street. There's pedestrian traffic—tourist traffic that looks promising, even if the season hasn't quite started yet.

"All right," Andrew says quietly. "Where to?"

o

Andrew stands when Milo does. "Lead the way."

Milo leads them to his usual walking route. They walk down Main, and Andrew tries not to notice the way locals notice them. He only sees two people he knows: Olivia Wood and Mr. Cavanaugh from the drug store. What gossip will this stir, if people remember them? Andrew shakes his head and tells himself not to care.

They go down side streets; Milo looks at the houses carefully. "I like to notice the details," he admits. "Nothing in Denver looks like home."

Home. How long has Milo called Santuit home? He didn't in college. Andrew lets Milo point out the details he likes and pretends he's not looking him over. Milo has changed, but it's subtle. His body is shaped differently: a little broader, but as muscled as Andrew remembers. His hair is still that lovely deep red that's almost brown that Andrew's never found a name for. His face is older: not old, but mature. Milo catches him looking, and Andrew darts his gaze elsewhere.

"So this is where you walk?" he asks.

"One of the places. Depending on where my mood is, sometimes the beach or the forest."

"Familiar haunts?" Andrew says.

"Not so much," Milo says softly. "Like I said, it depends on my mood. There's enough on my plate."

"Maybe I shouldn't have said that," Andrew says, stopping Milo with a hand on his arm.

"Don't worry about it." Milo looks him in the eyes. "There's a lot we don't know, and we..." he takes a breath. "Maybe a lot we can't talk about right now? I don't know."

"Yeah." Andrew looks away. The houses here are pristine with their curled accents on porches and captivating rich colors: proper Cape houses.

"Let's admit this is weird. I have no idea what to do."

"I don't either." Andrew admires Milo's candidness. "Milo, what is good for you right now? Like you said, you have a lot to handle. Is this—" he gestures between them, "is this going to be too much?"

Milo is quiet, and resumes their walk. He's thinking—Andrew can tell by the way his face settles.

"No," he says finally. "I think it could be good. What about you?"

"I want to try. To be friends again," Andrew blurts. Milo smiles; it's wistful and unexpected, the sweetness of his face when he smiles like that.

"All right. Me too." Milo looks to the sky.

Andrew sighs. They walk and walk and don't speak. Andrew breathes in home; everything here smells of comfort and familiarity. He could never find this quietness in Baltimore and felt suffocated without it. It was always different for Milo—every corner of this town oppressed him. How much is the same as it was then? And how much can Andrew help?

"We should do something," Milo says before Andrew takes off for home. "Maybe get together with Ted? I haven't seen him yet."

"Really?"

"Yeah. I really should. His wife is helping my mom—do you know her?"

"Yeah." Andrew doesn't mention he was one of the groomsmen in Ted's wedding.

"To be honest, I've been putting it off," Milo admits. "This is all..."

"A lot?"

"Yeah. But I think it'll be nice." Milo smiles a little. His hair is tousled, one lock curling onto his forehead. Andrew refrains from biting his lip and doesn't let himself linger on Milo's eyes, that dark blue he's never seen on anyone else.

"We can get something together. Invite Kathy, if you want. Even Sarah, if that's not too much."

"Sarah lives here still?"

"No," Andrew says. "But close, up in Norwalk."

"Oh yeah, my mom told me that." Milo glances around the neighborhood, then back at Andrew. "It's so foreign to me, everyone still being so close to home."

"Most of us left for a while. I guess the Cape has a way of drawing people back." Andrew regrets his words almost as soon as they're out. Milo's face shutters, then he takes a deep breath. His smile is forced, polite and strange.

"I guess so."

"That was thoughtless—"

"No, don't worry about it," Milo says. "Come on, it's late. You said you have something you have to do tonight. I don't want to keep you." They're back on Main. Andrew wants to linger, but a glance at his cell phone tells him he's dangerously close to being late to dinner with his parents and Dex.

"I'll text you?" he says.

Milo nods, waving when Andrew does, and walks back to his car. Andrew makes quick time getting back to his apartment. He lives close to downtown but now he has to book it to leave enough time to change and meet Dex.

chapter ten

MILO SETTLES DOWN AT A STARBUCKS AND CORRESPONDS with his boss on his phone, and then calls Zeke, whom he counts as his best friend back home. He's kept contact limited to text and emails until now, outlining what's going on. He's kept distant, but Zeke knows not to press.

"How's it going, man?" Zeke answers easily.

"It's been worse," Milo says.

Zeke laughs lightly. "Ready to spill your tender guts?"

Milo laughs; Zeke has an irreverent sense of humor that Milo appreciates and needs. "Not to you," he kids. "Just thought I'd finally grace you with my voice."

"I've been pining," Zeke says drily. "How I've missed you."

"I could tell; there was so much subtext in those late night texts."

"There's nothing to stir up longing like texting about a rousing Nuggets game."

"You know, that always sounds strange, throwing the word 'nuggets' into a conversation if you don't have context. They couldn't have come up with a better team name?"

"Are you trying to distract me from asking personal questions?" Zeke asks.

Milo sighs. "Yes. It's nice to hear a voice, but that's about all I need right now."

"Cool. So, poorly planned sports team names," Zeke transitions easily. "Top five, go."

○

"How was it?" his mom asks. She's waiting up in the kitchen. They have a couple on their honeymoon staying with them, so he's used the family entrance. There's no escape from this ambush.

He rolls his eyes. "Fine, Mom." Fondness, curiosity and something else brightens her eyes and he's not sure he can handle it.

"Tell me everything," she says. Her arms are crossed on the table; her tea is at her elbow. His place has a steaming cup of what he assumes is decaf coffee, and even a plate of cookies. She clearly expects a debriefing and maybe a gossip session. His conversation with Zeke may have provided a temporary distraction, but now his insides are roiling again, and confusion layers everything.

"We had lunch at Tribute," he says.

"And?" she leads. Milo sighs. Maybe he can give her enough to assuage her curiosity without having to talk about all the things he's not ready for.

"He had sangria. I ordered a beer. Is it weird that that seems weird, because we're old enough to drink at a restaurant and I remember when we had to use fake IDs to drink?"

"Fake IDs?"

He winces, then smiles sheepishly. He really should be over thinking he might get in trouble.

"Well..."

"I'm messing around, honey," she says, smiling widely. "It's nice to know you were doing stupid things kids do at that age."

Milo looks at her. Their gazes are naked, acknowledging truths they usually skirt. Her hand on his is soft and slightly cold.

"Not too much," he says.

"Andrew was always so good for you."

Milo considers this. Andrew was more than good for him. Andrew was the reason he survived. "Yes."

"I was sorry to hear you guys stopped being friends." She's leading, and he can tell she wants to know what happened between them, because he's never told anyone.

"Mom..." He sighs and runs a hand through his hair. "This is all... overwhelming."

"I'm sorry."

"No, don't be. I am not sure I am ready to talk about... that. It's so unnerving that he's here and I'm here; I wasn't expecting that at all." He shrugs and looks down, tracing the bumpy weave of the placemat.

"I shouldn't be prying."

"You aren't. You want to talk; that's good. This part...I need a little time, that's all. There's a lot more history between us than I can explain right now."

"Well, whenever you want to, or if you need to, I am here, all right?"

"That sounds great." He looks at her gratefully.

"And whenever you're ready, I'd love to have him over for dinner."

"I'll let you know," Milo says. Inviting him over probably means inviting his boyfriend too, and that's definitely too much. Milo isn't prepared to contemplate why, not just yet.

∘ ∘ ∘

"LET'S GO to the beach," Andrew says.

Dex is buried in work; his dark hair is a mess. He's in sloppy sweatpants and a ratty shirt and there's tension in his shoulders Andrew tries to soothe with open palms.

"Drew, I have a deadline."

"Just for a bit. Clear your mind, de-stress a little." Andrew's feeling incredibly hemmed in. They've both been working all morning, which is criminal on a Saturday, when they should be lazing around or getting errands and housework done.

"Why don't you go down," Dex suggests. "You know the sun on the water gives me a headache. I hate the feeling of sand between my toes. I'll read."

"I thought maybe we could talk. Reconnect? We've been buried in work."

Dex turns in his chair and grabs Andrew's hand. "So let's do dinner. I'll make a reservation at Ashe's."

Andrew bites back a sigh. They've barely talked about his lunch with Milo, and it seems like a secret, even though it's not at all. It's more frustrating that Dex doesn't seem terribly invested or worried. Andrew would like to unburden himself, but he's not sure what the burden is. After years of separation, the memory of the most painful part of his life is suddenly too close and too bright. Andrew kisses Dex's cheek.

"Have fun," Dex says. He catches Andrew's mouth in a kiss, then turns back to whatever spreadsheet he's tangled in.

Andrew heads to the harbor and wanders by the boats before making his way to the beach. It's getting crowded in the public access areas—tourists lugging bags of beach gear, children in tow. If he were to wander among them, he'd catch the scent of sunscreen and the chatter of children woven with the sound of the water and the call of gulls, maybe the shouts and laughter of an impromptu game of beach volleyball. Sometimes Andrew loves making his way through groups of strangers in spaces he knows like the back of his hand. He likes to see people at their best and worst—soaking in the sun and vacation freedom, harassed by toddlers and saturated with sand and slightly sunburned.

Today, though, he goes to the beachfront designated for residents and walks just above the water line. He sees a few boats. The sun really is bright—bright enough that, yes, Dex would have gotten a headache.

He needs to talk to someone, but Dex seems both too close and too far. He only knows bits of his and Milo's history. Andrew could tell him the whole story, and Dex would still never be able to empathize with what they went through. He pulls out his phone and dials Sarah: someone who knows the whole history, but is removed from it, hopefully enough to offer sound advice.

"Hey, Sarah." Andrew turns the phone, cupping it to keep the hush of wind off the beach from drowning him out.

"Drew! Long time no talk."

"I know, I know."

"Don't worry; I know you're settling in," she says playfully.

Andrew takes a deep breath. Asking someone for advice when you've hardly made time for them in months might be a jerk move. But he doesn't feel comfortable talking about this with Ted either.

"Are you busy? I... I need someone to talk to."

"Everything okay?"

"Yeah," he assures. "Well, sort of."

"I'm around. Where are you?"

"Pine. I can meet you somewhere in between."

"'Kay. How about Joe's Shack in thirty minutes?"

"Sounds great. Thank you." Andrew hangs up and looks back over the water one last time, then tries to shake the sand out of his hair. He heads back to his car, opens every window to let the trapped heat out and empties sand from each shoe.

o

"I heard Milo is home," Sarah says once they've worked through the *it's been so long* preliminaries.

"Grapevine?"

"Something like that." Sarah reaches over for his hand. "How are you doing?"

"Um... I'm not sure?"

"Look, I haven't spoken to Milo since right after his dad's funeral, so I really have no idea what his story is. But I have been your friend almost our whole lives. I don't want..."

"What?"

"No one should be hurt like you were."

"Sarah." He puts his fork down and meets her eyes. "Please believe me when I say that whatever happened at first, I did something after that hurt us both even more. I don't want to talk about it, and I don't particularly want to relive it. I'm just trying to figure out how to move forward."

Sarah takes her hand back and fiddles with her straw. "Well, the grapevine wasn't terribly specific. How did you guys run into each other?"

Andrew pushes his shrimp and scallop pasta around his plate, "Dex and I were walking on the beach and we ran into him."

"Ohhhh, awkward."

"Not as bad as it could be? I met Milo for lunch yesterday. It was nice. But..."

Sarah waits him out patiently.

"There's a lot I haven't told Dex. Milo's story is his own. But everything is starting to feel... I'm not sure. Dex is acting like everything's par for the course, but I know it's not. I feel weird about that."

"Why?"

"Because it relates to shit I worked through before we got together that he's never known the cause of. I don't want to share it but I'm annoyed that he's acting like this is *nothing*, which makes no fucking sense because I'm keeping him in the dark. Basically, I want Dex to guess that I want him to push me to talk about things he has no idea about." Andrew pushes his plate away. "I'm being crazy, aren't I? This is actually insane; I am so fucked."

"What exactly does he know about your relationship with Milo?"

"That we were childhood best friends but that we drifted apart."

"So… basically not the *in love* and *heartbreak* parts." It's said kindly, but he still doesn't want to hear it.

"Yes." He looks away. "Whatever. So, verdict: Does Dex need to know?"

Sarah thinks it over. "I don't know. It's your relationship. You get to decide what's best, long term, with Dex. You don't have to do it now, but at some point, something's bound to come to a head."

Andrew looks over the bar rail. They came early enough to get a beach front view, and down the sharp incline of dune, the water is high and agitated. His stomach feels like that, churning helplessly, grinding and crashing against the inevitability of the shore.

o

Dinner with Dex is a little strained. Despite Andrew's intentions, they don't talk about Milo or Andrew's lunch with him. Andrew doesn't have to try to avoid it; it just never comes up. They talk about a problem Dex is having at work. Dex is an easy-going guy; it's hard for him to understand the friction he's run into with one of the partners in his firm. Andrew spends dinner trying to help him come up with managing skills for future interactions, all the while trying to find the will to bring up Milo.

By the time they get home, Andrew is buzzed from the wine they shared and the frustration of his day; his energy is built up almost to a boiling point. Dex doesn't seem to mind the assertive and thorough way Andrew takes him apart as soon as they're past the front door. Andrew fucks Dex with all of that drive. Sex knocks Dex out like a light, unlike Andrew, who often feels as if he's riding out an adrenaline high after.

Andrew's trip to the beach was calming, and his conversation with Sarah was enlightening, but dinner did nothing to address his issues. He wasn't home long before he felt hemmed in and frustrated again. Dinner at a crowded restaurant was the opposite of a place where he thought he could open up some very painful wounds in order to enlighten Dex. A distance maybe only he perceives is settling between them.

Andrew kisses the top of Dex's sleeping head and climbs out of bed. He checks on Dex one last time, tucking the sheet around him, then goes into the living room and fires up his laptop. It's old and heavy and makes an ominous whirring noise, but Andrew's always had a strange attachment to it.

Dex knows he keeps a blog, but he doesn't know that Andrew keeps two. Sometimes a pang of guilt overcomes him, but he's tried hard to convince himself it's okay. He's had a secret blog, a second identity, since college, and it's often a life saver, a place for honesty he has needed but could never express as the Andrew he's cobbled together over the years. *Lingering* is a blog no one in his real life has ever known about, and secrecy seems to be the only way of keeping it exactly what it is.

In many ways Andrew shocked his readers as much as himself when he realized that the ache dogging him, despite his happiness with Dex in their first year as a couple, was a longing to come home. When he first went to college Andrew was painfully homesick, but also all whim and changeability, stumbling home night after night from sloppy parties and blurring laughter. Back then, Andrew saw his life stretching before him as a never-ending carousel of revelry, pleasure and touch and boys all helping him coast over a cavernous emptiness only one unattainable boy could fill.

The breaking apart of his friendship with Milo changed everything. Andrew felt it in his bones, in every molecule. After seven years, still, some nights, Andrew can't breathe through the echo of the love he had for Milo. Andrew spent years avoiding the place that held the imprint of the force of their heartbreak. When he was ready, when he grew up enough to trust someone with his heart and try to pull himself together, Andrew begged Dex to give Santuit a chance. And on their first day in Santuit, when Andrew's feet were buried in the grit of Chickopee's sand, he felt it. The air here breathed. It pulsed through his body and against his skin. Andrew is not a terribly spiritual man, but that day, he knew the truth in sayings about full-circle journeys.

Dex got sand in his eye.

That memory sums up so neatly the problem they're trying to work out. He gave his heart to Dex in Baltimore, one of a string of cities he'd tried on and discarded. For a while, it was okay. But Baltimore's air rubbed the wrong way. Andrew hated the unclean wind, how it channeled between buildings, heavy with the shared air of many. He loved Dex, but he hated Baltimore and, in the end, pleaded with Dex to settle on a compromise: a trial period back in Andrew's hometown.

Now, Dex sleeps easily and unburdened while Andrew spends an hour staring at the blinking cursor on his computer screen. *Lingering* has been where he's worked through the most painful and complex struggles of his life. But whatever is happening now—not just Milo, but with Dex—feels too big even for it.

∘ ∘ ∘

ONE WEEK after their meeting at Tribute, Milo finds himself at the corner of Second and Turnbull, a block from The Clover. He checks the time. He is five minutes late, but figures that's not a problem. Tonight he's going to see Andrew and Ted and Sarah again, meet Sarah's boyfriend and get to hang out with Dex as well as Kathy, whom he's learned to like a lot. Nerves buzz under his skin, but also curiosity and excitement. Santuit works at a slow pace that can be maddening. Working from his mother's kitchen, unable to fill time with his usual pursuits, is driving him stir crazy.

The inside of the bar is brighter than he anticipated from the heavy, dark wood of the exterior and the window sporting its name in careful script. Milo takes a deep breath when the door shuts with a soft whoosh and finds the hostess stand. He's about to ask if his party has arrived when he hears his name shouted.

"Miles Graham, get your ass over here!" Ted calls. He's standing with a large pint of beer in hand and a familiar, shit-eating grin on his face.

"Ted," Milo reaches out to shake his hand, then lets himself be pulled into a rough but tight one-armed hug. "How are you, man?"

"Amazing," Ted says. Despite the seven years since they last saw one another, Ted is much the same. A little more weight in the belly and a slightly receding hairline are the only indicators that so much time has passed. The smile on his face is a carbon copy of Ted's as a teenager: all mischief and joy. He pulls a chair out for Milo and sits next to Kathy, who is taking advantage of a baby-free evening and has a mostly empty martini glass in front of her. Her face is lightly flushed, and her smile is sweet. "You know Kathy, I hear."

"Yes." Milo smiles at her. "You're a lucky guy."

"About seventy percent of the time." Ted groans dramatically when Kathy pretends to punch his arm. "I was going to say that the other thirty I'm *really* lucky."

"You're so full of shit," Kathy says, then pushes the drink menu over to Milo with a disarming smile. Her hair is down, done in beachy waves. Like this it looks blonder than her usual ponytail. Between that and the makeup that makes her green eyes brighter, she looks like a completely new woman. "Here, take a load off."

"You look lovely tonight, Kathy," he says.

"Come on, man, don't make me look bad, here."

"Hey," Andrew's voice interrupts Ted's complaint. "Sorry we're late." He doesn't offer an excuse. His color is high. Milo finally gets a second look at his boyfriend, whom, now that Milo isn't floored with shock, he can see is cute. They make a good-looking couple. Andrew sits and nudges Dex's chair out with his foot. They share a smile that speaks of the secrets only couples share.

"No worries," Ted offers.

"Sarah's late, too," Kathy says.

"Of course," Andrew adds, rolling his eyes. Milo is comforted to know that Sarah is still perpetually late.

○

They've had a round of drinks before Sarah shows up.

"Christ, Sarah, wow." Milo holds her back at arms-length. A pretty girl as a teen, Sarah is stunning now. Gone is the fresh-faced girl who teased Lucy about her inability to apply eyeliner while refusing to put on her own. "What, are you a supermodel now?"

"Oh my god, shut up." She laughs. "Some of us grow into our looks," she says, and then gives Ted a teasing smile, "and, tragically, some of us grow out of them."

"Aw, fuck you." Ted throws a balled-up napkin, but misses.

With a beer in him and familiar faces around, Milo starts to feel comfortable in a way he hasn't in a long time. Sarah's boyfriend cancelled at the last minute, which explains why she's so late.

Through laughter and appetizers, Milo relaxes into a feeling of family. He's known Kathy for a little while now. Her care with his mother, and her unobtrusive kindness that always respects Milo's privacy, have endeared her to him greatly.

At first, Dex's presence seems intrusive. Even when Milo doesn't look at him, he always seems to be at the corner of his vision. People he doesn't know always make Milo a little wary.

It turns out that Andrew's boyfriend is a great guy. It took Milo a while to warm up to him, but by the end of the night he has. Dex is obviously good to Andrew. He's attentive and intelligent. They share an easy affection Milo never saw from Andrew with anyone else. It's a little strange, because Andrew-of-the-past is a shadow Milo can't help but see everywhere, and there's a huge gap between the boy Milo let go of and the man in front of him.

Next to Dex, Andrew sits perched at the edge of his chair. He's sipping his drink through the tiny cocktail straw and looking sideways, flirting with Dex. "So then I trip over the mic cord and fall off the stage," Andrew says. His laugh is bright and light as it has always been.

"Oh my god, I thought I'd never show my face there again," Dex adds.

Andrew touches his hand. "I know. My attempts at singing were bad enough before I almost broke the equipment."

"I probably wouldn't have gone back either," Sarah says, nodding at Dex.

"No shame, this one." Dex bumps Andrew's knee under the table. They're filled with funny stories about their lives together.

Milo swallows down small pangs of jealousy, because he has never achieved this ease with any of his boyfriends. He and Patrick came close, maybe, but more so at home, in private.

"All right, I think I'm going to give my darling here a last call before we have to relieve my parents of kid duty," Ted says. Kathy is slightly drunk, all big smiles and laughter. "Anyone up for another round?"

"Absolutely." Dex tips his glass in Andrew's direction. "Do you need anything, honey?"

Andrew smiles at him and then demurs. Milo checks his watch. It's getting late. His mother's surgery is in a few days, and he's been trying to stay home more, get everything lined up perfectly so she won't have to worry about the business.

"Maybe some water?" Milo asks. The reminder of what's coming this week wakes anxiety he's been trying to ignore. He's had one too many beers. The buzzing in his blood felt good a minute ago, but is too much, now.

"You all right?" Andrew asks. Milo changes his posture, wondering what gave him away.

"Yeah," Milo says. "A little buzzed is all."

"Still not big on drinking?"

"No, it never grew on me. I mean, I like a beer or two—"

"But not being drunk," Andrew finishes. Dex watches the exchange, but doesn't say anything, and Milo doesn't offer more. His secrets are always close to his chest. He carries them more lightly after the work he's done to manage them, but sharing is not an intimacy he offers many people.

"Oh, I don't know," Sarah says. Her smile is wicked. "I seem to remember this one time we all went out and you decided to try out those test tube shot things."

"Oh my god, I forgot about that," Ted says. He starts to laugh.

"It wasn't *that* bad," Milo protests.

"You spent all night saying, 'Trust me, I know what I'm doing,'" Andrew says. He turns to Dex. "He kept telling us the shots didn't have much alcohol in them—"

"And that he calculated how many he could have by his body weight," Sarah chimes in.

"Oh my god, you guys, remember, by the end of the night he was saying, 'Trust me'—" Ted is now laughing too hard to finish and Sarah quickly joins him.

"'I'm... I'm a professional,'" Sarah finishes. Milo shakes his head, but he's laughing too.

Milo turns to Dex, trying to include him in the conversation, "I spent the rest of the summer with these jerks whispering, 'Trust me, I'm a professional,' any time I did anything that didn't work out."

Andrew laughs suddenly, loudly, and Milo knows he's remembering an incident only they know about, when Milo was in a rush to get to a swim meet after spending an hour between school and competition at Andrew's house. He'd forgotten his bag upstairs and gone back to get it. Anxious about being late, he came tearing down the stairs toward the door, tripped on absolutely nothing and went into a cataclysmically ungraceful cartwheel of a fall that was absolutely destined for a blooper reel. Andrew laughed so hard he almost peed his pants. By the time he pulled himself together enough to ask if Milo was okay, Milo was laughing too. Andrew offered him a hand up, and at the last minute whispered, "Trust me, I'm a professional," in his ear. They both laughed so hard Milo cried.

"Milo." Andrew's voice brings him back from the memory; he bites back a chuckle. "Is there anything we can help with?"

"Right now?" Milo asks, surprised.

"No, with your mother's surgery coming up," Dex says. Milo feels unworthy of the kindness Dex offers. He can't pinpoint why, but it makes him mildly uncomfortable. He can feel his smile fade and feel the warmth of the laughter leeching from him.

"No, I think we're okay. She has help set up, and I'm pretty much done with her books."

"Her books?" Andrew asks.

"She was doing everything by hand, no filing system, anything."

"Oh god, that sounds like my worst nightmare," Dex says. Milo nods.

"Dex's in charge of that sort of thing," Andrew adds. "He takes care of our taxes and has a filing system I don't get."

"You should talk to my mom," Milo says. "Maybe you could make sense of it. She gets it, but it's beyond me, and there's a bunch of stuff missing that she probably needs."

"Was she doing her own taxes or having them prepared by—"

"Oh my god, can we talk shop later, boys?" Andrew interrupts. "I'll fall asleep in the guacamole if you keep this up."

"Mmm, then I'd get to eat it off your face," Dex murmurs.

"That's..." The intimate innuendo in the look Andrew and Dex share makes Milo feel like an intruder. "The weirdest come-on you've come up with yet."

"It was pretty winning," Dex admits. His eyes still hold Andrew's; there's a little heat and a lot of amusement in them.

Milo can tell it's time to go home. Sexy, weird, inside-joke flirting—he definitely doesn't need to stick around.

o

It's getting awkward Milo texts Zeke that night, in bed. *Being friends with Andrew, I mean.*

A few days after their last conversation he emailed Zeke an abbreviated, if somewhat honest, rundown of his friendship with Andrew.

Bound to be. Too much history. Zeke responds quickly.

Too much for friendship now, you think? Milo bites his lip.

That's up to you. Is it helping or hurting?
Confusing, Milo replies.
That's a thing to work out then.
You're so helpful. Milo frowns and tries to settle into the too-soft bed.
Not here to solve it man. Listening ear = helpful. As helpful as I can be.

Milo closes his eyes. Zeke is right, of course.
I think I miss therapy, he admits.
It's crazy, but I heard this rumor that they have that on the East Coast too.
Shut up.
Just food for thought.

Milo puts his phone down. It's late, not in Denver, but here. Finding a good therapist he had a rapport with had been a trek. He hasn't the energy for that right now. He's not sure he needs it. A coping strategy, or a way to think through the problem, maybe. But he's learned those skills; he just has to use them. Right before his mother's surgery is not the time to worry about anything else. The situation with Andrew doesn't require resolution right now; he's okay with waiting, because neither of them is going anywhere soon.

o

"How are you holding up?" Andrew asks.

They're at the Starbucks Milo frequents when he needs to get out of the house to work. Andrew ran into him on his break and decided to take a long lunch; Milo looked tired and pale, and it's not as if Andrew wasn't worrying anyway.

"Fine," Milo says. He shrugs, fiddling with a pen.

Andrew tilts his head. "Really?"

"Yeah." Milo rolls his eyes, but not rudely. "I promise. I mean, it's stressful. Taking care of my mom when she's like this... it's hard. It would be hard for anyone, probably."

Andrew tries to imagine it. He's seen Shelby a few times recently, and picturing his mother like that, weak and out of it, is hard. His mother is a force to be reckoned with, in her way. "Yeah, I imagine."

"Don't look at me like that," Milo says, smiling and kicking him lightly. "I'm not falling apart."

Andrew blinks and looks at Milo again, more carefully. He sees now—Milo really does seem okay. Tired, but put together. He resists shaking his head. *You'd think I would have outgrown this.* There's a long silence, interrupted only by the sounds of the foam machine and baristas calling customer names. The line is almost out the door.

"It's weird, right?" Milo says, breaking into Andrew's thoughts.

"Hm?"

"Sometimes when we hang out, it's like nothing's changed, and then I have to stop myself, because so much actually has."

"I know what you mean."

"I want to know who you are now," Milo says. "And I'd like you to know me."

"Okay..." Andrew says, pinned down by Milo's gaze.

"Part of that is trusting I'll talk about something if I need help. I mean, it might not be with you, but I've gotten really good at that."

Andrew forces a smile. He doesn't have a right to want to be the person Milo talks to. He doesn't know why he wants to *push* to be that person. "Would it be condescending to tell you that makes me really proud of you?"

Milo blushes and looks down. He's been clicking his pen. "No. It's nice."

"So…" Andrew says. There's so much he wants to ask: What changed; who Milo has in his life; how he met them. They've not really broached anything about the missing years—not the important things. But Milo is being very direct, and Andrew has been hoping that this—this tentative new friendship—is something they'll carry on when Shelby gets better and Milo leaves. At some point, he reasons, they should start to work through their histories. At the very least, they should assuage what he assumes is mutual curiosity.

Andrew has hundreds of questions: questions he's thought up during conversation and bitten back; questions that wake him in the night, then haunt him into dreams that hurt; questions born of seeing the truth behind Milo's changes.

"Yeah?"

"Tell me something," Andrew says. Milo waits, then raises an eyebrow. "Just something. Something I don't know."

Milo considers him for a minute. His brow is creased, more freckled than it was when he came back to Santuit a few weeks ago. Andrew wonders if he'll ever stop wanting to play with his hair. It must be the color, because Andrew's never suffered from a compulsive need to touch anyone else's hair.

"I once went to someone to have them try to balance my chakras," Milo says finally. Andrew bites his lip and tries not to laugh, because Milo looks dead serious. Then he smiles widely and Andrew lets himself crack up.

"This is probably rude," he says once he's caught his breath.

"No, it's cool. It's not a bad thing. It works for people? Or, they let it? I don't know. It wasn't for me. I had such a hard time keeping a straight face. She was so earnest, too!"

"I'm having a hard time imagining that, or you being so rude as to laugh."

"Well." Milo shrugs. His cheeks are still pink. "I didn't actually laugh, although I really wanted too. I bet it totally messed with the balancing."

"Hey," Andrew says, "don't knock laughter; I hear it's the best medicine."

There's a silence when they make eye contact, and then they burst into laughter loud enough to draw looks. Milo looks good with his face creased in laughter, shoulders shaking and body lighter in its lines. It's nice to be able to do this again.

"I have to get back to work," Andrew says eventually and with reluctance. "But I'm glad we ran into each other. I've been thinking about your mom. And you."

"Oh?"

Andrew can't read his smile. "I mean—" he stops. "I mean because of your mom, and her surgery." He shuts his mouth before he makes anything worse. "Anyway, yeah. We should hang out. I hear the weather is going to be great this weekend."

"Yeah, definitely. Text me, we'll figure something out. Ted said something the other day about a barbecue."

"Great." Andrew rubs the palms of his hands against the tops of his thighs and then shrugs awkwardly and backs out the door.

chapter eleven

"LET'S GET AWAY," DEX SAYS OVER DINNER THAT NIGHT.

"Away?" Andrew puts his fork down.

"Yeah. I don't know. Let's go to Boston or New York or D.C., or *somewhere*. Maybe next weekend. You can get the time, right?"

"Well, Milo and Ted and I were thinking about doing a barbeque thing that weekend."

"But that can be any weekend, right?" The insistence in his voice sparks a little alarm. Dex's eyes are wide; tension is tight around his mouth. "I can get all of next weekend free."

"Is everything all right, Dex?" Andrew doesn't resume eating despite his hand's desire to do something mundane and natural.

"I don't know. I feel..." Dex takes a sip of water and a deep breath. "Hemmed in. Restless?"

Andrew refrains from pointing out that they live in proximity to beaches and wide open spaces and nature. That a city, literally, is more hemming. Because he knows that's not what Dex means.

"Don't you ever just want to get out of here?" Dex continues.

No.

Andrew doesn't say that, though. He reaches forward to take Dex's hand and swallows his trepidation. There's a lot of unhappiness in Dex's tone, enough that Andrew wants to ask if a getaway is going to be a solution or a Band-Aid. He puts on a smile and squeezes his fingers.

"Where do you want to go?"

○

That night, Andrew watches Dex's back as he breathes deeply in dreams. He traces the constellation smatter of freckles lightly and thinks of how easily he gave in. He agreed with Dex's suggestion of New York, picked dates, shuffled work conflicts. He texted Milo, who was understanding, and decided to put off the barbeque until the following weekend, if Ted and Sarah were game. He pretended excitement and ignored the tension that sat between them the rest of the evening. Andrew is alone by the water more and more. The slow, steady beat of living in a Cape tourist town makes Dex crazy. Dex is in many ways like the boy Andrew was a long time ago: hungry for noise and the glitter and the bright wire nights of city living.

Andrew kissed Dex goodnight with every ounce of love and care he could muster. The long silence between the kiss and Dex's eyes closing in acquiescence was honest. Andrew touched Dex's eyebrow and ear lightly, and wished for words or deeds or changes that might fix something, anything. He held him carefully until he rolled away in sleep. The hushed night slipping through the open window whispers hopes he wants to cling to. Andrew tells himself it won't matter in the end. The strength of their commitment will help them find a compromise.

○ ○ ○

IT'S BEEN a long weekend alone; Shelby is up and around, mostly, and their guests have been remarkably easygoing and low maintenance; not much for him to do on that front. With the weekend, Milo promised himself a break, because he's been working nonstop. He has no desire to blur his personal and work lives until they can't be unglued.

He's unsettled by how many times he picks up his phone to text Andrew. It's not as though they've been seeing each other every day. But between responsibilities, the places he traverses are quiet in a way he's now beginning to find lonely, rather than haunting. Milo has no desire to interrupt Andrew's weekend with Dex, so he settles for upping his workouts, running farther and harder, harassing Zeke by email and going over to Ted and Kathy's for beer and a Red Sox game on TV.

Sunday Milo heads out of the house after a late lunch. He's restless, so he goes to the beach. It's the height of the season, so the public beaches are packed. He has to go to the end of Pine, almost around the tip of the peninsula, to get away from the noise. The tide is low, and there are many small treasures on the sandbar for him to collect. He has music pumping loudly through his iPod because the sound of the water seems grating. After several trips back and forth, Milo sits next to his pile of found objects. The sun is low and it's getting chilly with the waning light. He constructs a circle of stones and shells, alternating them, and then lets himself really look, he clears his mind and examines what he has and tries to let the objects choose him, and let the shape to be created speak to him.

A sudden movement on his periphery startles him. It's Andrew, who flops onto the sand next to him with a bright smile. Milo pulls his earbuds out.

"This is cool; what is it?" Andrew asks. Milo looks at his circle.

"It's a sand mandala with found objects," Milo explains, and Andrew looks at him as if he's crazy. Okay, so maybe not much of an explanation.

"Like the thing Buddhists do?"

"Uh, sort of, but not? There's more to the history than that."

"It's suddenly so clear," Andrew says, and Milo smacks his knee.

"It's something I picked up when I started therapy. At first it seemed eccentric or hokey. It's meant to be an exercise in mindfulness."

Andrew looks at him for a long minute, then at the sand. "Mindfulness? How?"

"Um, well," Milo says as he draws his fingers through the sand. "I'm not an artist—" Andrew snorts and Milo ignores him. "I can draw a circle, though. You're supposed to try to focus on *not* focusing on a plan and immerse yourself in that moment, or that activity, to quiet your mind."

"Quiet your mind," Andrew repeats. Milo's not sure how to read his tone.

"I mean, my therapist Janet had a whole spiel about the reason why, in the end, you choose what colors or shapes you do and what they might mean on a deeper level. That part was a little like the chakra thing for me."

He glances at Andrew, but sees no judgment, only interest.

"It was nice, though, otherwise. It helped me get the hang of meditating, which is really important for working on..."

"On?"

"Oh, well, you know." Milo fiddles with the shells between the pebbles in the circle. "Just... anxiety and stuff. I had a lot of anxiety."

He knows Andrew remembers that. He doesn't want to tell him how much worse things got before they got better. The sound of the water is picking up, and clouds are boiling in from the southwest. Milo tries to judge how long they have before weather drives them from the beach.

"I'm glad," Andrew says. "That it helped, I mean."

Milo considers asking about the sadness in the words, or why Andrew's face seems melancholy. He has some idea but he doesn't really want to address it right now.

"Anyway, this isn't quite like that. Obviously. I'm not anxious right now," Milo says, tries to cut back on the nervous babbling. "Just bored."

"Do you—" Andrew stops and clears his throat. The wind is whipping through his hair, making the collar of his button-down shirt flutter. He's more dressed up than usual.

"Do I?"

"Remember. That we used to do this stuff." Andrew picks up a shell.

"I remember." Milo's eyes on Andrew feel like kindness, as do his words: easily shared memories that don't hurt. Andrew's smile is bright and sweet, but there's something else behind his eyes.

"Do you want to finish it? Maybe it'll help."

"I don't need help," Andrew says.

Milo looks at him steadily. "Okay."

"I mean it," Andrew says a little sharply, and then looks away when Milo bumps their shoulders together.

"I mean it too," Milo says. "They're your feelings. You can still finish it, though."

Andrew looks back at him, then down at the sand, and pokes at the shells for a second, separating them.

"Show me how?" he asks at length, and even through the whipped-up wind, it's warm all through Milo's bones.

o o o

HOWEVER BENIGN the moment he shared with Milo on the beach seemed on the surface, it didn't feel that way to Andrew. At home he finds Dex methodically unpacking, and helps him silently, all the while wondering if he should tell Dex about it. Nothing happened, nothing that requires confession. Somehow those minutes with Milo are much too intimate to share. So he keeps quiet. If Dex notices, he probably attributes the tension between them to the way Andrew ran off to the beach the moment they got home.

That night he texts Sarah and asks her to meet him for a drink; his insides roil whenever he thinks of the conundrum he's caught himself in.

"Hey, babe." Sarah comes up behind Andrew where he's sitting at the bar. She kisses his cheek and plops down on the seat. Her hair is in a high ponytail, but curled. It's a girlish look—especially paired with the pink top she's somehow pulling off—but not immature.

Andrew smiles at her. "You look pretty."

"Aw, thanks." Sarah tips her head with a smile, then signals the bartender. "So, no Dex?"

"He had..." Andrew turns his wineglass by the stem. "Okay, so, I didn't ask him. I kind of needed someone to talk to."

"That isn't him." She states bluntly.

Andrew winces. "Is that terrible?"

"No, not at all." Sarah orders her drink, then turns her attention back to him. "Listen Andrew, I wanted to ask you this before, and please don't take this the wrong way, but why me? We haven't really been close in a while."

"I know; I'm sorry." He leans his elbow on the bar and puts his head in his hand. "It's not because I didn't want to talk to you."

"I'm not upset, honey. I'm just curious."

"I haven't really had someone to talk to who isn't Dex in a while."

"What about Milo?" Sarah gives him a look that is somehow innocent and suggestive at once. Andrew lets his exasperation show. "I'm just kidding. He's what you need to talk about though, isn't he?"

Andrew finishes his wine in one long swallow. "Yes. No. I don't know." The noise in the bar is rising a little. Sarah waits him out while he gathers his thoughts and calls for another drink. As much as he wanted to talk to someone about Milo, he can't bring himself to do it.

"I had a friend in college—Nat—who was the only non-home friend I ever talked to about Milo, you know?"

"And?"

"She was my only confidant, but she wasn't always a great one. At times, I did need some tough love, but still... Anyway, after Milo's dad died and things happened..."

"Things?" Sarah prompts. He knows everyone has always wondered what went down between them.

"Nat and my roommate were a big part of how I managed to get out of bed and move on. Still, being friends with her, compared to Milo, in terms of trust and feeling supported, was not remotely the same. I never trusted anyone that much. Until Dex." Andrew bites his lip.

"So it's not just Milo, is it? You need to talk about Milo *and* Dex."

"Yeah." He buries his head in his hands.

She rubs his arm. "Listen, everyone has boyfriend troubles. Look at mine!"

Andrew laughs along with her. "I can't because I've never met him."

"Yeah, I'm not sure I have either."

"Sarah—"

She waves it off. "Don't worry about it, Drew. That's a story for another day. Right now we're talking about your stuff. So, Milo or Dex?"

"Did you know that before we moved here, we lived in Baltimore?"

"Yeah, I think so. How was that? I've never been."

"At first it was okay. But it really wasn't for me. Dex loved it there, though, and I love him, and it was a compromise."

"But now you're here."

Andrew launches into a brief explanation of their time in Baltimore and their decision to move back to Santuit. "You know, he kisses me sometimes like I'm his air. Like I shape his happiness. And I feel it too, that safety that comes from a long-time relationship, those moments when we're totally in sync. But then something happens and I wake up and realize he might be happy with me, but he's not happy here."

"But you are, right?"

"Happy here, you mean?"

"If that's the part you want to talk about, sure."

Andrew makes a face at her. "He hasn't said anything yet, but we have a one-year deal, and I know he's thinking about it."

"Have you guys talked about this?"

"No."

"Why not? It seems like this is a big deal."

"Sarah, I have this beautiful man I've let myself love, after years of not letting anyone close. But now I'm wondering if love is enough. I don't want to give up, but something doesn't feel right. I can't tell what it is, but being here feels like a big part of it."

"Andrew," she says carefully, "Don't you think Milo could have something to do with that, too?"

Andrew closes his eyes; they are suddenly burning with the threat of tears. He shakes his head—not because she's wrong, but because trying to think about Milo and Dex and what's happening in his heart is too much.

"I know this hurts, but I think it needed to be said. You'll have to work this out eventually, right?" Sarah asks.

"You're right." Andrew struggles to compose himself and she tugs him over to put her arms around him. She doesn't offer him platitudes or solutions or try to make him talk any more. He's no closer to a solution, but the catharsis of saying things he's been afraid to think seems like a positive step.

o o o

ONLY DAYS later, Andrew contacts Milo to ask him to lunch.

"Hey." Milo interrupts his thoughts. "What's up?"

"I don't..." Andrew pulls his hand through his hair. "I don't know. I'm in a mood, I guess."

"I would have thought a weekend getaway would help pull someone *out* of a funk."

"You'd think," Andrew says. He plays with his silverware, lines it up perfectly, then knocks it all apart. He looks up at Milo and wonders what the limits of their new friendship are and if he can balance his changing relationships with the men in his life.

"But it didn't?"

"Not like he—*we*, I mean, wanted? He thinks of Dex, in bed in a nice hotel, eyes wide and voice quiet. *Will you talk to me?* he asked. *Don't I always?* Andrew replied, and then felt a pang at the sadness in Dex's eyes. When they kissed, and then made love, it was as if they both knew something was missing. "Sometimes I think he misses how I used to be."

"How's that?"

"Impulsive? Fun?" Andrew hazards. He smiles when Milo scoffs.

"Are you suddenly not fun?"

"No, I am..." He smiles. "I think."

"I think so too," Milo says. Andrew shrugs a little.

"But I don't know... we're older. I always wanted to come back, and when we did, I really felt..."

Milo waits him out patiently while he finds the words.

"Like the roots I always had here really grew. We're growing up. I want to settle down. I wanted that with him."

"Wanted?" Milo asks.

Andrew shakes his head. "I mean want. I want that."

"And he doesn't?"

"No, he does. Maybe not here. But he said he did. This place, though..."

Milo looks down at his plate, the sloppy pile of ketchup and the remnants of French fries he didn't eat, the tomato seeds that slipped out of his burger and the lettuce he removed. The sun is bright and the chatter of people surrounds them.

"It's transformative," Andrew finally says. Milo probably knows what he means. When he left, Andrew watched him set fire to their old lives and all their memories. The last month or so, though, he's seen a change in Milo's stance and posture and the way he touches the earth and sand here.

"It kind of is, isn't it?" he says. Andrew focuses on finishing his salmon, makes little piles of his rice and then presses them down with his fork. He picks out slivers of almonds, then finally eats. Milo works on his fries, but Andrew knows he hates the little leftover ones that are mostly the edges of the potato with tough skin and weird taste.

"How did you guys meet?" Milo asks after a long silence.

"Oh, you know, the usual for me, then." Andrew lifts a shoulder and scrambles to think of a way to encapsulate this story. "At a party."

"Really? Still?" Milo knows they've been together for about a year. He tries to hide his surprise.

"It was a while ago," Andrew says dryly, easily reading Milo's face. "We knew each other the way you do when you travel in similar circles for a long time. Then things changed a bit—" Andrew clears this throat; it's a vivid memory, that first time, when admiration moved from banked to blatant, when Dex, laughing, led him home, and they fucked just inside the door.

"So can I call you?" Dex asked an hour later, after shrugging back into his clothes.

"We'll see each other around," Andrew answered. Casual had always been good. Well, at least comfortable. Dex shrugged good-naturedly, smiled like as if he knew a secret, and kissed Andrew's cheek.

Three weeks later, this time in Andrew's bed, he asked again. "But we're friends now, right?"

"I don't do friends," Andrew joked from the doorway by the bathroom. He remembers forcing himself to smile through the pang that rose as soon as the words came out.

"You don't make them, or *do* them?" Dex lobbed back. Crawling into bed and breathing out old pains, Andrew whispered something dirty about *making* him and the conversation was forgotten. Until it wasn't. Until friendship felt natural, not anything he'd planned, but something… nice.

"Eventually… we became friends."

"And then more?" Milo says. They both fidget a little.

"It took a while." Andrew can't help but smile, because the day he finally caved to the obvious, when he thought through and dismissed every irrational and lingering fear with honesty he had rarely afforded himself, he felt lit with happiness in Dex's arms, and Dex's smile meant he felt the same. "But it did. It just…did. And it was amazing."

"That's really nice," Milo says quietly. "I don't know that I've ever really had that."

"What, a boyfriend?" Andrew teases, trying to pick through the undercurrent.

"No. A boyfriend who's also a friend. Like that." Milo looks away, and Andrew sucks in a breath. It's sad—the words make him ache. And it's not because they are talking around old, painful wounds they're picking at without acknowledging, but because he wishes Milo had had that. Has that.

"We're still young," he offers. It's a dumb thing to say.

"I know. Don't look at me like that." He laughs. "I'm fine. I've been fine. I've had a lot of good things, you know."

"Tell me about them," Andrew says. He very much wants to understand the years he wasn't with Milo, to feel the happiness he wasn't there to see. "Have you been in love?"

"Yeah." Milo bites his lip and looks into Andrew's eyes. "It was wonderful, for a while. But it wasn't... *it*. You know?"

Andrew nods.

"But it was nice; it didn't end badly. We were together for about two years. With Patrick... I think we both eventually knew it would never be quite what we hoped, and it was right, us breaking up. We were both searching for that something... more."

I know what you mean. Andrew averts his eyes, picks up the folder with the bill and concentrates on pulling out his wallet and ignoring the words resonating inside.

o

In bed that night, Andrew is honest with himself. Being friends with Milo hasn't helped heal old wounds as much as he hoped. Instead, he's sleepless and aching, remembering a longing so desperate it took his breath, and the bitter tang of heartbreak, the taste of ash from that bonfire on his tongue. Loving Milo was the most selfless, even if not the healthiest, act of his life.

Finally understanding the limitations of their friendship, despite everything else, was a gift. They both needed healing, but especially Milo, whose love and fear had matched each other and paralyzed him. They'd loved each other as boys, but in the moment they confessed that with naked honesty, Andrew knew they would never grow into the men they wanted to be if they were together. Being with him would hold Milo back forever.

Reluctantly, Andrew wonders if that was foolish.

o

"My mom called me today," Andrew says.

"Well, hello to you too," Milo replies. Raucous background noise almost obscures his voice.

"Sorry, hi. Hello, how are you this fine day?" Andrew says, facetious and sassy. The background noise suddenly disappears.

"Great. Sorry, we're all pitching in to clean; we have a last minute guest coming and Mom is just..."

"Is she okay?"

"Yeah. The radiation seems to be hitting her hard this week. She's very tired and nauseated. We've all come together to make her rest and stop worrying about guests, because she refuses to close down."

"Is there anything I can do to help? Should I let you go?"

"No, we're pretty much done. What's up? I'm assuming you didn't call to update me on your family correspondence."

"Ooh," Andrew says. "You're hilarious."

"A born comedian," Milo replies; this time Andrew actually laughs.

"Anyway, my mother called and is insisting you come over for dinner sometime soon."

A silence that lasts too long trips Andrew's nerves.

"That sounds great," Milo says.

"Really?"

"Yeah, of course. Only if she makes macaroons."

"Of course. Baked goods are her M.O. for enticing me into family dinners."

WHAT IT TAKES

THURSDAY AFTERNOON brings a sudden onslaught of worry.

"What is your deal?" Dex asks when Andrew changes his shirt for the fourth time and bemoans his choice of wine.

"Nothing, I'm fine."

"Drew—"

"It's fine," Andrew snaps, then closes his eyes and takes a deep breath. "I'm sorry. I'm nervous."

"Why? We have dinner at your parents' all the time."

Andrew smooths his shirt, evaluates himself in the mirror again and wonders how to explain this to Dex.

"Listen, I haven't really told you Milo's story—because it's his to tell—"

"Okay...?"

"But... look, he had a really hard life here when we were kids. A hard time. I worry about things that might remind him of that."

"Like going to your parents'?"

"Yeah." Andrew turns to Dex, puts his hands on his shoulders and kisses him fleetingly. "He was with us a lot, over at our house. It was a good place for him then, but I don't want him to have to re-live some of the stuff that drove him there in the first place."

Dex looks a little sad and a little drawn. "Did he seem worried when you invited him?"

Andrew thinks of that pause, the split second when Milo's hesitation resonated like the clang of a bell. Maybe it was something no one else would have noticed, and nothing he could really explain to Dex.

"Andrew, he's a big boy," Dex continues. Andrew bristles. "If it upsets him, I believe he knows how to ask for support, right?

He seems to have himself together with what's happening with his mother."

Andrew considers Dex's words. He does make a good point. "Yeah. I guess I'm still used to the way things were." He tries not to wince, worried Dex might take that the wrong way.

"Come on, honey. Good food, good wine and good company are waiting for us."

Andrew smiles because Dex is right. He grabs the wine and a light sweater and tries to leave his worries behind.

o

"Sweetheart." Dex pulls Andrew aside in the kitchen where Andrew's been scraping the remains of dinner from plates into the garbage. "It's late, and I have to work tomorrow. Do you think we can make dessert quick?"

Andrew stacks the last dish carefully and doesn't look at Dex. It is late—everyone lingered over dinner. Milo fits so seamlessly in a room with his family; no awkwardness popped up, and when his parents and Milo reminisced, it was about good things. It's a warm, wonderful feeling, not just because of Milo, but because he missed his own family when he was gone.

"I'm enjoying this," he says to Dex. "What if you go home, and I'll get a ride and come later? I don't want you to be too tired tomorrow."

Dex sighs, setting off both annoyance and chagrin inside Andrew. He's talked about missing his family before; what seemed to both of them like a checkmark in the 'pro' column for coming home now seems like evidence that things aren't quite right. Every reason Andrew wants to stay is a reminder that Dex isn't happy here. He doesn't want to ask Dex to be kinder, because he's scared they'll leave soon and he'll be going without his family again.

"Please?" Andrew reaches out to squeeze Dex's hand.

"Sure," Dex says. He doesn't look happy, exactly, but he doesn't seem upset either.

o

"You seem a little down," Milo observes later. They're sitting in the family room sharing the last of the wine. Andrew's parents begged off and went to bed half an hour ago. Andrew knows he'll be tired tomorrow too, but his job is flexible enough that he'll manage an extra hour or two of sleep.

"I'm fine," Andrew brushes him off. He's already confessed more of his problems with Dex than he wants to admit. Milo holds his gaze, then shrugs.

"Wanna go for a walk? Get some fresh air?"

"Milo, it's midnight."

"So? You'll navigate; I know you'd never get us lost." Milo points at the ceiling, as if they can see the stars from here. Andrew smiles, but it's bittersweet—Milo remembering Andrew's silly notions as a kid that he could make his own constellations from the stars, that they could navigate new adventures with secret maps.

"All right," he says. He's pleasantly loose from the wine and too many macaroons. They pull their shoes on at the door, and Andrew has to steady himself against Milo when he loses his balance.

"You all right, sailor?" Milo rights him.

"I'm fine. Smaller than you; pretty sure I had more wine."

"You're such a lush," Milo jokes, pulling open the door. Andrew thinks of himself a few years ago.

"If only you knew," he says under his breath. He locks the door and, when Milo offers, links their arms and lets Milo steady him on the gravel drive.

"All right captain, where to?" Milo says. When Andrew looks up, the sky is a covered with a dizzying blanket of stars.

o

"Can I ask you a question?" Andrew says out of nowhere. They've been walking in silence—Andrew's led them to Chickopee Beach. Milo hasn't been here since he's been back, but he doesn't tell Andrew. Many years ago, they met here. Milo isn't sure if Andrew is leading them here for a purpose, or if it's habit.

"Sure," Milo says. Andrew doesn't say anything; Milo elbows him a little. "You in there?"

"Yeah. It's just...personal. More than we've—"

"Oh," Milo says. This dance they've been in, on the edge of too-much-but-not-enough, is one he's been wishing away without knowing how. "Yeah. Anything."

It's too dark to read Andrew's face, but the moon is huge and bright, and he can at least see that he is watching him.

"When did you forgive your mother?" Andrew asks. Milo tightens his hold on Andrew's arm to steady him, and takes a deep breath; the scent of the water is sharp and clean and bracing.

"Oh, well..." The sand ripples in front of them, valleys of shadow, but peaked in light, brightly reflecting the moon's glow. It's otherworldly and beautiful.

"You have, right? You seem like it."

"Yeah," Milo says. "I have." He walks with Andrew to the edge of the water, then toes his shoes off; the water lapping at his feet is cold. Andrew fumbles and so Milo helps him with his shoes; it's startlingly intimate.

"How? I remember..."

"You remember?" Milo prompts.

"You were so angry, and so... I don't—I mean. Betrayed?"

"Yeah." Milo stands still, and lets the suck and pull of the waves bury his feet in sand. "You know, all that negative stuff... god, it was so much to carry. I had so much shit I was lugging around with me. And that anger, with her and with life and with—"

Milo cuts himself off before he admits how angry he was when Andrew severed the last of their ties, months after their goodbye. He blocked him on social media, changed his number and took the last of himself from Milo's life. Even if all he had then were small scraps and tiny, fogged windows into Andrew's life… they had been enough to keep him going. It's not the time for that conversation—maybe it won't ever be. "I had to move on," he says instead, gently. "And I couldn't when I was drowning in it."

"So… it's just gone? All of your anger?"

"No… I, I wouldn't say that. I'm still angry about a lot of shit. But her?" Milo shakes his head. "I tried for a long time to forgive her, but I couldn't. Because she was an adult and I was a kid: inherently helpless. She had options I didn't. She could have left or protected me, you know? So yeah, I was furious."

"But now you're not?"

"There was a day about four years ago, maybe? She called, and needed help with something—not anything big, just something I could walk her through over the phone? I can't remember. But I do remember talking to her and feeling more and more annoyed and short tempered. There really wasn't a reason for my response on that call."

"Just built-up anger, then?"

"Yeah. I barely got off the phone with her before I lost it. I threw my phone against the wall. Shattered the screen and everything."

"Wow."

Milo notices that Andrew is shivering a little. "You forgot your sweater," he says, then takes his off.

"No, no don't—"

"It's fine. I'm not cold at all." He drapes it over Andrew's shoulders and leads them away from the water. They walk a little way until they've crossed from the resident stretch of beach into the tourist one, then finds a bench for them to sit on.

"I was with Patrick then. Scared the shit out of him. I don't know that I'd ever been that angry before—" Milo stops and backtracks. "Well, acted that angry. It was like everything boiled over; it was huge and I was out of control."

"Did this have to do with why things didn't work out between you?"

"No, but the way I freaked him out—it's one of the reasons I went back to therapy. I'd tried it before, and it had helped, but I let it slide. I think I thought it had helped as much as it could, which wasn't really a lot."

"So you went back," Andrew says.

"Yeah. It took a while. I had to find the right person, which isn't something I'd thought about before—how important it would be to find someone I really could trust and connect with. I was with Janet for at least a year before her lessons really clicked."

"What was she teaching you?" Andrew asks.

Milo stops to think about how to phrase this. "That I wasn't my feelings."

"I... what?"

"I wasn't an angry person. I was a person who felt anger."

"No offense, but that sounds like the same thing to me."

"I know, right?" Milo smiles. "I'm telling you it took an age for me to really get it. What she meant was that I let my emotions control me. I was letting myself be helpless to them, and when we think we *are* our emotions, instead of our emotions being something we experience, or can let go of, or survive... they're in control."

He stops while Andrew thinks this over. The rising wind picks up the sounds of the water. Milo buries his feet in the sand and tells himself it's the cold that has him leaning into Andrew's space. On the breeze he catches the scent of Andrew's cologne. It's new—to him at least—but lovely. "I sort of get that." Andrew sounds dubious.

"I remember the day I figured it out. It wasn't as though she was saying it differently. We'd been covering it for a while, and she was very patient with me, but there was so much cluttering my head and fucking with me, I had to really persist, you know? And one day, Patrick and I got into this ridiculous fight."

"And?"

"And I stormed off. There was a small part of me that knew I was being irrational, but I couldn't help it, and I kept thinking, 'This is my whole life; this is what it's going to be like.'"

"What was?"

"Me, being angrier and angrier and more and more fucked up and never moving past anything," Milo says. The despair he felt then leaks into his words. Andrew lays his hand on Milo's forearm, gently, and Milo smiles. "I wish I could describe what that felt like, always thinking my life was going to be this hopeless mess. And then…"

Milo looks up; the stars are brilliant and the night is heavy around them. Andrew waits patiently.

"Patrick came and found me. He told me he was sorry, and he loved me, and there was this…I don't know. Dichotomy? Between what I wanted in my life, and what I saw as the only life I was actually going to get."

"Ooh, now you're breaking out the big words," Andrew jokes.

Milo smiles at him and appreciates the lessening of tension. "Just taking a page out of your book."

"So this dichotomy?"

Milo looks back at the water and tries to collect his words so that they will make sense.

"I guess… I lived all that time thinking happiness was out of reach. That it was something I had to wait for, passively. It was a beautiful idea that I didn't really believe in. But you know what?" He turns to Andrew. In the warm light from the moon he can see that Andrew's hair is falling and his eyes are intent on him. He knows he's the sole recipient of Andrew's attention; it's a wordless language relearned with ease.

"What?"

"Happiness in our lives and future are things we *can* have. We can choose them. The things holding me back—they seemed so tangible. Like… I was carrying this huge bag of rocks. And I could see how holding on to them was holding me back. Each grief… one rock."

"One rock?"

"Something I could take out of that bag and leave behind. Healing… isn't something that exists in the future, waiting to find us randomly. It exists at our fingertips."

"Huh," Andrew says.

"Being mad at my mom… that was something I knew I could work on. Maybe even let go of. And it wasn't immediate, but I could see how allowing myself be so angry was me holding on to things I could never change. I mean, I, I'll never be angry or resentful or damaged enough to change what happened. And he's not here anymore. But I am, and she is, and we both had to heal."

"But she—"

"Did the best she could," Milo interrupts. "I'm not excusing her. But when I imagine her life, and remember what it was like, I think… is that what she pictured for herself? When she was growing up, when she had dreams about her life… the life she had with him is nothing a person would choose. Now I can see how helpless he made her feel. And that she did try her best. I felt—when I really took the time to think about her life, and her regrets… I felt so sad for her. Forgiving her doesn't have to mean excusing what happened. It means accepting it and separating those events from my relationship with her."

"It's gone? Like that?" Andrew snaps his fingers.

"No. But I am learning that my capacity for forgiveness is bigger than my anger."

Andrew exhales loudly. His fingers tighten around Milo's forearm, and then he leans his head against Milo's shoulder. Against his better judgment but following a deep ache, Milo rests his head against Andrew's.

"Look at the stars," Milo whispers. "I haven't seen anything like this in years."

"I missed them too. They've never looked the same without you."

"*Drew—*"

"Maybe I shouldn't have said that." Andrew takes a breath. In the pause between sentences, Milo thinks of the years it takes for starlight to reach earth—the unimaginable time between the change and the perception of the change.

"Maybe I needed to hear that," Milo says.

"You really are something special," Andrew whispers. "You always have been."

Milo closes his eyes; the dark of two a.m. confessions is disorienting, and this connection, his body touching Andrew's, feels like the only thing connecting him in space.

chapter twelve

"ANDREW, WE NEED TO TALK," DEX SAYS AS SOON AS HE closes the door. He puts his briefcase on the floor and toes off his shoes, giving Andrew enough time to save the draft of his blog post, shut his laptop so Dex can't see it, and turn around. The words alone should be enough to worry him, and they do. What's more, there's Dex's face, serious as it never is.

"Um, okay." He fiddles with a button on his sleeve, then follows Dex to the couch at his gesture.

"Something happened, and we need to talk it over."

For a gut-dropping second, Andrew thinks maybe Dex knows about the moment he shared with Milo on the beach. *That was nothing,* he reasons. Maybe it seemed like more than nothing, but that was only for him, and something he quickly packed up and away.

"Michelle wants me to apply for a job in D.C.," Dex says. Andrew shakes his head, sure he's heard wrong.

"She did what?"

"Recommended me for a job. A promotion."

Andrew tries to read his face, and finds he can't. It's a terrible feeling.

"What did you tell her?" Andrew asks carefully.

"That I'd think about it. Talk to you."

Despite not wanting to, he does in fact feel a thread of anger. "Dex—"

"Hear me out, please," Dex pleads. Andrew takes a deep breath, and bites back the resentment that's bubbling. "It's an excellent opportunity, a big raise. It would be in D.C., yes, but there are so many nice places to live. We'd be able to afford a house, and there's so much culture—"

"And politicians," Andrew interrupts, trying to make light of what seems like a dangerous conversation. His tone is all wrong, though, acid and anger.

"Andrew, be reasonable—"

"Oh my god, do *not* patronize me right now," Andrew says, too loudly. "Dex, you *promised* me a year. You promised me you'd try."

"I have." Dex winces. "I am. It's been almost a year."

"No, you haven't. You're buried in work. You don't come anywhere with me unless it's for an unplanned, whirlwind weekend to some stupidly crowded and ugly city—"

"You loved New York. I thought you'd like that; I did that for you!"

"Oh, please," Andrew spits out, "that was as much for you as me. What was that, a trap? Some way to get me to realize how much I missed Baltimore?"

"No!" Dex paces back and forth between the armchair and the fringed lamp Andrew hates but puts up with because it was Dex's grandmother's. "I don't know," he says. "Not on purpose."

Andrew closes his eyes and modulates his voice. "I'm not who I was, Dex," he says, as gently as he can through his anger.

"I know. I don't want you to be. I don't want either of us to stagnate. But I want us to grow together and lately all I feel is us growing apart."

A silence clangs through the apartment with the words. It's not Baltimore, or D.C., or Dex hating Santuit. It's a distance articulated for the first time. Words have power: As a writer, Andrew knows this perhaps better than Dex. Spoken aloud, they mean so much more than Dex might have intended. Andrew's confessions to an anonymous audience on his blog are suddenly much more real and much too present.

"When do you have to decide?" Andrew asks finally.

"I have time," Dex says. Andrew nods and stands. They're both too emotional for rational conversation, and Andrew recognizes that in anger they'll say things they can't take back.

Dex doesn't come to bed when Andrew does; he pretends to be working, but Andrew knows better. He made the bed in the morning, and the imprint of Dex's head no longer shapes his pillow. Andrew lays his hand on it, wishes it was still bowled in, and pretends it's still there, that shape he knows so well.

He wants to believe in a happy ending with Dex. His constancy in love is a beautiful capacity, but right now it seems like a hindrance. He doesn't want to be a man pining for the impossible when love is at his fingertips with Dex, but in his heart, he can't walk away from home. In the dead quiet of his room, Andrew understands that, no matter what, someone will end up with a broken heart.

o o o

MILO DRIVES his mother to her first post treatment checkup, despite her insistence that she's well enough to do it herself.

"You've spent too much time caring for me. What about your job? You have a life you're neglecting."

"You're the most important," Milo insists. He doesn't want to say that the life he worked so hard for—independent, successful—somehow holds less appeal than it did. Other than his connection with Zeke, Denver now seems like a transient, distant phase of his life. He has no strong tethers to that life. He's becoming self-aware enough to note that this was by design: a life without roots, nothing to keep him in place.

It's not that Santuit has suddenly become home. But he wants to be here for now. With his mother. With open spaces he can lose himself in. Even with Andrew.

Dr. Schroeder has wonderful news for them, and the way Shelby's hand squeezes his, so hard he's shocked, tells him more about how scared she's been than anything she's said. It seems like a privilege to know her fears, even if it's after the fact. It's one of those moments when Milo sees himself as an adult in her eyes. They leave with pamphlets and information on life post cancer, outlines for follow-up appointments and support groups. It's a lot to digest, so Milo tucks them into his binder.

"Celebratory lunch?" he asks in the car.

"Absolutely," she says, laughing and buckling herself in. "Pick a place, and I'll pay."

"No you will not." He tucks her hair behind her ear. It's darker than it would usually be; she's not been out in the sun gardening. "You did all the hard work. I'm taking you out."

"Hard work? Hardly. Sat there and did what I was told is more like it," she grouses.

"Mom." He shoots her a look before turning into traffic. "It takes incredible strength to handle what you've been through. Don't play it down. I think you should be proud of yourself." When he looks at her again, she's gazing out the window. When she turns to smile at him, it's with damp eyes and a tremulous smile.

"Have I told you lately what an incredible man you are? I'm so proud of you. I haven't told you enough. I don't know how—"

"No sad stuff today. Today we celebrate." It's true that he wants today to be positive. But the truth is also that he's not ready to really talk about the things she's heading toward.

Milo is determined to spoil her as much as possible. He pulls her car door open and gives her a hand out. Opens the door, pulls out her chair at the restaurant and informs her that she is required to pick whatever she wants on the menu and to please not worry about prices. She shakes her head.

"I worry about your income, with your reduced work hours," she explains.

"Don't, Mom. I promise this is okay."

"Do you think you'll go back soon? Now that things are more settled here?" Milo shakes his napkin out and places it carefully on his lap. The truth is he has no easy answer. Thinking of Santuit as home seems dangerous and unreliable. He can't be sure what is influencing that feeling—a renewed relationship with his mother, or Andrew. Something unfurling in his heart is emboldened with every moment he spends with Andrew. At his most rational, Milo knows this is playing with fire—not because he thinks anything will happen, or because he has any desire to break apart another couple who are obviously in love—but because he's putting his own heart at risk.

"I don't know," he finally admits.

Shelby gives him a long, level look; it's assessing and knowing and disconcerting. She doesn't say anything, just taps his feet with her own under the table and smiles at him. "Anything I want?" She says, glancing at the menu again. "Really?"

Milo wonders when anyone last really treated her, just for the sake of spoiling her—not in years and years, probably. The thought makes him both sad and a little guilty.

"The world at your fingertips," he jokes, because he said today wasn't for sadness, and he meant it.

ANDREW SHOWS up to lunch twenty minutes late and without Dex. The look on his face is a cross between unhappiness and warning: Milo can tell he's not supposed to ask, but he can't help it.

"What's going on? Is Dex okay?"

"He's fine," Andrew says shortly, then sighs and runs his fingers through his hair, completely disordering it. "He's—you know, let's not. This is a celebratory lunch, right?"

Milo swallows concern and nods. If Andrew would rather not talk right now, Milo can respect that. "I probably should have picked dinner to celebrate, so everyone could come. Do you need to talk—"

"Milo, really, don't sweat it." Andrew looks away, composing his face. "So, good news?"

"Yes!" Milo says, and he can't control his own face, which is wide with a smile. "Dr. Schroeder had great results for Mom. Everything responded well to the treatments: She is cancer-free and doesn't have to go back in for three months."

"Oh my god, Milo!" Andrew gets up and leans down to hug Milo; it's awkward and unexpected, but in the wake of all the good news and the relief Milo's been carrying, the perfect note.

Andrew disentangles himself, tugs at the hem of his shirt and sits again. His cheeks are slightly red; it's lovely to see someone else who's so excited, someone who cares so much about his mother. After they've ordered drinks, they share a slightly awkward silence whose origin Milo can't quite pinpoint.

"So," Andrew starts. "What's your plan, then?"

"Oh, I don't know." Milo spent half of yesterday worrying over his confusion about his future. His head is a jumble of potential outcomes, and a nagging instinct that everything he's doing is wrong because he's not listening to the right parts of himself.

They're quiet again, and Milo studies his plate and silverware too intently. Andrew clears his throat.

"Milo, can I ask you something?"

"Of course."

Andrew pauses, as if he's coming to a decision.

"Did you do them?"

"Do what?" Milo asks. Andrew's cheeks are still red, and he's biting the inside of his cheek. His gaze is more direct, even if it does seem unsure.

"The things on your list?"

It's an unexpected enough question that it takes a moment for Milo to grasp what he's saying. "Why... what's bringing this up?" he says carefully.

"I don't know," Andrew says. There's a candor in the words Milo trusts. "There's a lot we don't talk about. A lot I wonder about."

"Me too."

"Maybe I want to ask now because I know you have much less worry on your plate." Andrew shrugs.

"I do, yes. This is something you really want to talk about?"

"If you want to."

Milo feels more relaxed than he has in a very long time, and he's not sure if this conversation will weigh him back down. But he's gotten to see Andrew's life now, and his happiness. When they parted all those years ago, it was with a complete devastation Milo knows he wasn't alone in feeling. He can't pretend he hasn't wondered what path Andrew took. They've touched on topics and moments in that gap in their histories. True to their promises, Milo has never forgotten Andrew's wishes for his future, nor his own.

"Did *you* do them?" Milo asks softly. Their eyes meet; it's intense, the secrets they're sharing here, together in a place that remembers them as the boys they were.

Andrew smiles. "Most of them."

"Me too."

"And you remember them all?" Andrew asks.

"Of course. Do you?"

Andrew's smile is challenging and fun, then. "Quiz me."

"Tell me. Well, I mean, ask me."

Andrew thanks their server when she drops off their drinks. He waits for Milo to order before ordering his own meal. When she leaves, he looks at Milo with soft eyes.

"Europe?"

"Paris, Prague, Athens," Milo answers, pleased with Andrew's choice.

"That's an interesting assortment." Andrew picks the lemon slice out of his drink with his fork and drops it into Milo's drink without asking. Milo stirs it in and wonders how to summarize all of the lives he lived while healing and learning about himself.

"I had the money from Dad's trust, and I wanted to do something that would piss him off."

"What?" Andrew asks, laughing.

"I didn't go for anything but pleasure. It wasn't for education or professional development. I didn't have a plan; I went to Paris first because it seemed like the thing to do. It was too civilized, in a way, for how I was feeling, or what I wanted. After a week, I booked a ticket to Prague. And it was everything I wanted. It was so many things; civilized, yes, sometimes almost not; startling in a lot of ways. It surprised me. It inspired me. It's such a beautiful place."

"And Athens?"

"I don't really know how to explain Athens," Milo admits. "In retrospect, the whole trip was what any post grad trip to Europe is—a spoiled rite of passage that's little more than a cloaked excuse to 'find yourself.'"

"Is that what Greece was about, then?"

"Yes and no." If they're going to talk about this, he has to do it with candor. "It felt like visiting a—a place of origin to try to figure *something* out. I hadn't let myself acknowledge this when I left for Paris, because it had been two years since we'd spoken. But a lot of why I took the trip was because I promised I would.

"And I didn't know what, but I was searching for *something*. I didn't find it. It wasn't a magical, eye-opening trip. It was beautiful," he qualifies. "But maybe not what I was looking for."

"And did you ever find it?" Andrew asks.

Milo wants to touch Andrew's hand, wants some sort of physical connection, because this moment is terrifying. "I don't think I could. What I wanted was what I couldn't have, and nothing I could find abroad."

o o o

WHEN ANDREW gets home, he can hardly pull himself together to act normal around Dex, or as normal as expected, given Dex's sudden refusal to come to lunch, and the resentment that shimmers and pops between them.

Somehow, he and Milo managed to make it through lunch after Milo's confession. The conversation was strained; they avoided anything that even tangentially touched the sore spot Andrew had exposed by asking and Milo struck by answering. That Milo wanted to be with him after James's funeral isn't a surprise. That he'd still been caught up in those feelings two years later is something Andrew hadn't let himself consider once he'd pulled himself together and ordered himself to move on. He didn't move on, really—not for a long time—but he pulled himself out of bed. He got through college despite a good ten months in which he almost flunked. He learned to live without Milo, and with the longing he buried deeper and deeper as the years went on.

Missing Milo—he perfected that, smothering longing with pragmatism for the sake of survival. He shoved it deep enough that after a while it was hardly noticeable, another background noise in the symphony of everyday life. For a very long time Andrew survived by reminding himself that Milo was moving on and that it was what he needed. Despite this, Andrew spent the first years without him fantasizing about surprise visits: Milo somehow suddenly at his doorstep, confessing that it had all been a terrible mistake.

Had he known that two years later Milo would still be missing him, searching for or wishing for him, Andrew isn't sure he'd ever have pulled himself together. But he has that knowledge now, and, despite his better judgment, Andrew can't help but wonder what might have been.

Although they hardly spoke of their lists through the rest of lunch, Andrew's been thinking about his since. When he gave Milo his list of dreams, a family had been one of his wishes. He's not sure why he wrote it down, because having a family isn't a wish to be crossed off a list, like sky diving, or even a more abstract one, like finding success as a writer. Having a family was something Andrew wanted with *Milo*. Even without adding that specific, unrealistic dream, why confess such a desire only at goodbye?

For a long time, having a family remained an abstract dream. He and Dex have spoken of it a few times, but mostly in the context of how young they are and how they have time to think about it later. What had once been a visceral, if too mature and foolish dream, faded over the years into something less urgent.

Until today, Andrew believed he and Milo were making it as friends, despite the subtext always vivid between them. But figuring out how to navigate this friendship that's so different from its childhood version, enmeshed and perfect and completely unworkable... Andrew has been kidding himself.

Milo will leave soon. Despite the quick subject change from Milo's future plans, Andrew is sure of this. Andrew would never wish Shelby illness for the sake of having Milo back in his life. But it's bittersweet, this good news, knowing Milo is going to slip back out of his life. For years Andrew built his whole identity around the idea of being Milo's savior. He loved, and thought himself lovable, only as a satellite.

Dex changed that. Dex was patient and devoted and helped Andrew grow out of his fears and into self-worth, taught him to believe in love and held Andrew through terrifying vulnerability. Dex is his first serious relationship, but in any long-term relationship, things will get hard, and persistence is what they both need. Milo's friendship is something Andrew can't imagine giving up, but he needs to banish any *what if's* because they'll break things.

o

"I'm going to interview for the job," Dex says.

It's the middle of a quiet dinner. Andrew's not particularly fond of cooking, and it's not a strength. But he planned this, a nice dinner, hoping for something sweet and intimate. Dex's words sink like stones in his stomach.

"What? I don't—"

"I'm sorry," Dex says, looking down. "I'm not deciding anything. I...I need to try, at least. I'll always wonder, because this job is an incredible opportunity."

"I... I don't want to hold you back," Andrew says. His lips feel numb, his fingers tingle and anxiety is cresting in his chest. Despite Dex's ambiguous assurance, Andrew senses the immediate threat of goodbye. He feels a flash of blinding anger, and then more anxiety, because for one moment, he's not sure he's really afraid of Dex leaving him.

"Would you come?"

Andrew starts to respond, an automatic *yes* on his lips, because he's supposed to want to be with Dex more than home. But he hesitates, for a split second unsure whether he would leave for Dex.

"Well, then," Dex says. He stands, folding his napkin on the table. "I guess that's what I need to know."

"No, no." Andrew grabs Dex's hand. "I would, please don't—I just..."

"Andrew—" Dex's hand is gentle on his cheek.

"I love you," Andrew says, pulling Dex into his arms. He wants the words to mean enough. Dex sighs and, after a moment, wraps his arms around Andrew. Andrew kisses his neck, behind his ear.

"Andrew, this won't solve anything."

"Go to your interview," Andrew says. He kisses Dex's cheek and grips the back of his shirt. "And we'll decide what to do when it's over."

"Okay." Dex kisses Andrew softly, then pulls away.

Dex doesn't come to bed until late, and then carefully keeps their bodies apart. Feigning sleep, Andrew wills himself with everything he has not to cry, not to turn over and yell at him for his selfishness. Not to let his resentment consume what he's worked so hard to have. Not to use their bodies to bridge a gap he's not sure how else to cross. For a very long time, Andrew used sex to cover things he wasn't ready to feel, or to create false intimacy. He can't stand the thought of doing that now, even when it's tempting, when in the silence he can hear his relationship falling apart.

o

Andrew should see it coming, but he doesn't. At least, not so soon. Not before he's made up his mind. Holding onto Dex because he's not ready to make a choice is incredibly selfish and disrespectful. Dex comes home from D.C. and informs Andrew he is taking the job, and that the time apart enabled him to really evaluate where they both are and what they want. And what they want, Dex explains, isn't the same any more. It's incredibly brave, Andrew knows, for Dex to be the one to acknowledge what they've avoided talking about. Somehow, in these last few months, Andrew has fallen out of love with him—Dex's final words were too true—but in their parting, he can't bring himself to tell Dex that not being *in love* doesn't mean he doesn't love him.

The resonant peal of the door slamming behind Dex vibrates in Andrew's imagination. When Andrew manages to really look around, through the blur of tears, he sees all the spaces Dex erased himself from.

He finds himself on the beach, trying to smooth the rough edges of his thoughts, which bounce from self-loathing to righteous anger to acceptance, knowing that Dex was right. *They* weren't right; it wasn't going to work. Maybe it could have; maybe Andrew could have found a compromise or a solution. Only with Milo back here, worming his way back into Andrew's heart despite every best intention, he can't deny that he didn't really want a solution. He was a fool to think Dex wouldn't know or see the role Milo has played in this.

"You won't admit it," Dex said, one hand already on the doorknob, "but you wanted me to do this because you couldn't. You can't bring yourself to love him again, but you can't let go."

"That's not true," Andrew protested.

"I know," Dex said, more gently, "that I'm the first person you ever really let yourself love. Other than him. So maybe I could understand your fear."

"Dex—"

"But the truth is, I don't want to. I can't. That's not enough for me, and it shouldn't be for you."

By the time Andrew gathered himself enough to stand, to go to him, Dex was gone.

The beach seemed the best place to go. It's where his roots run deepest, grounding the secret self Dex could never understand. Maybe Andrew never gave him the chance. It's cold, a deep chill that seems early for the season. He's dressed warmly for once.

A senseless, shapeless, helpless anger fills Andrew—at his stupid heart that won't unlearn Milo and let him appreciate Dex's warm, uncomplicated happiness. And Milo... god, storming back into Andrew's life, a changed, yet completely similar man. Contained enough not to need Andrew the way he had as a kid, but still so much himself that Andrew sometimes yearns for those days and old, familiar patterns.

He should have offered to leave. He should have seen into the heart of Dex's silence and known they could only work if he left. But even as he wishes it, he knows he doesn't really mean it.

chapter thirteen

ANDREW DOESN'T ANSWER HIS PHONE FOR THREE DAYS straight. Milo texts and calls, but saves his news for when he can actually talk to him. It's something to share in person. On the third day, he takes a chance and goes by Andrew's place. Things have definitely been awkward around Dex recently, but Milo is worried.

No one answers the door.

He waits for an hour, hoping they're out running errands. After a while it seems foolish and useless to stay. What nags isn't the silence, but a growing, subtle energy from Andrew that's been building to something Milo thinks might be visible to others, not just to him.

Finally, he slips a note under their door, then decides to take a chance. He drives to Chickopee and parks. It's verging on sundown; everything glows hazy pink and orange. October is really a little too cold to be out near dusk. He rolls up the collar of his sweater and begins his trek through the sand. It kicks up into his shoes and rubs against his heels, but it's slightly less irritating than frozen toes. The air is swiftly leeching the warmth of the day; the swell of west-facing sand dunes blocks the last of the sun.

When he finally breaks through the grasses into deep sand that bears the marks of wind and trespassing feet, leaving him unsteady in his gait, he scans for any figure on the beach. He almost misses the one lonely silhouette to the east; as Milo approaches, he sees that it is indeed Andrew.

"You haven't been answering your phone," Milo says when he's within range.

"I haven't been ready to talk," Andrew answers without looking at him. In the waning light, it's clear he's been crying.

"Are you now? What's going on?" Milo hovers awkwardly. Andrew looks up at him finally, and his smile is an invitation to sit down.

"I don't know," he admits once Milo is settled. Andrew leans into him a little, for warmth and shelter from the wind, Milo assumes. As the wind kicks up, so does the water. It's a long time before Andrew speaks. The sky is pregnant with twilight, purple and indigo. Venus shines brightly in the east.

"He left," Andrew says at length.

"What?" Milo turns to him, shocked—both by the words and by the calm.

"It was coming. We both knew."

"I thought you were happy... you said you loved him. Are you all right?"

"I don't think love is always enough," Andrew says, simple and easy and light. Too light.

"Of course it... I mean—"

"I mean, loving someone isn't enough to make a life complete," Andrew clarifies. "He wasn't happy here. I couldn't be happy anywhere else. It pulled at us until we couldn't ignore it: I think we fell out of love. He said—there were other things that—" Andrew stops and swallows.

"What?"

Andrew stares at him; they hold each other's gaze and there's truth in that look he hasn't let himself speak out loud: a sense of home, intangible but electrifying. It sets his heart pounding so he can feel it in his throat and ears and where his breath is fast—too fast. Dizzy, he wonders who will say it first.

"My heart wasn't there anymore. It was somewhere else." Andrew's words, caught breathless in his throat, almost get lost in the mutter of nature around them. Milo closes his eyes and feels the words lodge in his heart and stomach and buzz into his hands and lips. His own breathlessness pops colored pinwheels behind his eyes. When he opens them, Andrew's eyes are still on him, only his lips tremble. His body is shaking, a little: a constant hum Milo can see and sense, and he knows it's not all the wind.

"Andrew—" Milo reaches up to touch his cheek, or his lips, or to place his hand over what he's sure is a galloping heart. But Andrew's hands are already on his face, framing the sharp cut of his cheekbones, fingertips at the edge of his hair. Then his mouth is on Milo's, lips too frantic, a kiss too needful, heady and helpless and shocking, but everything, everything, everything.

Milo hauls Andrew over his lap before the next breath. He doesn't gentle the kiss and neither does Andrew, but they settle; they fit each other's mouths and it's nothing and everything to nip at his lips and taste his breath and feel the cold between their bodies disappear as the spaces between them grow incrementally smaller and smaller until they only exist where it's impossible to fit closer together.

"Andrew," Milo breaks away to whisper. Andrew's mouth under his ear is wet and warm, and his teeth on his earlobe feel like too much. It's almost full dark, but the wrong place for this, the wrong moment, because as in all his tucked-away fantasies, he wants to take the time to enjoy Andrew with steady touch and lasting kisses and enough light to discover every part of him. Even with Andrew in his arms, this feels like a dream, unreal and unsteadying.

"I know." Andrew shudders against him and Milo's fingers are in his hair, pulling him in for a few more stolen seconds. "Come home with me, please."

"Andrew," Milo says, thinking of a home Andrew shared with someone else days before, "I don't know—will that be—"

"Please, I know, I know what I need and it's you, please. I need to know this is real."

"Yes." Milo can give them permission to do this, and he can trust Andrew's want and his yes. He can make this real as it never was, even after the funeral. "Yes, *yes.*"

o

It's surreal, for a second, to be at the threshold of his apartment, key in hand, with Milo a few inches behind him. Without Milo's body touching his, without that connection between their eyes, their frenetic magnetism eases. When he brings Milo in, it will be with a deliberate intent he let himself sink into in the car.

"Andrew, it's okay if you change your mind," Milo says, almost a whisper. Andrew wishes he was so close he could feel the breath of that whisper, feel Milo's heat so close to his own. He *can* have it. He only has to open the door.

He reaches behind him for Milo's hand and finds it, pulls him in. Milo shuts the door and pulls him back, kisses the back of his neck softly at first, as his hands pull him closer by the hips. Gentleness gives way to hunger quickly, to biting kisses and short breath, fingers slipping down Andrew's pelvis over his pants, teasing and so, *so* close to where Andrew is starting to harden.

Andrew puts his hands over Milo's, spreading his fingers between Milo's and pushing them down. He tilts his head against

Milo's shoulder and whimpers out a *please*, pushing their hands over himself.

"God, Andrew." Milo's hands mold over him, squeeze him, and Andrew is sure he'll melt into it. He turns to crush their mouths together, coming up on his tiptoes to do so. It's fevered, messy, but somehow with sweetness between them that he'll never find elsewhere. He rushes his hands under Milo's shirt. Stumbling backward blindly, Andrew manages to steer them to the couch while simultaneously finding Milo's lovely brown nipples. He digs the nail of one thumb into one lightly and swallows Milo's excited exhale.

"Here, here," Andrew says, panting desperately. He pulls Milo over him onto the couch. Like this, on a couch a little too small for them, with Milo's big body on his, Andrew is completely sheltered, overwhelmed by Milo's touch and kiss and smell.

He tries to roll up into Milo's body; their clothes are too constricting; the denim of their jeans blocks the connection he needs.

"Pants," he says, wriggling a little to get his hands between them.

"Here." Milo bats his hands away. He has Andrew's pants undone and off incredibly fast. They hit the floor with a thump, and then Milo's eyes are all over him. He runs his hands up Andrew's legs, over the fuzz of his hair and then thumbing the vee of his pelvis. He kisses Andrew's hip, then spreads his legs to nuzzle the curve of his inner thigh.

"Fuck, *oh god.*" Andrew gets his hands into Milo's hair. It's beautiful in the lamplight, soft in his hands. He tugs on it to bring Milo up to kiss him. "Yours too, please."

Milo works his jeans off, a little more awkwardly. Andrew helps him kick them off, kissing Milo's shoulders and neck and whispering *yes, yes* against the skin blooming red and damp with pleasure-flush.

Naked now, so close, but not close enough, Andrew folds his legs up to wrap around Milo's hips.

"I didn't—" Milo says, then gasps when their cocks rub together. They rock out of rhythm, desperation for that peak of pleasure making them uncoordinated and hasty.

"You didn't?" Andrew asks, then digs his fingers into Milo's waist.

"I imagined slow," Milo says, then bites Andrew's lip and kisses him, licking into his mouth, lush and edging toward a tenderness that's slower than their bodies cry for. "I wanted to appreciate you."

"Okay," Andrew says with a smile, still grinding up against Milo. Their bodies start to move together more smoothly. "Next time. Fuck me any way you want, but now—oh shit, *yes*—don't make me wait."

Milo tucks his face close to Andrew's and rocks against him harder; everything is desperate, too hot, with too much friction and perfect, perfect heat: the coalescing of all his longing making him come faster than he has in years.

"Shit, shit, *shit*," he moans into Andrew's skin, shaking hard and pulled apart on top of him. Andrew cries out, legs tightening almost painfully, and comes too.

o

It's warm still, somehow, even when they come down with sweat cooling and come sticky between them. Milo is heavy, boneless on top of him. Andrew doesn't want to ask him to stir, but has to.

"You're heavy," he whispers eventually.

"Yes," Milo says without moving. Andrew starts to laugh, then Milo does. He kisses Andrew's ear tenderly, then rolls off. He grabs Andrew's shirt and wipes himself off. He folds it over and finds a dry patch to wipe Andrew off, too.

"Hey, my shirt!"

"We're at your place," Milo says with an unapologetic shrug.

"Good point." Andrew shivers without the furnace heat of Milo's body on him. Milo is fishing through their pants for underwear. He hands Andrew his and then pulls his own on. Andrew doesn't move. Everything happened so fast he didn't get a chance to really *see* everything.

"God, you're incredible," Andrew whispers, sitting up. He reaches out to touch Milo's toned stomach, then pauses. "Is this okay?"

"Of course. Why wouldn't it be?"

Andrew bites back any response that might give away uncertainty. Now that they've had this moment, he's not sure what comes next. He knows what he wants, but the Milo he remembers was always an unpredictable mess, pulling him in, then pushing away in a dizzying dance.

"Come here." Milo pulls Andrew up to his knees, kneels on the couch next to him and places Andrew's hands on his body. Andrew noses along the line of his shoulder and sighs at the gentle touch of Milo's hands, coming around to cup his ass carefully.

"I wanted to appreciate you, too," Andrew says, kissing Milo's bicep.

"Well then, let's do that."

"I'm not seventeen, you ass; I think I need a bit of recovery."

"I'm not asking for sex right now. I want to touch you and look at you and make you feel good."

"That sounds—" Andrew closes his eyes. Something heavy and bittersweet swells inside; Milo's words are so much what he's always wanted. He knows he has to take whatever he can now, though he'll probably get hurt in the end. "—Yes."

Milo laughs lightly. "Where's your room?"

"Come on." Andrew takes his hand and pulls him down the hall. There are blank spaces on the walls where Dex had hung cityscape prints. Half their bedroom is gone, making the space seem hollow. Milo hesitates, looking around.

"Is this—"

"It's okay." Andrew feels the awkwardness and hurt of what's gone. But stronger than that, more compelling, is Milo, with him, *finally*. It's the fulfillment of wishes and years of longing. "Come here."

They lie on the bed, facing each other for a moment, looking at each other without speaking. Andrew feels words in his chest, beating with his heart, questions he can't ask for fear of ending this moment. He reaches over and traces Milo's jaw. Milo kisses his fingertips when they brush his lips. His eyes don't leave Andrew's. He sighs, but it's a good sound: comfortable, like relaxing into something welcome.

"You're beautiful," he says. Andrew closes his eyes and shakes his head.

"Not really," he says. He smiles, though. "Not too shabby, but nothing exceptional." His fingers wander over Milo's collarbone, down the incredibly defined pectoral muscles. His finger alights over Milo's nipple. Fascinated, he watches Milo's skin prickle with goose bumps. The delicious line between his abs beckons his touch, all the way down to the curls of his pubic hair. His cock is lovely: soft, relaxed and tender under Andrew's fingers. Milo's body trembles for a moment before he takes his hand gently and moves it, rolling Andrew over, placing it on the bed by Andrew's head.

"No," Milo says firmly. "You are. Your eyes—" He kisses Andrew's eyelids when they flutter shut. "And beautiful skin, *god*, everywhere." His touch is different than Andrew remembers. It's open-palmed and sure and hot. He cups Andrew's neck and then his chest and stomach. Andrew's not a small guy, but Milo is big. His hand feels so encompassing over Andrew's stomach. He bends and kisses above Andrew's bellybutton. "Your body is beautiful," he whispers, kissing again. Andrew's hand finds its way into his hair. It's such a rich, dark red against his skin. Milo ghosts a kiss at the head of his cock, barely a tease, but a little too much just yet. Andrew tugs on Milo's hair.

"I'm thin and totally untoned and currently sporting what could be considered a farmer's tan."

Milo kneels and straddles him with both hands spanning his waist. "Stop," he says, kissing Andrew to soften the words. "I'm the one looking at your body. It's like you were shaped for my hands. To be under me and around me."

Andrew cups Milo's face in his hands. "Would you do that?" he whispers.

"What?" Milo kisses Andrew's nose, then looks into his eyes when Andrew nudges him.

"Be inside me. So I could be around you, so I can feel you like that?" *Like I've wanted.*

"God, Andrew," Milo says, obviously overwhelmed. "Of course. I—you—"

"Let me touch you. You can keep touching me. You can take your time."

Milo's lips meet his tenderly, over and over. They feast on kisses, slipping exhalations into each other, breathing rediscovery into each other's bodies. Milo gets his hands under Andrew and hauls him on top of him so easily it makes Andrew breathless with a tiny thrill of desire shocking electric in his stomach. Milo arranges him, draping Andrew over his body with his legs spread to straddle his hips. He brings Andrew down for another kiss— one that lasts, that they lose themselves in, slow and growing, unfurling something sweeter in the gradually building heat. Andrew can feel when Milo begins to come apart. They pull away to look at each other. Milo touches him with tenderness that could hurt him; the memory after this night might be too much tomorrow, but right now it's exactly what Andrew wants.

His vulnerability, his love for this man, a constancy that has ached in him for so long: it's a gift exchanged when he sees that same honesty, painfully exposed, in Milo's eyes.

Milo massages his fingers into the muscles of Andrew's back, between his shoulder blades, and Andrew relaxes into the touch. Any remaining tension melts until he feels as if his body is a lose wax structure molding to Milo's body. Milo's fingers knead down the length of his spine. Andrew breaks the kiss with a soft gasp when Milo's fingers start to trace gentle lines over and up his buttocks. It's skin-prickling and shivery good. Andrew lays his head on Milo's chest and lets himself soak in the touch. He wallows in the sensation. Milo's fingers slip up the line between his cheeks, and Andrew whimpers, then kisses Milo's collarbone. They are skin on skin, both sweating a little. There's something about that barely there touch that hovers on the edge of too much: too much want; unbearable desire.

"Milo, god, *please,*" Andrew begs, then sucks a nipple into his mouth.

"Do you have lube?" Milo whispers. His fingers press in, a dry touch not quite where he wants it, but it's enough to set Andrew on edge.

"In the drawer." Andrew pulls away long enough to open the drawer and search. "Here." He tosses a condom onto the pillow, then sits up, grabbing Milo's hand and slicking his first two fingers. "Don't worry about being gentle," he assures him, then leans forward and props himself up with hands next to Milo's head. Feeling the strain against his hips, he spreads his legs farther apart. Andrew leans into the next kiss, sighing against Milo's mouth—it's a breath that ends in a sharp inhale when Milo slides cool, wet fingers against him.

"God, fuck *ye-yes,*" Andrew hisses, groaning and feeling himself open with that sharp pleasure he loves so much.

"I can't believe—" Milo's eyes are closed and his brow furrowed in concentration. When he opens them, the indigo of his eyes is the last spark Andrew needs to feel his skin light with pleasure like fire. Milo's fingers slide in easily; he takes his time, drawing that pleasure from Andrew by increments. He pulls his fingers out and grips Andrew's cock with a sure hand. He uses the other with deliberation and confidence, cupping and pulling a little at his balls until Andrew is whimpering from the slight pain that's pleasure too, lips open and panting against Milo's mouth.

"I've got you, sweetheart," Milo whispers and slides his fingers back in, as deep as he can, swallowing Andrew's moans with open-mouthed kisses. Andrew's body bucks into the sensation; nerves light from his sensitive rim all through his pelvis. That feeling of fullness, that heavy need to have something inside, pulls and pulls until he's begging for more.

"I'll get you there; it's okay," Milo assures him. One more finger in and Andrew sits up, leans back until he's rolling onto them, working himself down.

"Now, now," he chants.

"I have to—just one more. I don't want to hurt you." Milo sits up and kisses the hollow where Andrew's shoulder and arm meet.

"God." Andrew pulls back with the last of his composure to joke, "I know you're big, but I didn't think you were that big... *headed*."

"Oh my god, shut up; that was awful," Milo says, laughing so his eyes crinkle at the corners and *oh*, something cramps in Andrew's heart.

"I don't care; it's fine; go slow and I'll tell you if it's too much." Andrew isn't sure his body can do this, but he wants that feeling, something indelible that he'll feel for days, in case this moment is all he gets.

o

Andrew is so tight it seems a near impossibility, but he's willing—flushed and eager, all sweet hands and begging voice. Milo holds him steady at the hip and waits, lets Andrew control the pace.

"You're okay, it's okay," he whispers, over and over. Andrew has Milo in hand, holding him steady against his hole. He exhales, calming himself, and opens his eyes. They burn when they meet Milo's. Something like his Andrew smirk, a look perfected and completely, uniquely his, crosses his face as his body relaxes, letting Milo in. Andrew works him in slowly, whimpering with each little rock of his body, and with his face screwed up in concentration.

"Don't—" Milo bites his lip through the pleasure of that tight, gripping heat. "Honey, don't hurt yourself."

"Shut up, *oh god*, shut up, you're—" Andrew groans and rocks and corkscrews his hips down and down. That thrill, the blissed-out slip of his face makes something almost primal crest in Milo's body, manifests as an almost uncontrollable desire to grab Andrew by the hips and make this rougher and faster than they want. Andrew finally bottoms out, sighs and relaxes and then tilts forward onto Milo and kisses him with lips like fever. "Now," he whispers against Milo's mouth. So close like this, deep inside Andrew where he throbs and sears with heat, with Andrew's arms next to his head, with his lips all give and invitation and naked need, Milo loses himself. He moves slowly, tries to read the shuddering mess of Andrew's body. Their foreheads grind together, and for one delirious moment Andrew writhes, frantic and reckless, until Milo puts his hand on the small of his back and gentles him.

They've done reckless. They've done tenderness, yes, those years ago. But not like this. This is something else. This is Milo laid open and willing to take in every moment, treasure every second, to be so much a part of Andrew they won't know how to break apart. He pulls his knees up for leverage. "Like this, sweetheart," he says, slowly sliding into him and out.

"*Sweetheart*," Andrew answers, voice thick, honey-dazed. Milo kisses him, feels the warmth of one tear drip onto his face. His arms band around Andrew, bringing him painfully close as they move by increments. He hardly dares to breathe.

"God, I wish…" Andrew starts, then stops when his voice breaks.

"Tell me," Milo says, trying to convey with his body and voice how safe he wants Andrew to feel right now—how safe he feels.

"I want this to last, *god*, you inside me like this," Andrew says after a few seconds.

"Take a breath, then." Milo smiles and rolls them over. He kisses the fine ridge of Andrew's cheekbone and down the curve of his nose and the corners of his mouth and lets his body pin Andrew's, barely moving.

"Oh." Andrew arches his neck, head driving into the pillow. He brings his knees up, and takes. He takes and takes, body trembling and pleasure laden and acquiescing to Milo's pace and Milo's body. There's a belonging, a subsumption of their bodies Milo could never have expected; something he couldn't have known existed.

"Andrew," he says, long minutes later, after bringing themselves to the brink of orgasm and down again, holding off, not wanting this to end, "Andrew, I love—" Andrew bites down on his lip, then; cuts off his words and his air and kisses him, ferocious and wracking, his body pulsing hard around Milo as he comes.

Andrew moans, falling apart in Milo's arms, then relaxing by increments. Milo barely moves, just lets Andrew's body wring from him what pleasure it needs. When Andrew's eyes open lazy and bright with tears, Milo smiles and starts to pull out.

"No, no," Andrew clamps his legs around him. "Stay, don't stop."

"Andrew." Milo thinks of the oversensitivity he's always felt after he comes; that sense of something incredible fading into something not quite comfortable.

"I like it," Andrew admits, pink cheeked and something like shy. "You can do more. Faster."

"Oh—" Milo swallows down against a flutter of need and thrusts a little harder, and when Andrew cries out he only stutters for a second, because the look on Andrew's face is pleasure, not pain.

"Harder, come on," Andrew goads, pulling his knees up almost to his chest. It's fucking, hard and fast and bruising, but intimate, somehow even more so, when Milo gives in and lets himself go.

Each thrust is met by a high-pitched noise from Andrew, driving Milo's body's instinctive and mindless drive to the cusp, the brink and then the blaze of orgasm. He feels Andrew deliberately clamp down on him, moaning his own encouragements as Milo comes and comes, until he is completely hulled, a trembling wreck in the safety of Andrew's arms.

Milo pulls out and kisses the slight wince off of Andrew's lips. He cleans them both up sloppily, wraps the condom in tissues and drops it on the floor; shaking hands and a hard-beating heart make practicalities difficult. Andrew's arms open for him before he's finished, and somehow, despite their sizes, he fits into them perfectly. Andrew's heart thrums where Milo's cheek rests, thumping rabbit-fast against his ribs. Against his scalp is the tender sweep of Andrew's fingers, combing and combing.

"Will you ever outgrow this obsession?" Milo jokes through a slightly slurred voice.

"It's beautiful," Andrew says softly. "Who would want to?"

Milo kisses his chest carefully, rests his hand in the safe bowl between Andrew's ribs and hip and feels when they both begin to slip, drifting off sweaty and sticky and still so exposed.

chapter fourteen

WHEN THEY WAKE IT'S BRIGHT MORNING; GOLD SPILLS through the open window and onto Andrew's bed. That's not what woke Milo, the sun's too-hot weight on his body. Andrew is no longer holding him; instead he is sleeping adorably with both hands tucked under his face. It's so innocent, this strangely angelic and child-like self that Andrew hides, demonstrably vulnerable in sleep.

Milo lifts the comforter and slips out of the bed as carefully as he can. He cleans up a little more in the bathroom, brushes his teeth with a spare toothbrush he finds in a drawer and drinks what seems like a gallon of water. When he re-enters the room Andrew is as he was, asleep and tucked up under the covers. He's less careful getting back in, hoping to catch the moment Andrew slides awake.

He does, just as he settles; Andrew's body seems to vibrate from stillness to energy. He doesn't move, exactly, but his body comes awake, his eyes slowly open, then shutter closed. They focus slowly on Milo, dazed and then aware—a flitter of alarm and then skin-brightening joy.

"Hey," Andrew says in a sleep-sandpapered voice.

"Morning," Milo whispers. He wants to touch Andrew, his face or shoulder or hair. He wants to kiss him. He wants to say words he's never dared allow himself.

Instead, he smiles. Andrew's face is buried in the pillow. Only one sleepy eye peeks adorably at him. His lashes flutter as he wakes, and Milo feels swamped with incredible love.

"I've thought of you like this a thousand times," he admits. "More, even."

Andrew's face falls; he rolls onto his back and pulls the covers up, speaks a little hollowly to the ceiling. "I made myself give up years ago."

Milo bites his lip as the words cut through him. Andrew sighs and rolls back toward him. "Drew," Milo says as he touches Andrew's face gently, "I'm—I didn't mean to make this… sex is just—all of this has always been a little hard for me."

Andrew snorts and moves away. "Unlike me, because I've always been so *easy*, right?"

"That's not what I mean." Milo sits up, snatching the sheet up to cover himself. "Are you trying to pick a fight?"

Andrew turns his face away and doesn't speak for the space of ten long breaths, which Milo counts with increasing worry.

"Look, why don't we call a spade a spade," Andrew says, sitting and swinging his legs out of the bed. He opens a drawer and pulls on a maroon pair of boxer briefs with his back to Milo. "You say you've thought of this; now you've had it, right? Now you've gotten what you wanted, unfinished business done now. Go home, then." Andrew turns to him and his eyes are too bright and fierce. "Finish your journey, find the right man—"

"Oh my god, listen to yourself for a second here." Milo doesn't move from the bed. "How are you being this irrational?"

"Do *not* talk to me about being rational, Milo. The last time you brought rational to a conversation it was to make choices for the both of us that almost killed me."

"Me?" Milo cries. "Are you kidding me? *You're* the one who—" He does get out of bed then, searching for his own underwear, then giving up when he can't find it. He storms into the living room in search of his jeans. Andrew follows, slamming the bedroom door behind him with a crack.

"I'm the one who what?" Andrew's voice is dangerously low.

"*You* told me I had to leave. You made me believe I had to move on; you took yourself away and I was so fucked up I didn't know how to think straight about it."

"Don't you dare rewrite history, Miles Graham. You were there. You said it yourself: that I'd only ever love you as some broken kid. You made that choice for me."

"I didn't—you said—I can't..." Milo stutters. "That's not how it happened! I couldn't think. It took me months to figure shit out, to wrap my head around everything that happened. And you didn't give me a chance to fix anything, or set you straight—"

"To set me straight?" Andrew's voice is climbing, matching Milo's now. "What the actual *fuck*!"

"And I couldn't because *you* broke it; *you* deleted yourself from my life, so don't you dare put this on me!"

"I couldn't get out of bed, Milo! I couldn't breathe; I felt like I was dying. I almost failed out of school—" Andrew stops and scrubs tears from his face; Milo swallows down a sick heaviness, tries to breathe and calm himself but can't; he can't, because Andrew has it all backwards, acting as if he was *fine* after it, that everything was his fault.

"Do you think you're the only one whose heart was broken?"

"You didn't come for me!" Andrew yells. "You let me do it!"

"You have to be kidding me." Milo forces calm into his voice, even though he's vibrating with anger. "How can it be seven years later and you're still making yourself the martyr?"

Andrew's face pales and his lips tighten; he takes a step forward—Milo can't help but flinch because there is so much anger in that movement. But Andrew pulls back and makes fists. "Get out. Get out, *get out*," he snarls. Milo finds his shirt in a pile of discarded clothes. Andrew is breathing hard—as is he—and not looking at him. He tosses Milo's shoes into the hall and turns away without a word when Milo passes him, helpless to do anything but leave.

The sound of the door slamming behind him is a finality that takes out the last of his defenses. Weak-legged and trembling, he navigates the stairs down from Andrew's apartment and then squints into the sunlight. His look is the epitome of the walk of shame: rumpled clothes, hair a mess, and what he thinks he caught sight of in Andrew's hallway mirror: a small, high hickey under his chin. He pulls his shoes on without socks and walks to the beach to get his car, buzzing in the blank haze that follows blind anger and shock.

He drives home on autopilot, then sits on the gravel by the rock wall in front of the house. His mom will be up, getting the Smiths lunch, chattering about what the town has to offer, giving advice on what they might be interested in seeing.

Milo cannot face walking in there, not sex-smelling, with shattering devastation all over his face. He's never been a man of words, not like Andrew. The way everything unraveled so fast he had no way to catch it is stunning; Andrew's words were slippery fish, desperately escaping his dumb, fumbling fingers, throwing them both into what he realizes was an irrational argument, though threaded with truths he's not ready to decipher.

Everything Andrew accused him of doing, the held-in anger they both harbored for years, the lives they built that were only a fraction of what they could have made together: it's all a shameful waste, but one he can't see having gone any other way. He's never realized how deeply he blames Andrew, or how much resentment he's carried by placing the burden of responsibility on Andrew. He's such a mess, battered by the whiplash of making love to Andrew with the hope of a future, to where they ended up by morning. He might be reeling, but Milo is still determined to fix this.

He gets out of the car, looks into the fecund woods to his left, and dives in. At first he walks blindly, following the whims of his feet. It's been a while since he's wandered this way. He could get lost. But he won't. Andrew taught him these woods. If he wants to pay attention, he's certain he can get out.

Despite everything—the months home coming to terms with what he'd originally seen as a prison sentence, the months in which he felt himself warming and accepting this town as his, as a place that could be a kind of home—he's not come this way before.

Dex and Andrew seemed such a unified presence. Milo had no wish to break that apart. When he left home years ago—for what he thought would be forever—he meant to ensure Andrew's happiness.

The sun at zenith above him, no helpful guide, dapples his skin like water skipping over stones. A tree fell long ago across the path he's taking. It's moss-covered, verdant and cinnamon brown, damp decay edging toward umber. The cicadas silence mid-note, reminding him that he's the intruder. These woods have moved past him; it's long since he's been a part of this song.

He veers right rather than climb over the log, then he's in a clearing. It's shadowed by enormous trees, but there's a nice ten-foot area with only scrubby bushes and bare space. Across from him is the fort they built fifteen years before. Milo expected some decay, maybe a fallen-in ceiling and rot. Instead he finds it in good condition, with recent repairs he thinks must be Andrew's.

He knows that's a far-fetched deduction; other kids must have found it and repaired it as they adopted it. He remembers the last time he was here, too tall and cramped in the space, saying a goodbye he never thought he would, wrenching his heart out for someone else's future.

High-handed, Andrew accused. *Martyr*, Milo said back. In the mire of his grief and fear, he's always thought Andrew forced something on them he would never have done or agreed too given time to think it over. It took Andrew completely cutting him off almost a year later for Milo to face that he'd been hoping they could reconcile, admitting they'd been stupid—that *he'd* been stupid. But Andrew's message seemed devastatingly clear, and Milo told himself that the last loving act of kindness he could extend was to respect what Andrew wanted.

Milo ducks into the doorway. The last time he saw this place, Andrew had painted stars in a night sky across the ceiling.

Now, he sees, anguish a crescendo clamoring inside, that the little room is covered in words. The walls are painted with layers of sloppy blacks and browns and, in places, a neutral, untouched tan. The words are stark white.

He was

then I

But it was love spoken

into ocean above empty sky

useless and lost

On the wall above the window frame:

he touches me

and it's debilitating

guilt you choke me with

the longing for

fingers fleeting in memory

memory, a haunting

And so small he can't read without the use of his iPhone flashlight:

I love I love I love

linger will always take his shape

○

Milo almost falls asleep, he sits there so long. There's no way to date these poems. In his dozing haze, Andrew's words peal like thunder, reverberating inside his head.

How should one unpack blame? They both martyred themselves in youthful idiocy. They both ruined something. But when he thinks of the life Andrew shared with him—travel and jobs, and learning to connect with an audience through words—could he have achieved any of that? While holding Milo's hand through anxiety and fear for years?

Each visit to a therapist, each time he talked himself through fear, learned to find that handle to hold onto inside himself, and the strength to be a better man: Milo knows he might never have done that with Andrew as his citadel of protection. Love—the kind that sprang from hope of being a different man, not some creature carrying that bag of rocks—could he have ever offered that to Andrew?

The forgiveness he learned in these years, the drive to learn it, sprang from his deep need to be a complete person, to have dreams and to achieve them. Empty years also clamor in memory, though. He worked, driven by a dream for more that he has yet to find. He's had relationships that never fit for long and a life he enjoyed, friends and fun and a job he likes well enough, but nothing completing.

Home was a thought that trapped him in anxiety and fear when he boarded the plane to Boston. It nearly drowned him that first week. Then he saw Andrew. Was it Andrew alone who sought and nurtured a love for this place in him? Or was it he himself who caused it to bloom?

He traces the words *linger will always take his shape.* Too true, for them both.

The sudden clatter of feet through the forest brings him from the reverie with a snap. Andrew's head pops in, then startles back so quickly with surprise that he hits his head on the low lintel.

"Ow, *fuck!*" he cries. Milo tries to stand on lifeless legs and flops onto his hands.

"Are you all right?" he calls.

"Yeah, shit." Andrew climbs in, awkward but careful, still rubbing the back of his head.

"Let me see." Milo leans forward to feel for a bump, but Andrew pulls away quickly and Milo drops his hand.

"It's fine," Andrew's voice is sharp, his eyes slanted with little warmth and a lot of anger. "What are you doing here?" He's definitely angry.

"Thinking," Milo says simply.

"I thought you'd forgotten about this place." Andrew's fingers rest on his knees, which he's tucked up close. He's wearing different clothes: a long, soft cotton shirt that drapes shapeless in blue. Distressed jeans that aren't frayed for fashion, but from actual use. Comfort clothes.

"No," Milo says, then looks around. The ceiling is that beige that says nothing. "I wasn't ready."

"Ha," Andrew says, bitterly. Milo closes his eyes and tries to take apart the instinctive anger into something small and manageable. Put it into a box for discussion later, so he can feel the most important things. Things he's layered over, things he didn't think he could let himself feel, not when Dex seemed to be what Andrew needed.

"Why that color?" He points up at the ceiling. Andrew's eyes shimmer with immediate tears.

"After... that night," Andrew says, wobbly with something he's barely managing, "I knew it had to be erased. I had to learn to find a way without you. Those stars were part of a dream for us, and we broke that. I couldn't stand to leave that dream behind with the constellations I made just for you, while I was still wishing for you."

"You were a wish, too," Milo admits.

"Don't do that—" Andrew says, closing his eyes. "Don't pretend it was close to what I felt. That you could understand what it was like to love someone like that. Someone who knew, but never could give it back."

"You're right," Milo says softly. Andrew's breaths are ragged and loud; he wipes tears off his face with his sleeves, a no-nonsense movement. "But not because I didn't love you."

"I think that might actually make it worse."

"I never wanted to hurt you. I can't feel what you went through. But you don't know what it felt like for me, either. I didn't know how to love you without leaving."

"We could have learned," Andrew says, sniffling. Crying always makes him congested.

"You told me you didn't want me to always be that boy. You said you thought it was for the best."

"I didn't know—" Andrew starts, then takes a breath and modulates his voice.

"Can you promise you wouldn't have always loved me as that broken boy?"

"I don't know, okay?"

"I did it for you, too. I'm angry that we said goodbye like we did, and you're right that it was high-handed. But I've been sitting here for a while, thinking, and I think that…that that's on both of us. So yeah, I'm pissed about the years we could have had," Milo says, trying to choose his words. "But who I am now? I'm different. You are too; we can't say what might have been, and we can't erase our pasts. I've learned a lot. And one thing I learned… is that I want to stop wishing for a different past. I want to start looking *forward*." He takes a deep breath, on the edge of a cliff with roiling water below. "Andrew," he says softly and looks at Andrew as plainly and honestly as he can, "I could be better for you this time."

"This time? Is it that easy?" Andrew tilts his head. Milo can't read his tone.

"That love I had that I didn't think I could trust, that I didn't deserve? I—" Milo swallows. He wants to touch Andrew so much, his palms tingle with the memory of Andrew's body in them. "I have that to give, now."

"*Fuck*," Andrew says, then puts his head on his knees. His shoulders shake, but his tears are silent.

"Andrew." Milo scoots in, takes that chance and puts his hands on Andrew's shoulders. "Please let me love you. Please give me the chance."

"I wished for this," Andrew says, sobs breaking the air and Milo's heart. "I wished and wished; I broke myself apart for you. For so long I was resigned to having you any way I could, because loving you was like breathing; it was what I needed."

"I couldn't give it to you then," Milo pleads, "not the way you deserved. You had so much beautiful love, and I was sure I would destroy you. I'm sorry about this afternoon. That I blamed you for it all."

"You did destroy me." Andrew's cheeks are blotched and wet and his lips are trembling. "I wasn't exaggerating earlier, Milo. After I went back to school... there were days I didn't leave my room. When I cried so much it came to a point it wasn't physically possible any more. Nat and Damien would find me staring at walls. I didn't eat; I couldn't sleep. I barely went to class and I lost my job. I held onto hope for months. My friends finally staged an intervention."

"Andrew," Milo says, helpless, self-recrimination lacing his breath and words, "I'm so sorr—"

"It was kind, what they did," Andrew continues without acknowledging Milo. "It was hard, but done with my best interests in mind. If I'd thought... if I had any hope that you really loved me—"

"Andrew, how could you not know? I told you—"

"You told me and left. You pulled me in and pushed me away for years, Milo."

"I know," Milo says. "I didn't mean to—I was so scared, all the time, and I didn't know how to let myself be loved."

"Yeah well, I didn't either." Andrew looks up at the ceiling. "If I'm being honest with both of us, I don't know that I could have trusted you even if you'd stayed, or I had."

Andrew looks at him then, finally. The only remnants of his tears are a dampness along his lashes and faint streaks down his cheeks.

"I wouldn't let myself be loved for years, Milo, because I didn't know how to be loved without paying in the devotion I gave you."

Milo winces and pulls away. Said like that—baldly, words ugly but not without truth—brings him back to a time when he struggled daily with guilt that edged on self-hatred.

"I'm not blaming you, exactly," Andrew says. He puts his hand on Milo's arm. "I know you loved me, the best way you could. But not the way I wanted. I guess it wasn't healthy, for either of us."

"No, it wasn't."

Andrew takes a deep breath and folds his hands back on his knees. "I want to be angry with you right now. I don't really know why, except that you make me feel like I'm seventeen again, and that hurts. I don't want to say that maybe we were right, and I don't want to admit that it was both our faults. I don't want to wonder if I made a mistake when I made myself say goodbye. I tried it, really loving someone, with Dex. I don't want to think that those years were a waste, or that I never really loved him. Because falling in love with him really was beautiful and I saw our future together clearly."

"I'm so sorry," Milo says.

"But then you were here, your beautiful stupid face and everything between us that never went away. I fooled myself into thinking what I'd severed was gone."

"I know. I felt that too," Milo says, quietly, and takes a risk, kisses Andrew's knee.

"And I couldn't help falling out of love with him, because no one is as bright as you, and I can't think of anything that could eclipse what I have inside for you."

"Andrew," Milo says helplessly.

"Milo, please, *please* don't hurt me."

"Come here." Milo pulls him forward, so awkward and not really fitting on his lap. "Please give me a chance. Please let me love you."

"Milo, I don't know." Andrew buries his wet face in Milo's neck.

"I'll love you every way you want. The ways you dreamt I could. The ways I wanted to be able to before. I'll love you like the man I've become, not like that stupid boy who thought the world wanted to hurt and break him."

Andrew takes his face into his hands and forces Milo to look at him. "You always deserved every ounce of love. You were worthy of it."

"But I didn't think so, then. And I do now."

Andrew shudders in Milo's arms, then tilts into a tender kiss that Milo deepens into a drawn out plea with his body. It's delicious and full when he feels Andrew unlock, when he feels the acquiescence and visceral *yes* exchanged between their bodies.

o

"What about this?" Andrew gestures toward the woods behind them and the beach before them. Their hands are clasped tightly between their bodies, hard, as if letting go would untether something incredibly fragile.

"What? It's a beautiful day." Milo glances up at the ash gray sky, fascinated by the texture of the clouds, bubbling and lumpy.

"It's about to rain."

"I don't care." Milo stops them to drop kisses like the promise of those raindrops on Andrew's lips.

"But still." Andrew pulls away with laughter spilling out.

"Still?"

"You can't stay here and work," Andrew says. "Where will you live?'

"Anywhere you are," Milo says simply, immediately.

"I can't do that," Andrew says. "Keep you somewhere that will make you unhappy. You can't work here."

"Andrew, I'm not unhappy here. And before you say it, it's not only because of you." Andrew leads them to the sand sits and pulls Milo down.

"You know what I learned in the last few years about my past?"

"That it sucked?" Andrew tries to joke.

"Well, that too," Milo says wryly. "But also that all that resentment and rage tied me down. They exhausted me, my shame and self-hatred and everything I couldn't let go of."

"Your bag of rocks," Andrew says, remembering the day when Milo had spoken of forgiveness.

"Yeah." Milo squeezes Andrew's fingers where they are clasped again. "Well, a lot of those were *his* fucking rocks. I had to figure out how to let them go. Then I had to find my way inside me, and to reach that anxiety and anger that I thought were *me*."

"You amaze me," Andrew says. "And it worked?"

"And it's a work in progress," Milo admits. "Coming home set me back a little. But I had a handle. I had skills I learned. Every day, at first, I had to go for walks, had to force myself to look around and notice every detail, to focus my brain anywhere other than on what made me anxious or mad or overwhelmed. I came down to the beach and meditated."

"You really did become a hippy," Andrew jokes. "You should write a self-help book."

Milo shoots him a fond look. "I think I'll leave the writing to you."

"Well, if you insist." Andrew's smile is flirtatious and fond. "Without the balanced chakras, though."

Milo smiles, but continues his original train of thought. "You—it was...that was like really coming home. Coming home without the same need. I could really feel you, for the first time. Differently."

"Oh—" Andrew looks at the water and bites his lip.

"But you had Dex, and I couldn't take what you had found away from you."

"Milo—" Andrew says softly.

"I'm sorry if I did."

"You didn't, no. I felt like that too. Maybe it would have worked with him, but compared to this...Everything with you fits without trying..."

"God," Milo puts his forehead against Andrew's.

"I'll go anywhere you want," Andrew promises.

"No." Milo pulls back and Andrew's eyes are chocolate in the lack of sun. He starts to laugh.

"What?"

"I can't believe I forgot to tell you." Milo takes a breath. "I applied for a job at the Cape Preservation and Development Foundation when I wasn't sure what would happen with Mom. I wanted to tell you; that's why I came looking for you."

"Because you were thinking about it?"

"Yeah, I was. But god, right now, I'm not just thinking about it."

"Why, why would you chose this place when everything—"

"This is where your heart beats happiest," Milo whispers. They're nose to nose, hands clasped still. "And where yours does, mine does too. You're teaching me to love this place like it's new, and I want that, with you."

epilogue

"Daddy, Daddy, *Daddy!*" Margo turns in his arms and chants repeatedly until Andrew has to turn away from his conversation with Milo.

"What, what, *what*?" Andrew says. Margo's eyes brighten at the teasing tone.

"Don't be sassy," she says in a prim and dead-on imitation of his voice. Next to him Milo cracks up.

"You were saying?" Milo reminds her. He tugs at one of her pigtails that's falling apart from rubbing against her wool scarf. She turns toward the water, wiggling her butt more firmly on Andrew's lap, and points to the horizon. To the west, the sun is finishing its inexorable slide into night, and to the east the sky is plum to lilac and magnolia pink.

"That's Venus. They told us in school." She points at the faintest twinkle of a star just beginning to prick through.

Andrew takes her little hand, cold from the October wind on the beach, and kisses it. "I think that one is Venus, honey." He extends both their hands and points in the right direction, where it's bright and big and low in the sky.

"Connor!" Milo calls out, "Uh-uh, not by the water."

Connor turns to shoot them a smile over his shoulder. "No." He says it clearly, and very firmly. Andrew hides a smile behind Margo's shoulder. Connor's fair hair catches in the breeze and Andrew knows his cheeks are pink from the sun he caught earlier that day. Connor squeals and runs away from the waves when they wash over his toes. He giggles and runs back in, but Andrew's not really worried. The water is too cold for him to go in too far. His toes might suffer, though.

"Hey, mister, you listen to your father," he calls out, perhaps not as seriously as he should.

"Nope," Connor says, popping the 'p' sound and laughing. Milo sighs when Andrew tries to hold back a laugh. Milo groans when he stands, but he's smiling too.

"You have no defenses against his cuteness," Milo calls over his shoulder.

Margo looks back at him over her shoulder and nods knowingly, as if she's in this with them. She's only six, but in many ways she is. Connor is a hysterical little handful, a complete contrast to Margo's serious and quiet nature.

Andrew kisses her cheek and hugs her close. By the shoreline he catches the low tones of Milo's voice as he catches up to Connor and laughs, scooping him out of the water. With the light fading, they're little more than silhouettes. The night sighs and lets go of the sun. Water droplets arc from Connor's feet when Milo scoops him up. He shrieks with laughter when Milo holds him close and tickles his neck with kisses, and the image and sound are an indelible stamp in Andrew's chest. Margo turns and tucks her face into Andrew's neck for warmth. Her nose is cold and she's putting one of his legs to sleep. Her sweet, trusting weight and the heat of her body alone keep him warm.

It's one of those perfect moments, a snapshot he'll always remember, even when every other detail from this night may be lost. Andrew will carry it tucked with so many more: the look on

Milo's face when Andrew proposed on a star-filled night in their tiny fort; the palest blue of the sky above him and the beautiful indigo of Milo's eyes when he laid Andrew down on a blanket in the sand and, between kisses, finally, finally told Andrew he was ready for children. Ted toasting them at a bonfire a few nights before Margo came into the world. Connor, too, early and tiny in Milo's cupped palms.

Milo carries Connor up the sand, cradled in his arms, and turns him upside down to make him laugh harder before depositing him on the blanket.

"Bud, you have to listen to your fathers," Milo says seriously, drying his little feet.

"Why?" Connor asks.

"Because we don't want you to lose your toes," Andrew says, pushing wisps of Margo's long red hair away where the wind tosses it across his face.

"Why?"

Milo bites back a smile and kisses the top of Connor's head. For all of the fear Milo harbored that he would damage any children they would have, Andrew is constantly moved by how beautifully Milo loves their children. "Because you need them."

Connor spreads out his toes and looks at them with the seriousness of a three-year-old trying to solve a puzzle. Finally he looks up at them. "Why?"

On his lap Margo giggles. "Because he loves you, silly," she says. "Remember, he loves your heart and your fingers and toes. He loves you to infinity—"

Andrew chimes in with her with the phrase they use at bedtime, when they tuck them into their rooms under glowing stars in the shapes of Andrew's invented constellations—each child with their own, and one for Milo on both ceilings: "He loves you more, the most, and always, always, always."

Acknowledgments

None of this would be possible without my Interlude Press family who work tirelessly to put these books together and get them out into the world. Above and beyond that, thank you so much to Annie for patience, gentle guidance and for constantly reminding me to believe in myself. To Candy for helping me learn to look forward and ignore what's in the rear-view mirror. To Lex, who introduced me to Cheyenne Jackson's *Xanadu* performance at the Tony Awards, made me laugh on bad days, and who couldn't wait to show me what he wanted for this one. I wish you could have seen this part.

Thanks to Cameron Salisbury and Nicki Harper for making my story shine; Kelby Harrison at USC for research help; Choi Messer who designed this book and the talented artist behind the beautiful cover, Nelli I.

Finally, from the deepest corners of my heart to Georgie, Riah, Heidi, Erin and April for believing in this book, cheering me on, lifting me up, and when needed, pushing me to get this story out. As always to my beautiful family for putting up with my artistic temperament and tendency to hole up in an office with imaginary characters who make me cry.

About the Author

Jude Sierra began her writing career at the age of eight when she immortalized her summer vacation with ten entries in a row that read "pool+tv." She first began writing poetry as a child in her home country of Brazil, and is still a student of the form.

As a sucker for happy endings and well-written emotional arcs and characters, Jude is an unapologetic bookaholic. She finds bookstores and libraries unbearably sexy and, to her husband's dismay, is attempting to create her own in their living room. She is a writer of many things that hope to find their way out of the sanctuary of her hard drive and many that have found a home in the fanfiction community.

Jude is currently working on her Master of Arts in Writing and Rhetoric and managing a home filled with her two cats, husband and two young sons. Her first novel, *Hush*, was published in 2015 by Interlude Press. Visit Judesierra.com for more.

Questions for Discussion

1. Milo and Andrew share a special connection with the fort they built. Explain how what it meant to each of them changed over time.

2. Both parts of the story begin with Milo arriving in Santuit. Both arrivals signify important events in his life. Explain how they are similar and how they are different.

3. Andrew becomes accustomed to being the person who puts "broken Milo back together". How could that be a problem in a long-term relationship for the two men?

4. Milo's dad's behavior had far-reaching effects in Santuit as well as in both Andrew and Milo's lives. How did the town's complicity in the abuse affect Milo's willingness to be there?

5. If Andrew hadn't waited two weeks to report Milo's dad in the first chapter, how would the story been different? What turning points did it create for the boys?

6. Several decisions led to Milo and Andrew losing contact for seven years. Trace the decisions that prevented them from declaring their love from the time Andrew came out until their ultimate separation after the bonfire.

7. Andrew and Milo react very differently to being in college. How does each man's choices affect their ability to stay friends, or connect on a deeper level than friendship?

8. Coming out was a very different experience for each boy, despite coming out to each other first. Who had the easier time with coming out and why?

9. Milo has to deal with both physical and psychological abuse from his father. Which one affects him more in the long run? Which one is harder to overcome? Why do you think that is true?

10. Describe the process it took for Milo to heal and be ready to commit to Andrew. Why did it take so long for the two men to truly be together?

Now available from

interlude 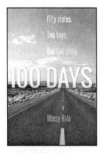 press™

100 Days by Mimsy Hale

Jake and Aiden have been best friends—and nothing more—since the age of six. Now college graduates, they take a road trip around the USA, visiting every state in 100 Days. As they start their cross-country odyssey, Jake and Aiden think they have their journey and their futures mapped out. But the road has a funny way of changing course.

ISBN 978-1-941530-23-8   EBOOK ISBN 978-1-941530-29-0

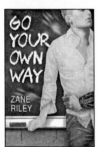

Go Your Own Way by Zane Riley

Will Osborne couldn't wait to put the roller coaster ride of his public education behind him. Having suffered bullying and harassment since grade school, he planned a senior year that would be simple and quiet before going away to college and starting fresh. But when a reform school transfer student struts into his first class, Will realizes that the thrill ride has only just begun.

Lennox McAvoy is an avalanche. He's crude, flirtatious, and the most insufferable, beautiful person Will's ever met. From his ankle monitor to his dull smile, Lennox appears irredeemable. But when Will's father falls seriously ill, Will discovers that there is more to Lennox than meets the eye.

ISBN 978-1-941530-34-4   EBOOK ISBN 978-1-941530-77-1

Lodestones by Naomi Mackenzie
Published by Duet Books, an imprint of Interlude Press

On the eve of a new school year, several groups of college students cross paths on their way to a secret end-of-summer lake party, including two inseparable best friends who discover over the course of 24 hours that their relationship is something much deeper than friendship.

ISBN 978-1-941530-37-5   EBOOK ISBN 978-1-941530-51-1

Platonic by Kate Paddington

Make me believe it, even if it's just for one night...

Mark Savoy and Daniel O'Shea were high school sweethearts who had planned their forevers together. But when Mark goes to college in California rather than following Daniel to New York, he embarks on a decade-long search for independence, sexual confidence and love. When Mark lands a job in New York and crosses Daniel's path, they slowly rebuild their fractured friendship through texts and emails. If they finally agree to see each other, will they be able to keep it platonic? Or will the spark of a long-lost love reignite just as Daniel accepts a job overseas?

ISBN 978-1-941530-02-3   EBOOK ISBN 978-1-941530-10-8

One **story** can change **everything**.
www.interlude**press**.com

CPSIA information can be obtained at www.ICGtesting.com
Printed in the USA
LVOW11s1524280116

472714LV00008B/961/P